Jilly Cooper is a well-known journalist, writer and media superstar. The author of many number one bestselling novels, including *Riders*, *Rivals*, *Polo*, *The Man Who Made Husbands Jealous*, *Appassionata*, *Score!* and *Pandora*, she and her husband live in Gloucestershire.

Jilly Cooper was appointed OBE in the 2004 Queen's Birthday Honours List.

CHILDREN'S BOOKS
Little Mabel
Little Mabel's Great Escape
Little Mabel Saves the Day
Little Mabel Wins

ROMANCE
Bella
Emily
Harriet
Imogen
Lisa and Co
Octavia
Prudence

ANTHOLOGIES
The British in Love
Violets and Vinegar

IMOGEN

Jilly Cooper

CORGI BOOKS

IMOGEN
A CORGI BOOK : 9780552158800

Originally published in Great Britain by
Arlington Books Ltd

PRINTING HISTORY
Arlington Books edition published 1978
Corgi edition published 1979
Corgi edition reissued 2005

1 3 5 7 9 10 8 6 4 2

Copyright © Jilly Cooper 1978

Set in 11/14pt Times by
Kestrel Data, Exeter, Devon.

Corgi Books are published by Transworld Publishers,
61–63 Uxbridge Road, London W5 5SA,
A Random House Group Company.

Addresses for Random House Group Ltd companies outside the UK
can be found at: www.randomhouse.co.uk
The Random House Group Ltd Reg. No. 954009.

Printed and bound in Great Britain by
CPI Cox & Wyman, Reading, RG1 8EX.

The Random House Group Limited supports The Forest Stewardship
Council (FSC), the leading international forest certification organisation.
All our titles that are printed on Greenpeace approved FSC certified paper
carry the FSC logo. Our paper procurement policy can be found at:
www.rbooks.co.uk/environment.

For Lyn Adams
with love

Author's Note

The idea for IMOGEN first came to me in 1967. I wrote it as a long short story called THE HOLI-DAY MAKERS and it appeared in serial form in *19*. In 1977 I took the story and completely re-wrote it, and the result is IMOGEN.

IMOGEN

Chapter One

The little West Riding town of Pikely-in-Darrowdale clings to the side of the hillside like a grey squirrel. Above stretches the moor and below, in the valley, where the River Darrow meanders through bright green water meadows, lies Pikely Tennis Club. In the High Street stands the Public Library.

It was a Saturday afternoon in May. Miss Nugent, the Senior Librarian, put down the mauve openwork jumper she was knitting and helped herself to another Lincoln Cream.

'I've never known it so slack,' she said to the pretty girl beside her, who was dreamily sorting books into piles of fiction and non-fiction and putting them on a trolley. 'Everyone must be down at the tournament. Are you going, Imogen?'

The girl nodded. 'For an hour or two. My sister's raving about one of the players – some Wimbledon star. I promised I'd go and look at him.'

'I'm sorry you had to work this afternoon,' said Miss Nugent. 'You're always standing in for Gloria. I wonder if she really was "struck down by shellfish". I'm going to ring up in a minute and see how she is.'

'Oh, I wouldn't do that,' said Imogen hastily, knowing perfectly well that Gloria had sloped off to Morecambe for the week-end with a boyfriend, 'The – er – telephone in her digs is in the hall, and I'm sure she's feeling far too weak to stagger down two flights of stairs to answer it.'

Feeling herself blushing at such a lie, she busied about stacking up leaflets entitled *Your Rights as a Ratepayer* and *What to do in Pikely*. Bugger all, Gloria always said, in answer to the latter.

Miss Nugent burrowed inside her cream rayon blouse, and hauled up a bra strap.

'Decided where to go for your holiday yet?'

'Not really,' answered Imogen, wishing some reader would come in and distract Miss Nugent's attention. 'My father's swapping with a vicar in Whitby in September. I might go with him.'

She dreaded discussing holidays; everyone else in the library seemed to have planned trips to exotic places months ago, and talked about nothing else. She extracted a romantic novel called *A Kiss in Tangier* from books destined for the Travel Section and put it on top of the Fiction pile. On the front was a picture of a beautiful couple embracing against a background of amethyst ocean and pale pink minarets. Oh dear, thought Imogen sadly, if only I could go to Tangier and be swept off my size seven feet by a man with a haughty face and long legs.

The library was certainly quiet for a Saturday. In the left-hand corner, where easy chairs were grouped round low tables, an old lady had fallen asleep over Lloyd George's letters, a youth in a leather jacket was browsing through a biography of Kevin Keegan, his lips moving as he read, and little Mr Hargreaves was finishing another chapter of the pornographic novel he didn't dare take home, for fear of his large wife's disapproval. Apart from an earnest young man with a beard and sandals flipping through the volumes of sociology and a coloured girl who got through four romances a day, desperately trying to find one she hadn't read, the place was deserted.

Suddenly the door opened and two middle-aged women came in, red-faced from the hairdressers opposite, smelling of lacquer and grumbling about the wind messing their new hair-dos. Imogen took money for a fine from one, and assured the other that Catherine Cookson really hadn't written another book yet.

'Authors have to write at their own pace you know,' said Miss Nugent reprovingly.

Imogen watched the two women stopping to browse through the novels on the returned books trolley. Funny, she thought wistfully, how people tended to look there first rather than at the shelves, how a book that appeared to be going out a lot was more likely to be in demand. Just like Gloria. Three boys had been in asking for her already that day, and had all looked sceptical on being told the shellfish story. But Imogen knew they'd all be back again asking for her next week.

You learnt a lot about the locals working in a library. Only this morning Mr Barraclough, who, unknown to his wife, was having a walk-out with the local nymphomaniac, had taken out a book called *How to Live with a Bad Back*. Then Mr York, reputed to have the most untroubled marriage in Pikely, had, with much puffing and blowing, rung in and asked Imogen to reserve *Masters and Johnson on Sexual Inadequacy*. And after lunch Mrs Bottomley, one of her father's newest parish workers and due to do the flowers for the first time in church next week, had crept in and surreptitiously chosen four books on flower arrangement.

'Vivien Leigh's going well,' said Miss Nugent, 'and you'd better put David Niven aside for repair before he falls to pieces. When you've shelved that lot you can push off. It's nearly four o'clock.'

But next minute Imogen had been accosted by a dotty old woman with darned stockings asking if they had any dustbin bags, which led to a long explanation about how the old woman's dog had been put down, and she wanted to throw its basket and rubber toys away as soon as possible.

'The dustmen don't come till Wednesday, and I'll be reminded of him everytime I see them int' dustbin.'

Imogen's eyes brimmed with tears. 'Oh, I'm so sorry,' she said. After devoting five minutes to the old woman, she turned to two small boys who came up to the desk looking very pink.

'Any books about life?' asked the eldest.

'Whose life?' said Imogen. 'Biographies are over there.'

'You know, facts'a life – babies and things,' said the boy. His companion started to giggle. Imogen tried to hide a smile.

'Well the biology section's on the right,' she said.

'Don't be daft,' snapped Miss Nugent. 'Run along, you lads, and try the children's library next door. And hurry up and shelve those books, Imogen.'

She watched the girl pushing the squeaking trolley across the library. She was a nice child despite her timidity, and tried very hard, but she was so willing to listen to other people's problems, she always got behind with her own work.

Imogen picked up a pile of alphabetically arranged books in her left hand – so high that she could only just see over them – and started to replace them in the shelves. The collected editions were landmarks which made putting back easier. *Sons and Lovers* was replaced at the end of a milky green row of D. H. Lawrence. *Return to Jalna* slotted into the coral pink edition of Mazo de la Roche.

Even working in a library for two years had not lessened her love of reading. There was *Frenchman's Creek*. She stopped for a second, remembering the glamour of the Frenchman. If only a man like that would come into the library. But if he did, he'd be bound to fall in love with Gloria.

A commotion at the issue desk woke her out of her reverie. A man with a moustache and a purple face, wearing a blazer, was agitatedly waving a copy of Molly Parkin's latest novel.

'It's filth,' he roared, 'sheer filth. I just came in here to tell you I'm going to burn it.'

'Well you'll have to pay for it then,' said Miss Nugent. 'A lot of other readers have requested it.'

'Filth and written by a woman,' roared the man in the blazer. 'Don't know how anyone dare publish it.' Everyone in the library was listening now, pretending to study the books on the shelves, but brightening perceptibly at the prospect of a good row.

Imogen returned *The Age of Innocence* to its right place and rolled the trolley back to the issue desk.

'Let me read you this bit, madam,' shouted the man in the blazer.

'Run along now, Imogen,' said Miss Nugent, hastily.

Imogen hesitated, embarrassed, but longing to hear the outcome of the row.

'Go on,' said Miss Nugent firmly. 'You'll miss the tennis. I won't be in on Monday. I'm going to Florrie's funeral, so I'll see you on Tuesday. Now, sir,' she turned to the man in the blazer.

Why do I always miss all the fun, thought Imogen, going into the back office where Miss Illingworth was clucking over the legal action file.

'I've written to the Mayor five times about returning *The Hite Report*,' she said crossly, 'You'd think a man in his position . . .'

'Maybe he thinks he's grand enough to keep

books as long as he likes,' said Imogen, unlocking her locker and taking out her bag.

'Twenty-one days is the limit, and rules is rules, my girl, whether you're the Queen of England. Have you seen Mr Cloth's PC? It's a scream.'

Imogen picked up the postcard of blue sea and orange sand and turned it over.

I wouldn't like to live here, the deputy librarian, who was holidaying in Sardinia, had written, *but it's a horrible place for a holiday. The pillows are like bags of Blue Circle cement. Wish you were here but not queer. B. C.*

Imogen giggled, then sighed inwardly. Not only had one to find somewhere smart to go on holiday, but had to write witty things about it when you got there.

She went into the ladies to comb her hair and wash the violet ink from the date stamp off her hands. She scowled at her reflection in the cracked mirror – huge grey eyes, rosy cheeks, too many freckles, a snub nose, soft full lips, long hair the colour of wet sand, which had a maddening tendency to kink at the first sight of rain.

'Why do I look so young?' she thought crossly. 'And why am I so fat?'

She removed the mirror from the wall, examining the full breasts, wide hips and sturdy legs which went purple and mottled in cold weather, and which fortunately today were hidden by black boots.

'It's a typical North Country figure,' she thought gloomily, 'built to withstand howling winds and an arctic climate.'

During her last year at school she had been unceasingly ragged for weighing eleven stone. Now, two years later, she had lost over two stone, but still felt herself to be fat and unattractive.

Her younger sister, Juliet, was waiting for her as she came out of the library. Far more fashion-conscious than Imogen, she was wearing drainpipe pedal pushers, brilliant coloured glove socks, and a *papier mâché* ice cream cornet pinned to her huge sloppy pink sweater. A tiny leather purse swung from her neck, and her blonde curls blew in the wind as she circled round and round on her bicycle like a vulture.

'There you are, Imogen. For goodness' sake, hurry! Beresford's on court already and he's bound to win in straight sets. Did you bring *Fanny Hill*?'

'Blast! I forgot,' said Imogen, turning back.

'Oh, leave it,' said Juliet. 'It doesn't matter.' And she set off down the cobbled streets, pedalling briskly.

'What's his name again?' said Imogen, panting beside her.

'I've told you a million times – Beresford. N. Beresford. I hope the "N" doesn't stand for Norman or anything ghastly. Mind you, *he* could get away with it. I've never seen anyone so divine!'

Last week, Imogen reflected, Juliet had been distraught with love for Rod Stewart, the week before for Georgie Best.

Although a pallid sun was shining, afternoon shoppers, muffled in scarves and sheepskin coats, scuttled down the street, heads down against the wind. Imogen and Juliet arrived at the Tennis Club to find most of the spectators huddled for warmth around Court One.

'I can't see, I can't see!' said Juliet in a shrill voice.

'Let the little girl through,' said the crowd indulgently and, in a few seconds, Juliet, dragging a reluctant Imogen by the hand, had pummelled her way through to the front.

'There's Beresford,' she whispered, pressing her face against the wire. 'Serving this end.'

He was tall and slim, with long legs, smooth and brown as a conker, and black curly hair. His shoulder muscles rippled as he served. His opponent didn't even see the ball. A crackle of applause ran round the court.

'Game and first set to Beresford,' said the umpire.

'He plays tennis champion,' said a man in the crowd.

'Isn't he the end?' sighed Juliet.

'He looks OK from the back,' said Imogen cautiously.

But as Beresford turned round and sauntered back to the baseline for the next game, she caught her breath.

With his lean brown features, eyes bluer than delphiniums, and glossy black moustache above a smooth curling, sulky mouth, he was the embodiment of all the romantic heroes she'd ever dreamed of.

'You win,' she muttered to Juliet, 'he's devastating.'

In a daze, she watched him cruise through the

next three games, without conceding a point. Then –
she could never remember afterwards exactly how it
happened – he was strolling back to the wire netting
to retrieve a ball, when suddenly he looked up
and smiled at her. He just stood there smiling, his
brilliant blue eyes burning holes in the netting.

The crowd was becoming restless.

'Beresford to serve!' snapped the umpire for the
third time. Beresford shook himself, picked up the
ball and went back to the baseline. He served a
double fault.

'At the first sight, they have changed eyes,'
crowed Juliet, who was doing *The Tempest* for
'O' Level. 'Oh, Imogen, did you see him look at
you? And he keeps on looking. Oh, it's too unfair.
Why, oh, why, aren't I you?'

Imogen wondered if she had dreamed what had
happened. She glanced round to see if some beautiful girl, the real object of Beresford's attentions, was
standing behind her. But there was only a fat woman
in a purple trilby and two men.

His game had certainly gone to pieces. He missed
several easy shots and every time he changed ends
he grinned at her.

'He'd better stop fooling about,' said Juliet, 'or
he's going to lose this set.'

As if by telepathy, Beresford seemed to pull himself together. Crouching like a tiger, he played four
games of rampaging brilliance to take the match
without dropping a set.

How the crowd – particularly Imogen – thundered

their approval. Beresford put on a pale blue blazer and gathered up his four rackets. As he came off court, he stared straight at Imogen. Suddenly she felt frightened, as though the tiger she'd been admiring at the zoo had just escaped from its cage.

'Let's go and find Daddy,' she said.

'Are you mad?' said Juliet. 'Stay put and Beresford'll know where to find you.'

But Imogen, seeing Beresford pause to satisfy the demands of a group of autograph hunters, had already bolted into the tea tent.

They found their father talking to the Club Secretary.

'Hullo,' he said, 'have some tea.' And went back to his conversation.

A savage example of the Church Militant, the Reverend Stephen Brocklehurst had one great secular passion – sport. He was now giving the Club Secretary a blow by blow account of why Beresford had played so badly.

'The boy was over-confident, of course; thought he had the whole thing sewn up.'

Juliet giggled and applied herself to the cucumber sandwiches. Imogen sat in a dream, until Juliet nudged her. 'Beresford's just walked in,' she hissed.

Imogen choked over her tea. Everyone was hailing him from all corners.

'He's seen you,' whispered Juliet. 'He's working his way in this direction.'

'Hullo Nicky,' said the Club Secretary. 'Whatever happened to you?'

Beresford laughed, showing very white teeth. 'I saw something I fancied on the other side of the netting,' he said, looking at Imogen.

'You ought to play in blinkers,' said the Club Secretary. 'Come and join us. Have you met our vicar, Mr Brocklehurst, and his daughters, Imogen and Juliet?'

'No, I haven't,' said Beresford, shaking hands and holding Imogen's hand far longer than necessary before he sat down between her and the vicar.

'Brocklehurst,' he said, reflectively, as he dropped four lumps of sugar into his tea. 'Brocklehurst? Weren't you capped for England just after the war?'

Mr Brocklehurst melted like butter in a heatwave.

'Yes indeed. Clever of you to remember that.'

After talking to the vicar about rugger for five minutes, and having wangled himself an invitation to lunch next day, Beresford turned his attention to Imogen.

'Well, you certainly threw me,' he said softly. 'It's a good thing there weren't any Davis Cup selectors about.'

'I'm so pleased you won,' stammered Imogen.

'And I'm pleased,' he looked straight into her eyes, 'that you're even more beautiful close up.'

So was he, thought Imogen. Far more beautiful, with dark smudges under his eyes, and damp tendrils curling round his forehead. His voice was low and confiding as though she were the only person in the world he wanted to talk to.

And although he asked the usual questions –

What did she do for a living? Did she enjoy it?
Did she ever come to London? – his smoky voice,
and the way his eyes wandered over her body and
her face, made even those familiar phrases sound
significant.

A pale youth with long mousy hair, wearing a
v-necked sweater with reindeers round the border,
came up and cleared his throat. Nicky looked up
without enthusiasm.

'Yes?'

'I'm from Yorkshire Television,' said the youth. 'I
wonder if we could have a few words with you?'

'When?' said Nicky.

'Well now?'

'I'm busy.'

'It won't take long.'

'I'll talk to you after the doubles. Now beat it,'
said Nicky curtly, and turned back to Imogen.

She gazed at him, bewildered by such perfection.
Perhaps it was the black rim round the iris or the
thickness of the lashes that gave his blue eyes their
intensity. His suntan was so even, it looked painted
on. And he'd actually called her beautiful. Later
that night she would bring out the remark like an
iced cake saved from tea murmuring it over and over
to herself, trying to remember exactly the husky
smouldering overtones of his voice.

'Where d'you play next?' she asked. The thought
of him going away was already unbearable.

Nicky grinned. 'Rome on Monday, Paris the
week after, then Edinburgh, Wimbledon, Gstaad,

Kitzbühel, and then the North American circuit, Washington, Indianapolis, Toronto, finally Forest Hills, if I don't die of exhaustion.'

Imogen gasped. Scotland was the most abroad she'd ever been to.

'Oh, how lovely,' she said. 'Think of the postcards one could send.'

Nicky laughed. 'I could face it if you came with me,' he said, lowering his voice.

Imogen blushed and gazed into her tea cup.

Nicky watched her for a second. 'Trying to read the tea-leaves? They're telling you that a tall, dark, tennis player has just come into your life,' he said.

'Hi,' said a voice behind them. 'I see you've got yourself stuck in as usual, Nicky.'

They had been so engrossed, they hadn't noticed the arrival of a stocky, grinning young man. He was chewing gum and wearing a gold earring, a pale blue tracksuit top and a blue towelling headband to keep his blond hair from flying about.

'I came to see the reason you dropped three games in the singles,' he said.

'This is it,' said Nicky.

Once more Imogen felt herself colouring painfully.

'Congratulations,' said the young man, giving Imogen a comprehensive once-over and shifting his gum to the other side of his face. 'You always had good taste, Nicky.'

'This is Charlie Painter,' said Nicky. 'My doubles partner. Fancies himself as a tough guy.'

'I don't take anything lying down, except pretty girls,' said Painter, winking at Juliet. 'Look, if you can bear to tear yourself away, we're on court in a minute.'

'I can't,' said Nicky, turning his steady, knowing smile on Imogen again. 'You don't need me. You can thrash those two creeps with your hands behind your back.'

'The light's terrible. It's going to be like playing in a coal cellar,' said Painter, peering out of the tent.

'Well, appeal against it,' said Nicky. 'You know I'm frightened of the dark and I want to go on chatting up Miss Brocklehurst.'

Imogen shot a fearful glance at her father, but happily he was still nose to nose with the Club Secretary, rhapsodising over Hancock's try.

The loudspeaker hiccupped and announced the finals of the men's doubles. Reluctantly Nicky got to his feet.

'There's a party here this evening, I wonder if you – and your sister, of course,' he added smiling at Juliet, 'would like to come?'

'Oh, yes please,' began Imogen, but the vicar promptly looked round.

'Good of you to ask them,' he said blandly, 'but I'm afraid they've already been booked to help at the Mothers' Union whist drive. We shall look forward to seeing you at lunch tomorrow, any time after half past twelve.'

Both Imogen and Juliet opened their mouths in protest, then shut them again. They knew their father. Just for a second Nicky's eyes narrowed. Then he smiled.

'I shall look forward to it too,' he said, and followed Painter out of the tent.

'Sod the Mothers' Union,' muttered Juliet.

'I know you like them below the age of consent,' said Painter, as they walked towards the No. 1 Court, 'but isn't she a bit wet behind the ears?'

'Older than she looks, left school two years ago,' said Nicky, pausing to sign a couple of autographs. 'And very nice, don't you think?'

'Sweet,' agreed Painter, signing them too.

'And entirely untouched by human hand,' said Nicky, 'which makes a change.'

'We were the first that ever burst into that sunless sea,' said Painter and laughed. 'All the same, you'll never get your spoon into that pudding. Bet the old Rev locks them both in chastity belts every night.'

'He's asked me to lunch.'

'So what? He'll still never let you get near enough to pull her.'

'Want to bet?' said Nicky, taking a racket out of its press, and making a few swipes with it. 'Bugger, my shoulder's playing up again.'

'A fiver,' said Painter, taking off his blue jacket.

'Make it a tenner,' said Nicky, flexing his shoulder.

'All right, you're on.'

As he and Painter took the first set 6–0, Nicky was aware of the vicar and his daughters watching him. He was glad his first serve went in each time, and for once volleys, smashes, lobs, drop shots, everything, worked. He was getting to the ball so quickly he had time to examine it for bugs before he hit it. This was the kind of barnstorming form he'd got to maintain for the rest of the season. He flashed his teeth at Imogen and saw she was about to go.

Nicky had reached the age of twenty-six without ever falling seriously in love. He had had affairs by the score – there were endless temptations on the tennis circuit. If you were superbly fit, you didn't just go to bed and read a book in the evenings. If you won, you wanted to celebrate, if you lost you needed cheering up. But on the whole his heart was more resilient than his self respect. From broken affairs he recovered rapidly without any need of convalescence. They left no scars and no regrets and sometimes he was sorry they didn't, thinking he was missing out on something other people had and seemed to value, although it caused them anguish at the time.

Recently, too, he had felt a vague dissastisfaction with his life. There had been trouble about his knocking off another player's wife, a Mexican beauty, whose insanely jealous husband had rumbled them. The reason Nicky was playing in Pikely this week rather than Hamburg was in the hope that the whole thing might blow over. Then last week an offer of an advertising commercial which would have brought him in several thousand a year had suddenly gone instead to another British player, who, although less glamorous than Nicky, had reached the finals of the big tournaments more often than Nicky had the preceding year. Finally, the night before he'd driven up to Pikely, his Coach had taken him out to dinner.

'What are you playing at, Nicky boy?' he had asked after the second bottle, with his usual mixture of bluntness and concern. 'You've got everything going for you, but you're not getting any younger, and you'll never make it really big unless you cut out the birds and the booze and the late nights. Haven't you ever thought of settling down?'

Nicky had replied that he had too much trouble settling up in life to think of any permanent commitment. His debts were crippling at the moment, he said, and they had both laughed. But the Coach's remarks had stung and Nicky had not forgotten them.

As the crowd clapped approvingly at the end of the set, Mr Brocklehurst dragged his protesting daughters away, saying they mustn't be late for the whist drive. Nicky had looked so sensational on court that Imogen could hardly believe their tête-à-tête in the tea tent had ever taken place, but as she left he had waved his racket at her, so it must be true.

As they drove home to the vicarage with Juliet's bike perched precariously on the roof rack, they passed a school friend of Juliet's riding home from a gymkhana festooned with rosettes, who gave them a lordly wave with her whip.

'Just showing off, silly bitch,' muttered Juliet.

'10p in the swear box,' reproached the vicar, but mildly, because he doted on his younger daughter.

As he crossed the River Darrow and took the road up to the moors, he, too, felt a faint dissatisfaction with life. Watching Beresford today had reminded him of his youth on the rugger field. He had been good looking too, and had experienced the same adulation from women and hero-worship from men.

'Having achieved the ultimate glory of playing rugger for England,' said an unkind fellow clergyman, 'Steve Brocklehurst spent the rest of his life in exhausted mediocrity.'

Mr Brocklehurst was also only too aware that another great athlete, David Shepherd, had made bishop. But no such promotion had come his way. No doubt he would be left to moulder away the rest of his life in Pikely, where the adoration of the spinsters of the parish was no substitute for the stands rising at Twickenham. In his more gloomy moments the vicar thought there was a great deal to be said for an athlete dying young, cut off in his prime, rather than growing paunchy and rheumaticky.

Life, however, had its compensations. He was well respected in the district; no local committee was complete without him; he loved his garden and his games of golf, and his vague, charming wife, probably in that order. His two sons, both at boarding school and costing the earth, were shaping up as excellent athletes. Michael was already in the fifteen. Juliet, adorable, insouciant, the baby of the family, could twist him round her little finger.

But as a man of God, it had always nagged his conscience, like a bit of apple core wedged in one's teeth, that his elder daughter, Imogen, got on his nerves. In the beginning he'd resented her not being a boy; as she grew up he was irritated by her clumsiness, her dreaminess, her slowness, her tender heart (how easily he could reduce her to tears), her inability to stand up to him, and her complete lack of athleticism. He still remembered a humiliating gym display at her school a few years ago, when Imogen had been the only one in her class who totally failed to get over any of the apparatus. He had also been deeply ashamed of her lumpiness, but at least she'd slimmed down a bit lately, and she'd kept her job in the library, which helped out with the housekeeping. (Money was very tight, with three children still at school.) But why did she have to agree with everything he said, like one of those nodding doggies in the back of cars?

There was no doubt, though, that young Beresford seemed taken with her, and needed keeping an eye on. The vicar might not love his elder daughter, but he wouldn't let her come to any harm. He had been a bit of a lad himself in his day and, like most reformed rakes, he veered towards repressive puritanism where his daughters were concerned. He was only too aware of the lusts of young players after too much beer.

Next moment he caught sight of his curate on his

shiny new red racing bicycle, with its drop handle-
bars which the vicar thought both undignified and
far too young for him. He waited until they were
only a few yards behind the curate, then sounded his
horn loudly, which made the poor young man nearly
ride into the ditch.

The vicar chuckled to himself and turned up
the drive. The vicarage was one of those draughty
Victorian houses, made only slightly less forbidding
by the creepers and rambler roses surging up its
dark grey walls, and the wallflowers and purple
irises in the front flower beds. At the back of the
house was a lawn long enough for a cricket pitch,
where Imogen bowled endlessly to her younger
brothers when they were home. On either side were
herbaceous borders, and at the end long grass and
bluebells growing round the trunks of an ancient
orchard.

As they opened the front door, Homer, the golden
retriever, his eyes screwed up from sleep, greeted
them, singing with pleasure, looking frantically
round for something to bring them and settling for a
pair of socks lying on the floor.

Going through the hall, with its old coats hanging
on a row of pegs and a pile of parish magazines
waiting to be delivered, Imogen found her mother
in the drawing-room, looking rather pious and
virtuously sewing buttons on one of her father's
shirts. She knew perfectly well that her mother had
been reading a novel and had shoved it under the
shirt the moment she heard wheels on the gravel.

'Hullo, darling,' she said vaguely. 'Had a nice time at the tennis?'

'Yes, thank you,' said Imogen, kissing her. She knew there was no point in saying any more; her mother wouldn't listen to the answer.

'I suppose we ought to get changed for the whist drive,' said Mrs Brocklehurst with a sigh. 'What time does it begin?'

'Eight o'clock,' said the vicar, coming through the door. 'Hullo, darling. Just time for me to plant out my antirrhinums.'

'Well, of all the blooming cheats,' said Juliet to his departing back, as he went out of the french windows. 'We could have stayed and watched the last set after all. I hope his rotten snapdragons never come up.'

The whist drive seemed to last an eternity, but eventually the final chair had been stacked in the church hall, and the last *vol-au-vent* crumb swept away.

'Don't you sometimes wish Daddy had been an engineer?' said Juliet, as she and Imogen trailed home.

'Yes,' said Imogen, listening to the lambs bleating in the field behind the house, and praying that Nicky wasn't enjoying his party too much. 'I say, Juliet,' she felt herself blushing, 'it did happen, didn't it? This afternoon I mean.'

'Course it did,' said Juliet. 'Even Daddy got the wind up and whisked you home. Normally he'd never leave in the middle of a match.'

When she got home Imogen washed her hair, undressed and got into bed. Then she filled the rest of May and the whole of June in her diary ecstatically describing her meeting with Nicky, shivering with excitement and wonder at the imperious way he'd dismissed Yorkshire Television, and told his partner to appeal against the light to give him more time with her.

Why me? why me? she kept saying over and over again, burying her hot face in her pillow, and squirming with delight. She must get some sleep or she'd look terrible in the morning. But it only seemed a few seconds later that she was woken by Homer barking at the paper boy and the church bell tolling for Holy Communion, and the Sunday morning panic of her father calling from the depth of the hot cupboard that he couldn't find a clean shirt.

Chapter Two

Imogen sat clutching a cup of black coffee at breakfast. The vicar, mopping up egg yolk with fried bread, was deep in the sports pages of the *Sunday Times*, while Juliet, who was eating toast and marmalade, peered across at the headlines.

'What a dreadful world,' she sighed. 'I don't think I shall ever live to see twenty-one.'

'What are we having for lunch?' asked Imogen.

'Macaroni cheese, plum tart and custard and then, I suppose more cheese,' said her mother vaguely.

'But we can't give him that!' said Juliet aghast. 'I mean he's famous. Can't we have a joint?'

'I'm afraid the shops aren't open on Sunday,' said her mother. 'I'll try and persuade Daddy to open a bottle of wine.'

Imogen wondered how on earth she could last through the morning. But in the end there seemed to be lots to do, frantic hoovering and dusting, bashing lilac stems and arranging them with irises in a big bowl in the drawing-room, laying the table, trying and failing to find matching wine glasses, making a crumble top to liven up the plums, mixing a dressing for the salad, and praying that the vicar, who disapproved of frivolous culinary refinements, wouldn't notice the addition of garlic. Then she had to go to Matins. It was a beautiful day. The cuckoo was calling from the beech wood beyond the churchyard, and the trees were putting out acid green leaves against a heavy navy blue sky, which promised rain later.

'Defend us with thy mighty power, and grant that this day we run into no sin,' prayed the vicar, addressing the congregation in a ringing voice.

Juliet grinned and nudged Imogen, who went pink and gazed straight in front of her. She had already prayed fervently to God to grant her Nicky, but only, she added hastily, if *He* thought it was all right.

Her father was getting to his feet. A hymn and a sermon and another hymn, thought Imogen thankfully, and they would be out in the sunshine again. She mustn't forget to pick up the cream for the crumble from the farm.

Then she gave a gasp of horror, for she saw that her father, with what seemed a suspiciously malicious glance at their pew, was walking over to the Litany desk.

'Oh, no,' groaned Juliet. 'We had the Litany last week. Beresford will have come and gone by the time we get out of here.'

'And what about my pie in the oven?' muttered Mrs Connolly, their daily woman, who was sitting in the pew behind. The congregation knelt down sulkily.

Never had Imogen found it more difficult to concentrate on her imperfections.

'From fornication, and all other deadly sin; and from all the deceits of the world, the flesh and the devil,' intoned the vicar.

'Good Lord, deliver us,' Imogen chorused listlessly with the rest of the congregation. Oh, why hadn't she had a bath beforehand?

'From lightning and tempest; from plague, pestilence and . . .'

The sun was shining outside the church, but inside it was freezing. The vicar, who never felt the cold, insisted on turning off the radiators in April. It was twenty past twelve by the time she got home, and Nicky was due at a quarter to one. To warm herself up, she had far too hot a bath.

Having tried on every dress in her wardrobe, and hating them all, she settled for a black sweater and skirt which at least slimmed her down a bit. Her legs looked red and fat through her pale stockings. If only she'd got out of the bath sooner. There was no doubt, she thought sadly, if there was less of you, people thought more of you.

Going out of her room, she nearly fell over Juliet who was lying on the floor in the passage pulling up the zip on her jeans.

'How do I look?' said Juliet, scrambling to her feet.

'Familiar,' said Imogen. 'That's my shirt.'

Juliet looked her over critically.

'You look nice, but I think you should tone down some of that rouge.'

'It's not rouge,' sighed Imogen, 'it's me.'

It was five to one. Imogen checked that everything was all right in the kitchen and went into the drawing-room to wait. She picked up the colour magazine. There was a long piece on Katherine Mansfield, which she vowed to read later, but knew she never would. She had read the report of a tournament in Hamburg three times at breakfast, particularly the bit about 'The British contribution being severely weakened by the absence of Beresford, who was playing at Pikely, where he triumphed in the singles, doubles and mixed doubles, as was to be expected.' Nicky was so illustrious, it was as though the sun was coming to lunch. Once more she got her compact out of her bag, and powdered her pink cheeks with more energy than success. Oh, to have been born pale and interesting.

It was five past one now. Perhaps he wasn't coming after all, perhaps after all that winning he'd forgotten or met someone at the party last night. She put down the magazine and wandered nervously round the room rearranging the lilac, plumping cushions, straightening Juliet's music which was littered over the top of the piano.

The clock that had dawdled all morning suddenly started to gallop; it was edging towards a quarter past one now. Her father always kicked up a fuss if lunch was late. It was quite obvious Nicky wasn't coming. I can't bear it, she thought in anguish. Then suddenly she heard the rattle of a car on the sheep track and Homer barking.

Next minute her hands went to her face in terror and excitement, then frantically she smoothed her hair, pulled down her sweater and put on more scent, most of which went over the carpet. In a panic, she rushed into the hall and locked herself into the downstairs lavatory. Next moment Juliet was shaking the door.

'Come out quickly. Nicky's just rolled up in a Porsche looking too fantastic for words. Go and let him in.'

'I can't,' squeaked Imogen. 'You go.'

'I'm putting on the broccoli, and Mummy's still tarting up. Go *on*, he's your lover.'

Imogen came out wiping her sweating hands on her skirt. She could see a man's figure through the bubbly glass panel of the front door. The bell rang.

'Anyone for tennis players?' cried Juliet.

'Oh, shut up,' said Imogen.

'Go *on*. He'll think we've forgotten and go away.'

With a trembling hand Imogen opened the door. Nicky was bending down to pat Homer, who was wagging his blond plumy tail and carrying a stick.

'You're not much of a watchdog,' said Nicky, rubbing his ears. 'Hullo, angel.' He straightened up and smiled at her. 'Sorry I'm late. I took a wrong turning and got stuck behind a convoy of Sunday motorists.'

'Doesn't matter. It's lovely to see you,' said Imogen.

She had wondered if he'd look less glamorous out of tennis things, like sailors out of uniform, but he looked even better, wearing a scarlet shirt which set off his suntan, and jeans which clung to his lean muscular hips even more tightly than Juliet's.

'Come in here,' she muttered, going towards the drawing-room. Nicky stepped forward to open the door for her, reaching the handle the same time as she did, letting his hand linger on hers far longer than necessary.

'Would you like a glass of sherry?' she said. 'It's quite dry.'

'I'd prefer beer, if you've got some. I'm supposed to be in training.'

'I'll go and get it. Won't be a second.'

'Don't be, I'll miss you,' said Nicky, picking up the paper and turning to the sports page.

Imogen rushed into the kitchen. Fortunately there were six Long Life in the fridge.

'How's it going?' said Juliet, dropping broccoli spears into boiling water.

'I don't know,' said Imogen rushing out, nearly falling over Homer. 'Promise you won't leave me alone with him too long.'

'What I like about this house is its relaxed atmosphere,' said Juliet.

'Nastase won at Hamburg,' said Nicky, putting down the paper and taking the can and a glass from Imogen.

'Do you know him?'

'Yes, he's a great mate of mine.'

He walked over to the french windows.

'This is a lovely house.'

'It's a bit scruffy,' said Imogen, acutely aware of the worn carpets, the cat-shredded armchairs and the faded red cutains, which had shrunk in the wash and hung three inches above the window ledge.

Nicky, however, used to the impersonality of hotel bedrooms, only noticed the booklined walls, the friendly dog, the fat tabby cat asleep on the piles of music on top of the piano, the *Church Times* scrumpled up under the logs in the fireplace, waiting to be lit on a cold night, and the apple trees snowed under with blossom at the end of the garden.

'It's a family house,' he said. 'My father was in the army so I spent my childhood being humped from one married quarter to another. I always longed for a real home.'

He glanced across at Imogen, gazing at him with such compassion. He had also seen how deeply moved and delighted she'd been when he arrived. He was touched. He liked this solemn little girl with the huge eyes.

'You smell marvellous,' he said, moving towards her.

'It's not me, it's the carpet,' confessed Imogen.

There was a pause. What could she say next? If only she had the badinage and ready-made phrases like Juliet or Gloria.

'Lunch won't be long,' she stammered, as Nicky sat down on the sofa. 'Would you like some peanuts?'

'No thank you,' said Nicky softly, 'I want five

minutes alone with you. Come and sit beside me.'
He patted the sofa.

Imogen sat down. There was another pause.
She stared at her hands, aware that he was watching her. Then they both jumped out of their skin
as the large tabby cat leapt off the Beethoven
Sonatas on to the treble keys of the piano, and
proceeded to plink plonk his way down to the
bass clef, and walk with dignity out of the french
windows.

They both burst out laughing. It broke the ice.

'Was it a nice party, last night?' asked Imogen.

'How could it be? You weren't there,' said Nicky.
'I drank too much cheap wine, and nearly came and
broke up your whist drive.'

'I wish you had,' said Imogen wistfully. 'When
d'you go to Rome?'

'Tonight. I'm driving straight to Heathrow from
here. Might reach the quarter finals this year. I've
got an easy draw.'

And a friend of Nastase's too, thought Imogen.

'Doesn't it frighten you, so much success so early?'
she asked.

Nicky laughed softly with pleasure. She'd fed him
the right cue.

'I don't frighten easily,' he said, taking her hand
and spreading the fingers out on his thigh.

She heard a step outside and, terrified it might be
her father, snatched her hand away, but it was only
her mother in a crumpled flowered dress, smelling
faintly of mothballs, which she'd obviously just got

out of the drawer. There was also too much powder on one side of her nose.

'Mr Beresford, how nice to see you,' she said, teetering forward on uncomfortable and unfamiliar high heels. 'Has Imogen given you a drink? She's awfully forgetful.'

Oh God, thought Imogen, I do hope she's not going to be too embarrassing.

'She's looked after me beautifully,' said Nicky, as Mrs Brocklehurst helped herself to a glass of sherry, 'and I love your house.'

She was followed by Juliet, who sat on the piano stool, patting Homer and grinning at Nicky.

'Hi,' she said.

'That's a nice dog,' said Nicky. 'What's his name?'

'Homer,' said Juliet. 'Short for Homersexual. He's always mounting male dogs.'

'Really darling, that's not true,' said Mrs Brocklehurst mildly.

'Who plays the piano?' asked Nicky.

'I do,' said Juliet. 'I'm thinking of taking up the cello as my second instrument.' And next moment she was bombarding Nicky with questions about tennis stars. Was Nastase as difficult as everyone made out, and Stan Smith as dead-pan as he looked, and did Borg have lots of girls?

To have a better look at Nicky, Mrs Brocklehurst removed her spectacles, leaving a red mark on the bridge of her nose. Goodness, she thought, he really is a very good looking young man, and he seems nice too.

'What's Connors like?' said Juliet.

'Darling, poor Nicky,' remonstrated her mother. 'Give him a chance and go and mash the potatoes. Daddy'll be in in a minute. When did you first decide to become a tennis player?' she said to Nicky.

'When I was a child I used to go down to the courts at seven o'clock in the morning, hanging around hoping for a chance to play. Every time I seemed to get a rapport with a coach my father was posted somewhere else. I used to spend hours playing imaginary matches with myself hitting a ball against the garage door.'

'How splendid! I suppose if one wants to do anything badly enough in life, one usually does.'

'I like to think so,' said Nicky, shooting an unashamedly undressing glance in Imogen's direction, and rubbing his foot against hers behind the safety of an occasional table.

The vicar came in, rubbing his hands and looking quite benevolent, spectacles on his nose.

'Ah, good morning Nicholas. Lunch not ready yet? Preaching's thirsty work, you know.'

'It won't be a minute,' said his wife soothingly. 'Juliet's just doing the potatoes.'

'Is there time for a quick look round the garden?' asked Nicky.

'Of course,' said the vicar with alacrity. 'Bring your drink out.'

'What a nice young man,' said her mother.

'Unbelievable,' sighed Imogen.

There was an embarrassing moment before lunch.

'I expect you'd like a wash,' said the vicar, pointing to the door of the downstairs lavatory. He always liked male visitors in particular to go in there so they could admire his old England and Harlequin rugger groups hanging on the wall.

'I'm not sure there's any loo paper,' said Mrs Brocklehurst.

'There wasn't,' said Juliet, crossing the hall with the macaroni cheese, 'so I tore some pages out of the parish mag.'

Lunch, however, was a success. Nicky had two helpings of macaroni cheese which pleased Mrs Brocklehurst, talked at length to the vicar about the British Lions and regaled them with gossip about tennis players and the various celebrities he'd bumped into on the circuit.

'I'm afraid I'm talking too much,' he said.

'No, no,' said Mrs Brocklehurst eagerly. 'We lead such sheltered lives in Pikely. Fancy Virginia Wade reading Henry James between matches!'

'Have you really met Rod Stewart!' sighed Juliet.

The vicar surprisingly opened a second bottle of wine.

'I wish we could have wine at the Mothers' Union,' said Mrs Brocklehurst. 'It would make things so much less sticky.'

'What about hash rock cakes?' said Juliet, taking a slug of wine.

*   *   *

'Eat up, Imogen,' snapped the vicar. She was still struggling with her first helping. The food seemed to choke her.

'Picking away like a sparrow,' went on the vicar, his voice taking on a bullying tone, 'or more like a crow in that colour. I do wish young people wouldn't wear black.'

Imogen bit her lip.

'Bastard,' thought Nicky. He turned to the vicar. 'How d'you think England'll do against the West Indies?' That should keep the old bugger gassing for a few minutes. Out of the corner of his eye, he examined Imogen, mentally undressing her. He would take her later in the heather, and be very gentle and reassuring. He was certain she was a virgin.

'They ought to bring back Dexter,' the vicar was saying.

'Don't bother to finish, Imogen,' whispered her mother. 'I should clear if I were you.'

Thankfully Imogen gathered up the macaroni cheese and the plates. As she took Nicky's he stroked the back of her leg, the one farthest away from the vicar.

She went into the kitchen and, licking macaroni cheese off her fingers, dumped the plates in the sink. She picked up a drying-up cloth, bent down and opened the oven door. As she was just easing out the plum crumble, she heard a step behind her.

'Isn't he the most utterly fantastic man you've ever seen?' she murmured from the depths of the oven.

'Glad you think so,' said a husky voice behind

her. Appalled, she swung round. Nicky, holding a vegetable dish in each hand, was standing, laughing, in the doorway. The crumble was burning her through the drying-up cloth. She shoved it down on the kitchen table. Nicky put down the dishes and ran a finger caressingly down her cheek.

'Sweetheart, you must learn not to blush. It's terribly pretty, but it'll give you away to your unspeakable father.'

Imogen, terrified he'd try and kiss her when she tasted of macaroni cheese, hastily handed him the plates.

'We must go back.'

But Nicky waited in the doorway, holding the plates and still grinning at her. Imogen stared fixedly at the door hinge, where generations had cracked the paint screwing off the tops of refractory bottles.

'It'll get cold,' she stammered.

'I won't though,' said Nicky, and brushed her cheek with his lips as she scuttled past him.

'You've forgotten the plates,' snapped her father.

'I've got them,' said Nicky. 'Must say, I'm dying to sample Imogen's – er – pudding.' He winked at Juliet who giggled.

'Don't you get nervous before a big match?' she said.

'No.' He shot a glance in Imogen's direction. 'The suspense turns me on.'

'What's Goolagong like?' asked Juliet.

'Sweet; much prettier in the flesh.' Nicky poured cream thickly over his crumble. 'Always humming to herself and laughing if she does a good shot. She never knows what the score is.'

He then told them a story about one of the linesmen falling asleep in a big match. 'He'd had too good a lunch,' he went on. 'The crowd were quite hysterical with laughter.'

His eyes are as dark as pansies now, thought Imogen, trying to memorise every feature of his face. His hands were beautiful too, so brown and long-fingered. She suddenly felt quite weak with longing. Then she felt a gentle pressure against her ankle. It *must* be Homer rubbing against her, but he only begged during the meat courses. He was now stretched out in the sun under the window, twitching fluffy yellow paws in his sleep.

Nicky continued to talk quite calmly to her father, but the pressure against her ankle became more insistent.

'Good congregation?' he asked, draining his wine glass.

'Pretty good,' said the vicar.

He looks sensational in those jeans, thought Imogen. In spite of their tightness and, although he was sitting down, not an ounce of spare flesh billowed over the top. Her mind misted over; she didn't even hear Nicky asking her father what he had preached his sermon about, or her father replying:

'Ask Imogen, she was there.'

'What *was* it about?' asked Nicky, smiling wickedly at Imogen.

'What, sorry,' she said, startled.

'Wake up,' said her father.

'I'm sorry, I was thinking about something else.'

'Nicky wants to know what my – er – sermon was about.' There was a distinct edge to the vicar's voice.

She felt the blood rushing to her face; they were all looking at her now.

'Nicodemus,' muttered Juliet.

'Oh, yes,' stammered Imogen gratefully. 'The wind blowing where it listeth, and people who believe in God having everlasting life.'

With a shaking hand, she reached out for her wine, praying the storm was over.

Nicky looked at his watch.

'Good God, it's nearly quarter to three.'

'I've missed Gardener's Question Time,' said the vicar.

'I hope I haven't gone on too much,' said Nicky modestly, in the sure knowledge that he hadn't. 'If you care about something, you tend to bang on about it.'

'Oh, no,' said Mrs Brocklehurst. 'It's been fascinating, hasn't it, Stephen? We shall all enjoy Wimbledon so much more, having met you.'

'I must drive back to London soon,' said Nicky. 'But I wouldn't mind a walk on the moor first.' He increased the pressure of his foot on Imogen's ankle.

'I must write my Evensong sermon,' said the vicar regretfully, 'and someone's coming at four to borrow a dog collar for the Dramatic Society's play.'

'I must bath Homer,' said Juliet.

'Imogen will take you,' said Mrs Brocklehurst.

'That's what I hoped,' said Nicky, smiling at Imogen.

'Why has Imogen painted her eyelids bright green to go walking on the moors?' asked the vicar, as he helped his wife with the washing-up.

'I'm afraid she's fallen in love,' said Mrs Brocklehurst.

'She's for the moors and martyrdom,' muttered Juliet.

The wind had dropped since yesterday and, as they climbed up the moor, the hot sun had set the larks singing and was drawing them up the sky. The bracken uncurled pale green fingers. Lambs ran races and bleated for their mothers.

'Bit of a sod to you, your pa, isn't he?' said Nicky.

'He was disappointed I wasn't a boy,' said Imogen.

'Jesus, I'm bloody glad you're not.'

He slid an arm round her about six inches above the waist.

'Very, very glad,' he repeated, as his fingers encountered the underside of her breast. Imogen leapt away; they could still be seen from the house.

'Don't know if you're more frightened of me or him,' said Nicky.

'Oh, I don't feel at all the same way about you,' protested Imogen. 'It's just that I've never met a famous person before.'

Nicky laughed, 'I'll introduce you to lots more if you promise not to fancy them.'

Imogen, not nearly as fit as Nicky, was soon puffing. Fortunately, he did most of the talking. 'It's a lonely life being a tennis player. Here today, gone tomorrow – thousands of acquaintances, very few friends. Never in one place long enough to establish a proper relationship.' He gave a deep sigh.

Imogen, her perceptions a little blunted by wine at lunch, did not smile. She looked at him sympathetically.

'Will you think of me occasionally when you're beavering away in your little library?'

'Oh yes, all the time.'

'That's nice,' he said, taking her hand and pulling her down beside him in the heather. Close to, she smelt of toothpaste and clean shining hair – rather like his little nieces when they came downstairs after their baths to say goodnight, thought Nicky sentimentally. He raised Imogen's hand to his lips.

Across the valley, the khaki hillside was latticed with stone walls, the fells glowed a misty violet. You could just see the mill chimneys, a dingy shadow in the distance.

'Isn't it beautiful?' said Imogen, desperately trying to remain calm.

'Not nearly as beautiful as you are,' said Nicky. 'And your pulse, my darling,' he added, feeling her wrist, 'is going like the Charge of the Light Brigade. Do you believe in love at first sight?'

'I don't know,' stammered Imogen truthfully.

'Well, I do. The moment I saw you yesterday – pow – it happened, as though I'd been struck by a thunderbolt. I don't know what it is about you. But it's something indefinable, quite apart from being beautiful.' He put his arm round her, holding her tightly so she couldn't wriggle free. After a minute she ceased to resist and lay back.

All the sky seemed concentrated in those blue eyes and, as he kissed her, she felt the stalks of the heather sticking into her back. It was all so smooth, so practised, so different from the grabbing and fumbling of the few local boys who had made passes at her, that it was a few seconds before Imogen realised what was happening. Suddenly his hand had crept under her sweater and snapped open her bra, and her left breast fell warm and heavy into his other hand.

'No, no, Nicky! We mustn't.'

'Why not, sweetheart? Don't you like it?'

'Oh, yes! Yes, I do. But . . .'

'Well, hush then.'

He was kissing her again, and his free hand was inching up her thigh. Paralysis seemed to have set into her limbs. She was powerless to fight against him. Then suddenly a tremendous crashing in the bracken made them jump out of their skins. Rescue had appeared in the form of a large black labrador, which stood lolling its pink tongue, its tail beating frantically.

'Heavens,' said Imogen in a strangled voice. 'It's Dorothy!'

'Who's Dorothy?'

'The churchwarden's dog.'

'Which means the churchwarden must be in the vicinity,' said Nicky, smoothing his hair. The dog charged back into the bracken.

Horrified, Imogen wriggled back into her bra, which had ridden up, giving her four bosoms like a cow, and went and sat on a moss-covered rock a few yards away, gazing down into the valley. Beneath them, the churchwarden was taking his afternoon stroll. Far below she could see her father walking back and forth in the orchard memorising his sermon.

'I must be crazy,' she said, and buried her face in her hands. Nicky came over and put his arms round her.

'It's all right, love. All my fault. I just want you too much, and you want me, don't you?'

She nodded dumbly.

'But not in front of the whole parish, eh? We'll have to find somewhere more secluded next time.' He looked at his watch 'I must go now.'

'You will write to me, won't you?' he said as he slid into his sleek silver car.

Imogen didn't know if she could bear so much happiness and unhappiness in one day. Against the joy of his wanting her was the utter misery of his going away. Look thy last on all things lovely, she thought, her eyes filling with tears. Nicky rummaged about in the glove compartment. 'I've got something for you.' He handed her a small box and watched her bowed head and the incredulous smile on her pale lips as she opened it. She took out a red enamel bracelet, painted with yellow, blue and green flowers.

'But it's beautiful,' she gasped, sliding it on to her wrist. 'You shouldn't – I can't believe – no one's ever given me – I'll never take it off except in the bath. It's like a gipsy caravan,' she added, moving her wrist so the painted flowers flashed in the sunshine.

'That's because it's a present from a gipsy,' said Nicky, turning on the ignition. 'See you when I get back from Paris.' And, kissing her lightly on the lips, he drove off with a roar of exhaust which set the cat leaping in horror out of its comfortable bed of catmint on the edge of the drive.

Imogen, Nicky reflected without a flicker of conscience as he headed for the A1, had been far more delighted with the bracelet than his Mexican beauty, who, after a few shrieks of pleasure, had asked Nicky to keep the trinket for her, in case her husband noticed it and kicked up a fuss.

Chapter Three

Imogen couldn't wait to get to the library next morning and tell Gloria all about Nicky. Fortunately Miss Nugent had gone to the funeral, Mr Clough, her deputy, was still on holiday, and the only other senior, Mr Cornelius, was busy making a display of fishing rods, nets and flies in the main entrance to encourage readers to take out some of the new sporting books, so Gloria and Imogen more or less had the place to themselves.

'This is him,' said Imogen, opening the 1977 *World of Tennis Annual* and showing Gloria a photograph of Nicky stretching up, muscles rippling, to take a smash. 'And here he is again coming off court after beating Mark Cox.'

'Oh, I know him,' said Gloria, peering at the book. 'Seen him on telly playing at Wimbledon. Wasn't there some row because he threw his racket at a linesman?' She turned the book round to the light. 'He's certainly fantastic looking.'

'But so much better in the flesh,' said Imogen, dreamily putting a pile of romances on the non-fiction pile. 'He's got this way of looking at you, and

56

the husky way he drops his voice and says things that no one but you can hear. And then we went for this heavenly walk on the moors, and he said when he saw me it was like being struck down by a thunderbolt.'

'Did he try anything?' said Gloria.

Imogen blushed. 'Well he couldn't do much, because the churchwarden suddenly came round the corner walking his dog.'

Gloria looked at the photograph again, and then incredulously at Imogen, who was so unsophisticated. How could a man like Nicky possibly fancy her? She felt slightly irritated too – *she*, Gloria, was the one who had the adventures, Imogen the one who listened in awed amazement. She wasn't too keen on such role reversal.

'When are you going to see him again?' she said, picking out a Catherine Cookson novel and putting it aside to be repaired.

'Well, he's playing in tournaments most of the summer, but he said it'd be soon and in a more secluded place this time,' said Imogen, fingering her red bracelet. She was disappointed that Gloria wasn't more enthusiastic. Then she added humbly, 'But just think, Gloria, if you hadn't gone to Morecambe,' she looked round nervously, 'I mean, been struck down by shellfish, you'd have come down to the Tennis Club with me, and it would have been you he'd have fallen for instead.'

She suddenly felt faint with horror at the thought.

'Don't talk so daft,' said Gloria, patting her curls

and cheering up because, secretly, she agreed with Imogen.

'Anyway he's promised to write to me,' sighed Imogen. 'Oh, Gloria, you've no idea how beautiful he is.'

In fact Nicky proved an extremely bad correspondent. He sent her one postcard from Rome saying he wished she were there. Imogen wrote back by return of post, a long passionate letter which took her hours to compose, pouring her heart out with the aid of the *Oxford Dictionary of Quotations*.

The Rome tournament ended, and Imogen glowed with pride as she read in the paper that Nicky had reached the quarter finals, and then only been knocked out after a terrific fight. Then he moved on to Paris, working his way steadily down the singles draw, and even reaching the semi-finals of the men's doubles. Every paper commented on his improved game, but no letters arrived.

'He'll ring you when he gets back to England,' said Juliet soothingly. But Imogen was in despair. It had all been a dream, probably her last letter had been too soppy and put him off. What right anyway had anyone as dull and fat as she to expect Nicky to fancy her? She couldn't eat, she couldn't sleep, and mooned around in her room playing the gramophone and reading love poems. Nicky had turned out her heart as one might scrabble through an old chest of drawers throwing everything into confusion.

On the third Monday after their first meeting, Imogen walked to work in despair. There had been no letter on Saturday and, after an interminable 48 hours' wait, no letter this morning. She daren't ring up home to see if anything had arrived mid-morning in case she got her father yet again. She was on until eight this evening; she wondered how she'd ever get through the day. Her black gloom, if anything, was intensified by the beauty of the day. A slight breeze had set the new grass waving and catching the light; cow parsley frothed along the verges, white candles still lit the darkening chestnuts, and the hawthorns, exploding like rockets, gave off a soapy sexy smell in the warm sun. It was all so bridal, rioting and voluptuous. She was glad to reach the narrow streets of Pikely with their blackened houses and dingy mill chimneys, and escape into the cool gloom of the library.

She was met by Miss Nugent in a maroon dress and a foul temper.

'You're ten minutes late. There's two trolleys of books to be shelved. You didn't finish half those withdrawal forms on Saturday, and you sent the Mayor an overdue notice when he returned the books weeks ago. It's not good enough, you know. There are plenty of others who'd like your job.'

'Can't say I know any,' muttered Gloria, whisking up in yellow shorts and a tight chocolate brown sweater and dumping a pile of books on the trolley. 'The old bag's on the warpath this morning,' she whispered to Imogen. 'No one can do a thing right. Old Cornelius should have been back from his holiday, but he sent her a cable saying: "Stranded in

Gib." I expect he's fallen for one of the monkeys. Did you get a letter?'

Imogen shook her head.

'That's a shame,' said Gloria, with all the enthusiasm of the secretly relieved. 'Don't fret, all men are lousy letter writers. I went to a terrific party on Saturday night. Tony Lightband was there; he really fancies you. He wants me to fix up a foursome.'

'That's nice,' said Imogen, failing to sound enthusiastic. Tony Lightband was five foot three, wore spectacles thick as the bottom of beer bottles, and was inflated with his own importance.

'Clough's back from his hols, looks lovely and brown,' said Gloria.

'Will you girls stop gossiping?' snapped Miss Nugent, bustling out of the inside office. 'And turn off the lights, Imogen, or Mr Brighouse will be over in a flash complaining about his rates.'

The day got progressively worse. Imogen didn't seem to be able to do a thing right. Even the sky began to cloud over.

It was early afternoon. Imogen was on the request desk, answering queries, finding books for people. Miss Nugent had also given her the least favourite task in the library of chasing up unreturned books.

'Lady Jacintha's had the new Dick Francis six weeks,' she said, handing Imogen the list, 'and Brigadier Simmonds has still got the Slim biography, and you must get on to Mrs Heseltine at once. She's got twelve books out, including *The Wombles in Danger* and *Andy Pandy*. I want the whole lot dealt with today. Tick them off as you telephone.'

'Yes, Miss Nugent,' said Imogen listlessly.

Miss Nugent relented a little. The last thing she wanted was to bully Imogen into giving in her notice.

'I only keep on at you because I think you're worth taking trouble with,' she said, offering Imogen a Polo. 'There's no point bothering with Gloria. She'll just go off and get married. But you've got the makings of a good librarian. Have you thought any more about taking the library diploma? You'll miss it this year if you don't sign on soon. It's always a good idea to have a training if you can't bank on finding a hubby.'

Imogen knew Miss Nugent meant it kindly, but it only made her feel more depressed.

'How's it going?' said Gloria half an hour later.

'Awful,' said Imogen. 'Brigadier Simmonds would like to court-martial me; Mrs Heseltine keeps pretending to be the Spanish *au pair* and not understanding, and Lady Jacintha's butler obviously has no intention of passing on the message.'

'Nugent always gives you the lousy jobs. Look, why don't we go to the pictures tomorrow night?'

This was a great concession, Imogen realised. Gloria didn't believe in wasting evenings on girl-friends.

'I can't. I've got to go to my first aid class,' she said gloomily.

'Don't say Nugent's pressganged you into that.'

Imogen nodded. 'We're doing the kiss of life tomorrow. I do hope Mr Blount doesn't use me as the model. Finish me off altogether.'

'I say,' said Gloria, lowering her voice, 'Judy Brighouse's just been in and taken out *Understanding Cystitis*. She only came back from her honeymoon last night. Bet they've been at it all the time. Oo, look, he's back.'

A good-looking man in a green velvet jacket came through the swing doors and up to the desk. 'I think I left Richard Strauss behind,' he said.

'You did,' said Gloria, giving him the book and the benefit of one of her hot stripping glances, which sent him crashing back against the doors, nearly falling over the fire bucket on the way.

'It says pull, not push,' said Gloria, smirking at the effect she'd had on him. 'Wish he'd try and pull me. He's lovely.'

'No good to you, lass,' said Mr Clough, on his way to a NALGO meeting. 'He's on his third marriage, and he's already got four children to support.' He turned to Imogen. 'Tell your Dad I've just got that gardening book in. If he'd like a quick look before we put it into circulation he can keep it until Wednesday.'

'There's something rather attractive about Cloughie,' said Gloria, shoving a couple of requested books into a side shelf. 'Here's just the thing for you, Imogen: *How to Stop Feeling Depressed and Inadequate*.'

'I *am* inadequate,' sighed Imogen.

'Oh come on,' said Gloria. 'Do cheer up. We don't want you dripping over everyone like a Chinese water torture all week.'

A man in dungarees came reeling up to the desk. 'Where can I find books on starting one's own business?' he said.

'Over there,' said Gloria, adding in an undertone, 'Absolutely reeked of drink, didn't he?'

'Expect he's just been fired,' said Imogen. 'Oh look, Mr Passmore's fallen asleep over the *Financial Times*.'

'No one's allowed to sleep in a library,' said Gloria. 'It's in the by-laws. Go and wake him up.'

'Telephone, Gloria,' said Miss Nugent, bustling up. 'Reader with a query. It's come through in my office. Can you go and man the issue desk, Imogen? Miss Hockney's gone to tea and there's a queue waiting.'

Gathering up her papers, Imogen went and sat down at the desk at the entrance of the library and began to check people's books in. Once she'd dealt with the queue she went back to her overdue list. Susan Bridges had kept *Colloquial German* and *Scaling the Matterhorn* out since February, when she met that Austrian ski instructor. She picked up the telephone and dialled Miss Bridges's number, but there was no answer – probably at work. She looked at the pile of cards in front of her. '*If you have returned the books in the last few days, please ignore this letter.*' The words blurred before her eyes.

Outside the sky was darkening. Oh Nicky, Nicky, she thought desperately, will I ever see you again? She looked at the red bracelet on her wrist, tracing the pattern of the flowers with her finger, shivering at the memory of that day on the moor.

'Thus have I had thee, as a dream doth flatter,

In sleep a king, but, waking, no such matter,' she whispered sadly. Nicky was the black Rowntree's fruit gum everyone wanted. How ridiculous to think that he could ever have fancied her for more than a moment.

She was so deep in thought she didn't see a large bad-tempered woman in a trilby with a snarling boxer on a lead, until they'd come pounding through the door.

Imogen steeled herself for a fight.

'I'm terribly sorry, you can't bring dogs in here.'

'Where am I supposed to leave him?' snapped the woman.

'There are dog hooks provided outside the door. You could tie him to one of those.'

'He'd howl the place down and break his lead. It's not safe in this traffic. I've come all the way from Skipton. I'll only take five minutes.'

'I'm sorry,' said Imogen nervously. 'Shall I hold him for you?'

She advanced towards the dog, which bared its teeth and growled ominously. She backed away.

'Have your hand off,' said its owner. 'Now are you going to let me in, or do you want me to go over your head?'

Imogen had a lunatic vision of the woman and dog taking off and flying over her head through the room.

'I'm sorry. Dogs simply aren't allowed,' she repeated.

'I need the books for my work. I'll complain to the council. I've got fines on all these books.'

Imogen looked hopelessly round for help. Miss Nugent had disappeared, Gloria was on the telephone, Miss Hockney was surreptitiously making wedding lists on the request desk.

'If we allowed one dog in, we'd have to let the whole lot,' she said firmly.

'That's what's wrong with this country,' snapped the woman, straightening her trilby and storming through the doors. 'Bloody civil servant,' she shouted back at Imogen.

'I must not cry,' said Imogen, gritting her teeth. 'I must not drip like a Chinese water torture.'

'I say,' said Gloria, rushing up and patting her hair, 'that Richard Strauss man in the velvet jacket's just phoned up from a call box and asked me out. Goodness, what's up with you?'

'A woman with a boxer just called me a bloody civil servant.'

'Old cow, she's not allowed to swear in a library, it's in the by-laws too, and anyway we're not civil servants, we're local government officers.' She switched back to the Richard Strauss man. 'He didn't even know my name, just asked for the "glamorous one",' she said, squinting at her reflection in the glass door. 'Didn't think I was looking very good today either.'

Imogen went wearily back to her overdue postcards, laboriously filling in the computer number of each book.

'I say,' breathed Gloria, 'get a load of him.'

'Don't bother me,' said Imogen. 'I've got to finish these beastly things. Anyway I'm not interested in men any more.'

'You'll be interested in this,' said Gloria faintly.

'No I won't ever again. My life is over,' said Imogen. Then a familiar husky voice said very softly:

'Have you got a book called *"Would the Assistant Like to Come out to Lunch"*?'

Imogen looked up and gave an unbelieving cry. For there, resplendent in a white suit and dark blue shirt, was Nicky. She gave a whimper and a gasp and, getting clumsily to her feet, ran round her desk and crashed into him, burying her face in his shoulder.

'I can't believe it,' she said, her voice thick with tears.

'Hey, hey,' said Nicky, lifting her chin with his finger, and smiling down at her. 'There's no need to cry, little one. I said I'd come back, didn't I?'

'I didn't think I'd ever see you again.'

'Didn't you get my postcard?'

'Yes, I did. It was lovely.'

Nicky shook his head. 'Oh ye of little faith,' he said gently and, well aware that there was now a gaping audience, including Miss Nugent, watching him, he bent his head and kissed her lingeringly.

'But what are you doing here?' said Imogen, wiping away her tears with the back of her hand, 'I thought you were in Edinburgh.'

'Got a walkover. Chap I'm playing pulled a muscle. Wants to rest it for Wimbledon. I don't have to play till tomorrow afternoon. Can I have a bed for the night, preferably yours?'

Imogen laughed joyfully, 'Of course you can. I'll ring Mummy. The only problem is the boys have been home for half term, so the place'll be in a bit of a shambles.'

Nicky was stroking her face now, tenderly smoothing away a smudge of mascara with his thumb. 'Can you get out for some lunch now?' he said softly.

Imogen eyed a disapproving and approaching Miss Nugent.

'Not really. I've already eaten and I'm on till eight. Oh, isn't it a drag?'

'Well, that works out quite well,' said Nicky. 'I'll go and have a work-out down at the club, and then I've got to do a short interview for Yorkshire Television. This afternoon seemed a good opportunity. I'll be through by eight. I'll come and pick you up and we'll go and have dinner somewhere.'

'But I'm not dressed for it,' wailed Imogen, conscious of her old grey sweater and jeans.

'You look beautiful,' said Nicky who only noticed how her grey eyes shone at the sight of him and how the stitches of the old sweater gaped over her bosom and how, with no make-up on, she looked about fourteen. 'You could never look anything else.'

There was a disapproving cough behind them. Nicky turned a dazzling smile on Miss Nugent.

'You must be Imogen's boss,' he said. 'I've heard so much about you.'

He was so lovely to everyone thought Imogen as she introduced him. Miss Nugent was now patting her crenellated curls, and simpering like a schoolgirl. Even Miss Hockney had put down her shopping list. Gloria was smouldering so hard she'd burst into flames any minute.

'Would you like a cup of tea?' she said.

Nicky shook his head. 'I must get down to the club.'

Outside the swing doors he kissed Imogen again.

'It's been a very long three weeks,' he said. 'I'm glad you're still wearing my bracelet.'

Funny, he thought, as he drove down the High Street, how pleased he was to see her. If Painter hadn't nagged him about not winning his bet, he doubted if he'd have bothered to look her up again. But now he had he was glad. He felt all the satisfaction of a dog with a number of bones buried round the garden, who suddenly unearths one unexpectedly and discovers it's matured much better than he had hoped.

He'd liked to have taken her straight up on to the moors and screwed her now, but he didn't particularly want to cover his new suit with grass stains before the interview. Anyway, there'd be plenty of time tonight, and it'd be more of a turn on pulling her under the old vicar's nose.

It was quite an achievement washing oneself from top to toe with gritty soap and a face towel in the ladies at the library but Imogen managed it. She also nipped across the road and bought a new pair of black pants which cut into her. And now she was sitting in the Dog and Duck enveloped in a cloud of Gloria's *Babe* being eyed by Pikely locals, drinking champagne with Nicky and wondering if she'd ever been happier in her life.

'This is the first champagne I've had this year,' she said.

'Then you must wish,' said Nicky.

Imogen shut her eyes, and took a gulp. 'Oh please,' she wished silently, 'give me Nicky.'

Nicky laughed and kissed her cheek. 'You'll get me if you play your cards right,' he said.

'How did you know what I was wishing?'

'You're totally transparent. That's what I like about you.'

'Did you think Gloria was pretty,' said Imogen wistfully.

'Who's she?'

'The sexy one in yellow shorts who offered you a cup of tea.'

'Didn't notice her, but then I only have eyes for you.' He filled up her glass. As they worked their way down the bottle he told her about Rome and

Paris, but she was so longing and longing to have his arms round her again, and yet panicking where it would all lead to, she could hardly concentrate.

'And what have you been up to?' he said, ordering another bottle.

'Nothing really.'

She told him about Juliet having to write out the 23rd Psalm ten times for saying bugger. But she didn't really think he'd be very interested in hearing about the second-hand book stall she had to organise for the church fête in aid of a new spire, and even spires seemed so phallic at the moment.

'How is your dear father? Still on the one day week?' said Nicky.

Imogen giggled and knew she shouldn't.

'Oh come on, darling, you know he's a pig.'

'Only to me,' said Imogen.

Nicky emptied the remains of the first bottle into her glass.

'Who's at home this evening?' he said carefully.

'No one,' said Imogen without thinking. 'Juliet's staying the night with a friend, and Mummy and Daddy are taking the boys back and stopping for dinner with the vicar of Long Preston.'

Nicky picked up the unopened bottle of champagne.

'Let's go then.'

Outside it was pouring with rain, street lamp reflections quivering in the cobbled streets. People huddled in the dorway of the fish shop. The smell of frying fat wafted towards them.

'Are you hungry?' asked Nicky.

'No,' said Imogen.

The powerful headlamps of his car lit up the cow parsley flattened by the deluge. The rain rattled against the windscreen. In the light from the dashboard she could see Nicky's profile.

'I went for that drop shot at the right moment,' he was saying. 'I was beginning to get the right length, and make friends with the ball again.'

A vast pile of unopened letters and cables were scattered on the back seat. 'Goodness, you get a lot of post,' said Imogen. 'It's last week's fan mail,' said Nicky.

As he swung up the moorland road leading to the vicarage, he put his hand on her thigh, caressing her through the thick stiff material. She lifted her legs slightly off the seat, hoping to make them seem thinner.

The house was dark and empty except for Homer who welcomed them ecstatically, charging off upstairs and, returning with a pair of old grey pants Imogen had been wearing yesterday, deposited them at Nicky's feet.

'Extraordinary pants,' said Nicky. 'Not yours, are they?'

'Goodness, no,' lied Imogen. 'They're probably jumble.'

'Look as though they belonged to your grandmother,' said Nicky. 'Go and get a couple of glasses, sweetheart.'

As Imogen threw the offending pants into the

dustbin, she heard the champagne cork pop. She felt like a gas fire that had been left on unlit for too long – Nicky's touch would be like a lit match, making her explode in a great gushing blue flame, singeing everything around including Homer's eyebrows.

They sat drinking on the sofa. Nicky had turned off all the lights except one lamp in the corner. She was shaking with nerves again, quite unable to meet his eye.

'It's been awfully wet the last few weeks,' she said.

'It's been awfully dry abroad,' said Nicky, picking up the bottle.

'No,' squeaked Imogen putting her hand over her glass.

'Don't be silly,' said Nicky, so the champagne trickled through her fingers, and spilled icy cold down her sleeve, meeting the rivulets of sweat that were coming the other way. Desperate for something to do, she drained her glass and felt slightly dizzy.

'Let's get down to business,' said Nicky and took her in his arms. 'You like me, don't you?'

'Oh, yes,' she stammered, 'I haven't thought about anything else for a single minute since we met.'

She was achingly aware of him, his mouth over hers, his hands in her hair.

'Come on,' he whispered. 'Let's go upstairs, much more comfortable. We've got hours of time. Homer will bark if anyone comes.'

'Not at Daddy and Mummy, he won't.'

'They won't even have started dinner yet.'

Imogen gazed up at Nicky with huge troubled eyes.

'It'd kill my father.'

'Hooray,' said Nicky. 'I'll come and sell tickets at his funeral.'

Imogen tried and failed to look shocked. He put his hands round her waist. She came towards him, dissolving into him. He moved his hand under her sweater, and closed it over her breast.

Imogen started to struggle.

'It'd be so awful,' she muttered, 'if I got pregnant.'

'You're not fixed up?' he asked sharply. 'When are you due?'

Imogen swallowed. She'd never discussed things like this with a man. 'Tomorrow or the next day.'

'No problem,' said Nicky, relaxing, launching into the attack again. 'That's why your tits are so fantastic at the moment.'

She was glad to be able to hide her embarrassment in his shoulder. Now she felt his hand on her back. She'd never known anyone with such warm hands. Next moment he'd slipped it under her jeans, and was stroking her bottom.

'You must stop,' gasped Imogen as he pushed her back on the sofa, and removed her sweater. 'I've never done it with anybody before,' she said, emerging from the fluff.

'I'm not just anybody,' said Nicky. 'And you can't

stop, sweetheart, any more than I can.' Oh, help, thought Imogen, what's happening to me. But next minute she froze with horror as the back door opened and Homer bounded out with a crash.

'Yoo hoo,' said a voice. 'Anyone at home?'

'*Ker-ist*,' said Nicky, then with incredible presence of mind he seized Imogen's sweater, turned it right-way out and pulled it over her head.

'Keep cool,' he murmured, kicking her bra under the sofa and tucking in his shirt.

'We're in here,' he called.

'Hullo Nicky,' said her mother, walking into the room carrying a large marrow. 'Hullo darling, what a beastly night. Isn't it a shame, poor Mrs Westley's got shingles? They tried to ring us but we'd already left. We didn't stop to dinner, and came straight home. They gave us this.' She waved the marrow. 'Daddy's putting the car away.'

'Well, have some champagne to cheer you up,' said Nicky.

Imogen rushed off to get more glasses, her heart hammering, feeling quite faint with horror. Just think if her father had found her and Nicky at it on the floor, in front of Homer too, she thought with an hysterical giggle. Thank God it was her mother who'd come in first.

As she went back into the drawing-room she heard her mother asking Nicky, 'Do you think there's any hope of Virginia Woolf winning Wimbledon?'

The rest of Nicky's visit was disastrous. They'd all gone to bed early and Nicky had whispered to

Imogen on the stairs, '*Courage, ma brave*. As soon as all's quiet on the West Riding Front, I'll creep along to your room.'

But alas, the vicar, suffering from one of his periodic bouts of insomnia, had decided to sleep – or rather not sleep – in his dressing-room, which was equidistant between Imogen's room and the spare room. There he lay with the light on and the door ajar, pretending to read Donne's sermons, but actually brooding on former glories, a row of silver cups on the chest of drawers and framed pictures of muscular men with folded arms round the wall.

Imogen lay shivering with terror in bed. And every time Nicky tried to steal down the passage, the vicar, who had ears on elastic, called out, 'Is that you, my dear?' So Nicky had to bolt into the lavatory. By one o'clock, mindful that he might rot up his chances in the Scottish Open tomorrow, he gave up and fell into a dreamless sleep. Imogen, who didn't sleep at all, could hardly bear to look at his sulky face next morning.

'Well that was a lead balloon, wasn't it?' he said, getting into his car. Tears filled Imogen's eyes. This was obviously good-bye for good. Then, noticing the violet shadows under the brimming eyes, Nicky relented. It wasn't her fault. If the vicar hadn't come home unexpectedly, she'd have dropped like a ripe plum into his hands. 'You couldn't help it. I shall be much freer once the American Open's over. Would your parents ever let you come away for a week-end?'

Imogen shook her head. 'I doubt it.'

'Have you got any holiday left?'

'A fortnight in September.'

'Anything planned?'

'No – nothing really.'

How few girls would have admitted it, thought Nicky, taking her hand. She was as transparent and as wholesome as Pears Soap.

'Well the only answer's to go on holiday together then.'

All heaven seemed to open. 'Oh, how lovely!' gasped Imogen. Then it closed again. 'But my father would never allow it.'

'H'm . . . we'll see about that.'

Chapter Four

A fortnight later, during Wimbledon week, Nicky
had a drink with his friend Matthew O'Connor in
Fleet Street. He had known O'Connor on and off for
a number of years. They bumped into each other
abroad – Nicky playing in tournaments, O'Connor
covering stories – and they had got drunk together
and been slung out of more foreign nightclubs than
they cared to remember.

'Are you going to France this year?' said Nicky.

'In September. Why?'

'Any room in your car?'

The big Irishman looked at him shrewdly. 'Depends
who you want to bring.'

Nicky grinned. 'Well, I met this bird in Yorkshire.'

'What's she like?'

'Got a pair of knockers you can get lost in.'

'What else?'

'Well she's adorable, like a puppy. You want to
pick her up and cuddle her all the time. But terribly
naïve. Dad's a vicar and a bloody tartar – like that
Mr Barrett of Walpole Street.'

O'Connor grinned. 'And you see yourself as Robert Browning?'

'Well something of the sort. Anyway, I can't get within necking distance on home ground.'

'Green is she? So you fancy an away fixture?'

'An away fixture is what I fancy.'

O'Connor ordered another round of drinks.

'I've always believed,' he said, 'that if a bird's worth doing, she's worth doing well. But a fortnight's a hell of a long time. Don't you think you better take her away for a week-end first?'

'I've got tournaments every week-end for the next two months. Besides I doubt if the old vicar would let her.'

'Well, he's not likely to let her go on holiday, is he?'

'He might. I can say we're going in a large party. Parents seem to have some totally mistaken idea that there's safety in numbers.'

'Will she fight with Cable?' asked O'Connor.

'You've never allowed me to meet Cable.'

'No more I haven't. Come and have a drink with us this evening.'

The next day Nicky wrote to Imogen's parents. He was planning to go to France for a fortnight in September with a couple of friends who were engaged, and there would also be another married couple in the party taking their own car. He'd thought Imogen was looking tired last time he'd stayed. She needed a holiday. Could she join their party?

To Imogen's joy and amazement her parents agreed. Even her mother had noticed how down she was, and her father, who was looking forward to his three weeks' exchange stint in the North Riding in September (the golf course was excellent there), had no desire to have his elder daughter slopping around with a February face spoiling the fun.

'I'll never, never be unhappy again,' vowed Imogen. She dialled Nicky's number in London to give him the good news.

All the same, it was a very trying summer. Wimbledon fortnight came, and Imogen and Gloria spent most of it with the transistor on or with a pair of binoculars surreptitiously trained on the television in the Radio Rentals shop opposite the library. Nicky was in coruscating form, reaching the last eight of the singles and only being knocked out after a marathon match, and the semi-finals of the doubles with Charlie Painter. Everyone commented on his improved game. And whenever he appeared on the television screen, clothed in white tennis clothes, mystic, wonderful, whether he was uncoiling like a whiplash when serving or jumping from foot to foot as though the court were red hot beneath his feet, waiting to whistle back a shot, he seemed a God infinitely beyond Imogen's reach.

She had also seen him in the players' stand, laughing with some of the more beautiful wives. Nor could she miss the way the tennis groupies (pert little girls with snake hips and avid eyes) made every match he played a one-sided affair by screaming with joy whenever he did a good shot, even cheering his opponent's double faults, and mobbing him every time he came off court. Could this really be the man who'd eaten her mother's macaroni cheese and wrestled with her on the sofa?

After Wimbledon he moved on to ritzy places all over the world and Imogen found that a diet of almost illiterate postcards and occasional crackling telephone calls was not really enough to sustain her. Oh ye of little faith, she kept telling herself sternly, but found herself increasingly suffering from moodiness and then feeling desperately ashamed of herself.

Even worse, everyone at work, having glimpsed Nicky and learnt they were going on holiday together, had turned the affair into a sort of office *Crossroads*. Not a day passed without someone asking her if she'd heard from him, or how long was it until her holiday, or how was he getting on in Indianapolis. Gloria's attitude was ambiguous too. On the one hand she liked to boast, when out, of how her greatest friend Imogen was going out with a tennis star, and let slip crumbs of tennis gossip passed on by Imogen. But on the other she was wildly jealous, particularly when the word got round and several of the local wolves started coming into the library asking Imogen for dates.

'They ought to provide wolf hooks as well as dog hooks outside,' Gloria said, with a slight edge to her voice. 'Then they wouldn't be able to come in here pestering you.'

Stung by Gloria's sniping (You shouldn't put all your eggs in one basket. I bet Nicky's playing round with all those foreign birds), Imogen gritted her teeth and went out with one or two of the wolves. But when the evening ended, remembering Nicky's beautiful curling mouth, and the caressing deftness of his touch, she couldn't even bear to let them kiss her; then felt mean when they stormed off into the night.

Finally, the weather had been terrible. Throughout July, August and early September, it deluged without stopping. The River Darrow flooded the water meadows and the tennis courts, and endangered the lives of several flocks of sheep. Imogen's hair crinkled depressingly, and she had absolutely no chance to brown her pallid body before her holiday. And the vicar, whose garden and golf had been almost washed away, was in a permanently foul mood and vented most of his rage on Imogen.

At last September arrived. By scrimping every penny, she'd managed to save a hundred pounds. Nicky had told her not to worry about money, that he'd take care of everything, but she knew France was terribly expensive, and she wanted to pay her way. As most of her wages went towards the housekeeping, it didn't leave much for her wardrobe.

'What am I going to do about beach clothes?' she said.

'You won't need much in a small fishing village,' said her mother. 'Which reminds me, Lady Jacintha sent a lovely red bathing dress for jumble. Red's in this year, isn't it? It's perfect, except for a bit of moth in the seat.'

The jumble was also deprived of two of Lady Jacintha's wide-bottomed cotton trousers, which didn't really fit, but Imogen thought she could pull long sweaters over them. Her mother bought her two kaftans in a sale in Leeds.

'This phrase book isn't much good,' said Juliet, lounging on Imogen's bed the night before she left. ' "My coachman has been struck by lightning," "Please ask the chambermaid to bring some more candles." I ask you!'

Imogen wasn't listening. She was trying on Lady J's red bathing dress for the hundredth time and wondering if it would do.

'My legs are like the bottom half of a twinset and pearls,' she sighed.

'You ought to get a bikini. Bet it's topless down there,' said Juliet. 'I think Mummy and Daddy are so funny.'

'Why?' said Imogen, folding up a dress.

'Thinking you'll be safe because you've got a married couple in the party to chaperone you. Ha! Ha! To egg you on more likely. I hope you're on the pill!'

'What on earth do you mean?' snapped Imogen.

'Well, you won't be able to hold off a man like Nicky once he gets you in France.'

'Don't be ridiculous,' said Imogen, storming out of the room.

But it was all too near the knuckle. Nicky's last letter – the only one he hadn't written on a postcard – had ended . . . *and, darling, for goodness sake go and get yourself fitted up. We don't want to spoil the whole fortnight worrying about you getting pregnant.*

Time and again during the past month Imogen had walked up and down in front of Dr Meadows' surgery, and each time she had funked it. Dr Meadows was one of her father's oldest friends and well over sixty. How *could* she ask him?

In the end, once more egged on by Gloria, she had gone to a family planning clinic in Leeds on the pretext of looking for holiday clothes. Unfortunately her two brothers, Michael and Sam, still home for the holidays, had insisted on coming with her, in the hope of catching a Gillette Cup match at Headingley. But this, predictably, had been rained off, and Imogen had great difficulty shaking them off, even for a couple of hours.

'I've got to buy lots of boring things like underwear,' she said.

'We'll come too,' said Sam, who at fourteen had only recently become interested in girls. 'We might be able to see into some of the changing rooms.'

'I don't like people hanging round when I'm buying clothes,' said Imogen quickly. 'It muddles me. Look, here's a fiver. Why don't you go and see the new James Bond? I'll meet you at the barrier at five o'clock,' and, blushing violently, she charged through the glass doors of Brown and Muff. Rushing straight through and out the other side, she set off at a trot towards the clinic.

'Where's old Imo really going?' said Sam, as they shuffled off to the cinema.

'F.P.A.,' said Michael, who was concentrating on lighting a cigarette in the rain.

'Blimey, is she pregnant?'

'Course not, just getting fixed up before her holiday.'

'How d'you know?'

'Left the address lying around in her bedroom.' He began to cough. The cigarette went out.

'Hope to Christ Dad doesn't find it,' said Sam. 'Fancy old Imo getting round to sex at last.'

'Just as well she's taking precautions. They're randy buggers these tennis players, even worse than rugger players.' Michael's cigarette, sodden now, obstinately refused to be lit. 'I hope she'll be all right, won't get hurt I mean,' he went on, throwing it into the gutter.

'Do her good to grow up,' said Sam, who was staring at a couple of giggling typists who, under one umbrella, were teetering by on high heels, heading towards the pub. 'I say, shall we skip James Bond and go and have a drink instead?'

'They'd never serve us.'

'It's pretty dark in there; you'd pass for eighteen anywhere. Fancy old Imo going on the pill.'

*　　*　　*

'Buy anything good?' said Sam innocently, as Imogen came rushing up to the barrier with only a few minutes to spare.

'I'd forgotten the sales were on. There's nothing nice in the shops,' stammered Imogen, failing to meet either of her brothers' eyes.

'Got your ticket?' said Michael, waving his. 'We'd better step on it; they're closing the doors.'

'Oh goodness,' said Imogen, 'I've got it somewhere.'

And as she was nervously rummaging, her shaking hands slipped, and the entire contents of her bag, including six months' supply of the pill crashed on to the platform.

'I wonder if scarlet women are called scarlet because they blush so much,' said Sam, bending down to help Imogen pick everything up.

And now on the eve of her holiday, the mauve packets of the pill were safely tucked into the pocket of her old school coat hanging at the back of her wardrobe. She'd been taking it for eight days now, and she felt sick all the time, but she wasn't sure if it was side effects or nervousness at the thought of seeing Nicky. It was such ages since their last meeting she felt she'd almost burnt herself out with longing. Then she was worried about the sex side. She'd been taking surreptitious glances at *The Joy of Sex* when the library was quiet, and the whole thing seemed terribly complicated. Did one have to stop talking during the performance like a tennis match, and wouldn't Nicky, accustomed to lithe, beautiful, female tennis players, find her much too fat?

She put her hot forehead against the bathroom window. In the garden she could see her father talking to the cat and staking some yellow dahlias beaten down by the rain and wind.

'That's what I need,' she thought wistfully. 'I'll never blossom properly in life unless I'm tied to a strong sturdy stake.'

She wondered if Nicky was really stake material. Her father was coming in now. He looked tired. He'd been closeted with members of his flock all afternoon.

She went back to her room and found Homer dispiritedly pulling her underwear out of her suitcase. He hated people going away. 'I'll be back soon,' she said, hugging him.

She also packed a pile of big paperbacks she'd never got round to reading, *Daniel Deronda, Lark Rise To Candleford*, Scott Fitzgerald and *Tristram Shandy*. On the bed lay a box of tissues (they don't have the kind of loo paper you can take your make up off with in France, Miss Hockney had told her), a cellophane bag of cotton wool balls and a matching set of Goya's *Passport* she had won in the church fête raffle. They didn't look very inspiring as beauty aids. She imagined Nicky's other girlfriends with the whole of Helena Rubinstein at their disposal.

There was a knock on the door. It was her mother. 'Hullo darling, how are you getting on? Daddy wants a quick word before he goes down to the jumble sale pricing committee.'

As she went into the vicar's study, Imogen started to shake. He was sitting behind his huge desk, lighting his pipe, a few raindrops still gleaming on his thick grey hair. All round him the shelves were filled with Greek and theological books, which the vicar never looked at, and gardening and sporting works which were much more heavily thumbed. On one ledge were neatly stacked volumes of the *Church Times* and the parish magazine. On the wall the vicar allowed himself one modest photograph of himself surrounded by the England team. On the desk was a large inkwell. He despised biros.

Now he was looking at her over his spectacles. Was his jaundiced air due to the fact she'd been wearing the same skirt and sweater all week to save her best clothes for France, or was he remembering all the countless times he'd called her in to lecture her about inglorious reports, or misbehaviour at home?

'Sit down,' he said. 'Are you looking forward to your holiday?'

'Yes,' said Imogen.

'Wish I'd been lucky enough to gallivant off to the sun when I was your age,' he went on heavily, 'but times were harder then.'

Oh God thought Imogen, he's not going to start on that one.

But instead her father got to his feet and began to

pace the room. 'I don't think your mother and I have ever been oppressive parents – we've always tried to guide you by example rather than coercion.' He gave her the chilly on-off smile he used for keeping his parishioners at a distance. His flock-off smile Michael and Juliet always called it.

'But I can't let you depart without a few words of advice. You are going to a foreign country – where there will be temptations. I trust you follow me, Imogen.'

'Yes,' she whispered.

'We are letting you go because we trust you. We know Nicky is an attractive young man, and a celebrity, used to getting his own way in life, but we still trust you.'

He stopped by the window, absent-mindedly stripping yellow leaves off a geranium on the ledge, testing its earth for sufficient moisture.

'It's been a trying afternoon,' he went on. 'Molly Bates and her daughter Jennifer were here for over an hour. Poor Molly. Jennifer suddenly revealed she was three months pregnant and the young man concerned has disappeared. Of course every attempt will be made to trace him and persuade him to marry the girl, but if not, she will spend the next months in an unmarried mothers' home – not the most attractive of dwelling places – but Molly Bates feels, as a member of the Parochial Church Council, that Jennifer cannot have the child at home. Whatever the outcome, the girl's life is ruined. She is second-hand goods now.'

Poor Jennifer, thought Imogen, perhaps she'll be sent off to the jumble sale.

'When you're in the South of France,' said her father, 'remember the fate of poor Jennifer Bates and remember you're a clergyman's daughter, and they, like Caesar's wife, must be above suspicion.'

Imogen had a momentary fantasy that the packets of purple pills must at this moment be burning a hole in her old coat pocket, that her father's outrage was like the sun on glass. Fortunately he construed her crimson face as embarrassment at the topic of conversation rather than guilt.

He sat down and moved the inkwell on the desk. 'Remember the words of Milton,' he said in sepulchral tones, 'She that has chastity is clad in complete steel.'

Imogen suddenly had a vision of herself clanking around the beach in the South of France in a steel suit of armour. Her father, she decided, must have been very much like Milton. She also suspected that he was rehearsing his sermon for next Sunday. She had a horrible feeling that he was going to make her kneel down and pray over her.

'You are entering the school of life,' he said, dropping his voice dramatically. 'All I can do is pray for you night and day. Now go back to your packing and have a wonderful holiday in the sun. I must away to the jumble pricing committee.'

The contrast between her gadding, sybaritic existence and his modest, selfless toil was only too obvious. Imogen went out of the room, closing the door quietly behind her. She went upstairs feeling hopelessly depressed. Her father had brilliantly succeeded in taking all the excitement out of her holiday. Sex with Nicky would be even more of a moral battlefield than ever. Whatever she did, bed or not, her father would be standing at the bottom of her bed in spirit, shaking his finger at her.

Oh hell, it was time to have the pill, lying in its little capsule like one of the lights round an actress's mirror. She felt like Persephone about to take her pomegranate seed and be condemned to an eternity in Hades.

She shut her bedroom door and started groping through her half-empty wardrobe to find the thickness of her old tweed coat at the back. She couldn't find it. She pushed aside the rest of the clothes; it wasn't there, not even slid off its hanger on to the floor. She burrowed frantically through the landing cupboard, then ran downstairs. Her mother was peeling potatoes and reading a novel at the same time.

'My old school coat, it's gone,' gasped Imogen.

'Surely you're not taking that to France?' said her mother.

'No, but where is it?'

'I gave it to the jumble, darling. As we'd taken out Lady Jacintha's bathing dress and those trousers I thought it was the least we could do.'

But Imogen had gone, out of the house like a rocket, belting down the garden path, slipping on the wet pavement, tearing along the moorland path, bracken slapping against her stockings, twigs scratching her face.

The coat had her name in it, the pocket contained the pills and Nicky's last letter, the one about getting fitted up and telling her most explicitly all the delicious things he was going to do to her when he got her to France. Visions of what her father would do swept over her. He'd stop her going. Suddenly the thought of not seeing Nicky again filled her with such horror she thought she'd faint. Her breath was coming in great sobs.

There was the church hall, light, laced with raindrops, streaming from its uncurtained windows. Inside Imogen found scenes of tremendous activity and was nearly knocked sideways by the smell of moth balls, dust and none too clean clothes. Ladies of the parish in felt hats stood round laden trestle tables, rooting through other people's cast-offs, searching for possible bargains, subtly pricing down garments they pretended they didn't know had been sent in by fellow sorters.

'I don't think she's even bothered to launder these corsets,' said the butcher's wife, dropping them disdainfully into the nearest bin. 'And this hostess gown is quite rotted under the armpits.'

'Lady Jacintha has sent in a fox fur without any tail,' said the local midwife. 'Rats, rats,' she added, waving it at the caretaker's cat, who, giving her a wide berth, leapt on to a pile of old books and records.

'Hullo, Imogen love,' said the butcher's wife.

'Come to lend a hand? I thought you were off on your holidays tomorrow.'

'I am,' said Imogen, frantically searching round for the piles of coats.

'If you're looking for your Dad, he's over there.'

Imogen peered through the dusty gloom and froze with horror. In the far corner, in front of a long freckled mirror, Miss Jarrold from the Post Office was trying on Imogen's school coat, which came down to her ankles, and being encouraged on either side by Mrs Connolly, her mother's daily woman, and the vicar.

'There's still some wear in it,' Miss Jarrold was saying. 'I could get my sister from Malham to turn it up.'

'Oh very becoming, Miss Jarrold,' the vicar was saying jovially. He had his hearty 'flock-off' smile on again.

'Not sure about the colour, Elsie,' said Mrs Connolly. 'It never did anything for Miss Imogen either.'

'I'm only going to use it for gardening and walks, seems a bargain for 50p,' said Miss Jarrold, and turning back to the mirror, she adopted a model girl's stance, shoving her hands into the pockets. 'Oh look, there's something inside.'

Imogen was across the room in a flash, just as Miss Jarrold pulled the purple packets and Nicky's letter out of the pockets.

'Whatever's all this?' she went on.

'They're mine,' said Imogen, snatching them from her.

Miss Jarrold was so startled she stepped back with a resounding crack on some 78s of the Mikado.

'Imogen,' thundered the vicar, 'where are your manners, and what have you got there?'

'Nothing,' she muttered, going as red as a GPO van.

'Love letters and photos,' said Mrs Connolly calmly, who disliked the vicar intensely, and had seen exactly what was inside the pocket. 'No girl likes to lose those, do they, love? Oh look, there's Lady Harris at the door. I expect she wants to discuss the refreshments with you, vicar.'

'Ah, yes, indeed. Welcome, welcome,' said Mr Brocklehurst in a ringing voice, finishing off the Mikado altogether as he went towards the door.

For a minute Imogen and Mrs Connolly looked at each other.

'Thanks,' stammered Imogen. 'That was terribly kind.'

'Better to be safe than sorry,' said Mrs Connolly. 'My Connie's been on them things for years. I'd beat it if I were you, before your Dad has second thoughts. Have a nice time. 'Spect you'll come back brown as a berry.'

'Seems in a hurry,' said Miss Jarrold innocently. 'Is she courting?'

'Happen she is,' said Mrs Connolly, who knew perfectly well Miss Jarrold read all the cards that came through the Post Office. 'She hasn't told me owt about it at any rate.'

*   *   *

The last few hours were a torment, but at last Imogen was on the train to London, her small suitcase on the rack. Her mother, Juliet and Homer, drooping and looking gloomy, stood on the platform. Suddenly Imogen felt a great lump in her throat. 'I'm sorry I've been so awful and boring the last few weeks. I'll make it up to you, really I will,' she said, leaning out of the window. 'I wish you were coming too.'

'We'll all miss you,' said her mother.

'Don't forget to send me a card,' said Juliet.

'Be careful about drinking the water,' said her mother.

'Remember chastity begins and *ends* at home,' said Juliet. 'Here's something to read on the train,' handing her a parcel as the train drew out. In it were copies of the *Kama Sutra* and *The Sun is my Undoing*.

Gradually the dark stone walls, the mill chimneys, the black-grimed houses, the rows of washing and dirty white hens in the gardens were left behind. She was on her way.

Chapter Five

An hour and a half from London she started doing
her face. Half an hour away she decided she looked
awful and took all her make-up off and put it on
again. The new, very cheap dress, ivy green with a
white collar, which had looked so pretty when she'd
tried it on in the shop, was now crumpled like an
old dishcloth. Her new tights were making spiral
staircases round her ankles. The train drew into
King's Cross. Imogen was one of the first off, pushing her way through the crowd, radiant smile at the
ready like a British Railways' ad. She had lived
this moment so often in her mind. People rushed
forward to kiss people and gather up their suitcases.
No one came forward to claim her. The kissers
dispersed and still no Nicky. She was sure she'd told
him she was arriving on the eight-thirty train.

The station clock jerked agonisingly round to
nine-ten. Two drunken sailors lurched up to her and
lurched away when they saw the frozen expression
on her face. She struggled not to cry.

Then, like an Angel of Mercy, loping aross the
station, in the same white suit and an orange shirt,

came Nicky. 'Darling, sweet love! God, I'm sorry. What can I say? There's the most God-awful traffic jam in Piccadilly. Are you all right? Has half London been trying to pick you up?'

'Oh,' said Imogen, half-laughing, half-crying, 'I'm so, so pleased to see you.'

As he kissed her, he smelt of drink and, she thought, of scent. Perhaps it was her own scent, new yesterday, which she wasn't yet used to.

'Come on,' he said, picking up her suitcase.

In the taxi he took her hand. Imogen was too besotted to realise the roads were quite clear.

'We're going straight to Matt and Cable's, the people we're going to France with. You'll like them. He's a lunatic Irish journalist and she's a model.'

'A model?' Imogen tugged surreptitiously at her wrinkled stockings. She hoped she wasn't too glamorous. Then she remembered with relief, 'Oh, but they're the engaged couple.'

'Well, not engaged exactly, just co-habiting. But I had to bend the facts a bit to reassure your father.'

They arrived at a huge block of flats. Imogen was disappointed Nicky didn't kiss her. There would have been plenty of time as the lift climbed to the tenth floor. Instead he smoothed his hair in the lift mirror. There was no answer when he rang the door bell, so he pushed open the door and shouted, 'Anyone at home?'

Footsteps came from the back of the flat, a waft of scent flooded the hall. 'Darlings! You've arrived,' said a girl in a light drawling voice. 'How are you?'

Her red dress was slit to the thighs. Her lips were as crimson as her painted toe nails, which peeped out of high black sandals. She had delicate cat-like features, sly, slanting eyes the colour of watercress and carefully tousled inky-black hair snaking down her back. Except for her suntan she might have stepped out of a Beardsley drawing. There was something serpentine, too, in the way she coiled herself round Nicky, kissing him on the cheek and murmuring:

'Darling, marvellous to see you.'

'Imogen, this is Cable,' he said, disengaging himself too slowly for Imogen's liking. The girl stared at Imogen incredulously for a minute and then a slow smile spread over her face. 'Welcome to London,' she said. 'Did you have a good journey? I've been packing since dawn and I'm completely exhausted. Where's your luggage?'

Nicky held up Imogen's dog-eared suitcase.

'Heavens,' said Cable. 'Is that all? Matt will adore you. I've filled three suitcases already and he's griping about my taking a fourth. Come and have a drink.'

'Can I go to the loo?' said Imogen, who didn't want to, but was desperate to repair her face before Nicky could compare her any more with this ravishing creature.

'Down the passage on the left,' said Cable. 'We'll be in here. Do you think five bikinis will be enough, Nicky?'

What price Lady J's motheaten red bathing dress

97

now? thought Imogen savagely as she combed the
tangles out of her hair. Her face was all eyes in a
for-once pale face. She pinched some of Cable's
rouge, but it made her look like a clown so she
rubbed it off again.

She found Nicky and Cable in a room where
everything seemed scarlet – carpet, curtains, and
every inch of wall that wasn't covered by books
and pictures. Even the piano was painted red, and in
one corner stood a huge stuffed bear wearing a
scarlet regimental jacket.

'Oh, what a heavenly room,' sighed Imogen.

Cable looked at her with surprise. 'Do you think
so? Matt's taste – not mine. He'd been here a year
when I moved in, so the damage was done. It's hell
to keep tidy,' she added, pointing to the papers
billowing out of the desk, and the piles of books and
magazines on every available surface.

In one chair sprawled a basset hound who
thumped his tail but made no effort to get up, and
on the sofa, snoring gently, lay a very big, very long
man.

'He was playing poker all night,' said Cable sourly.
'He's been lying there since he came in at half-past
eleven this morning.' She kicked him, none too
gently, in the ribs. 'Come on, Sloblomov, wake up.'

The man groaned and pulled a cushion over his
face.

'He even sleeps standing up,' said Cable. 'I've
seen him at parties propped on one leg like a horse,
patiently waiting to be led home to his stable.'

The man removed the cushion and opened a bloodshot eye. 'Stop beefing for God's sake. I'm on my holiday. I'm entitled to kip if I want to.'

'Not when we've got company,' said Cable.

He opened the other eye. 'Hullo, kids,' he said, and yawned without bothering to put his hand over his mouth.

Imogen was astounded that such a beautiful girl should go for such an ugly man. He had battered features, a very sallow skin, dark heavy-lidded eyes that turned down at the corners, and a streaky blond mane, much in need of a cut. He got up and shook himself like a dog. Beside Nicky's gleaming beauty he looked thoroughly seedy. She also had a vague feeling she'd seen him before.

'How are you, Nicky boy?' he said.

'He needs a drink,' said Cable. 'We all do.'

'Well, run along and get me some Alka Seltzer.'

'You do look a bit rough,' said Nicky. 'Did you make a killing last night?'

Matt drew a large wad of notes out of his hip pocket.

'It'll buy us a few snails,' he said.

Nicky grinned. 'I'll go and help Cable with the ice.'

'Bring the evening paper with you,' Matt shouted after him. 'I want to see what won the three-thirty.'

He turned to Imogen, looked her over lazily and gave her a surprisingly attractive smile. 'Just come from Leeds, and covered in coal-dust are you? I went there once, a terrible dirty place it was. I thought I'd been misrouted to Hell.'

Imogen giggled. 'The part where we live is very pretty. I like your flat.'

'Come and look at the view.' He went over to the window and drew back the curtains. All London glittered before them.

'There's Big Ben, Westminster Abbey, the Shell Building. On a clear day you can see Margaret Thatcher.' He had a nice voice, too, thought Imogen, leisurely, with a faint trace of Irish. Perhaps he wasn't so ugly after all – just different-looking from other people. She was still trying to work out where she'd seen him before.

'Now, what are you drinking, beauty? Whisky, gin, anything you like.'

'Oh, whisky, please, with masses of water.' She sat on the arm of the dog's chair and stroked his ears. 'What's his name?'

'Basil. Never get a basset hound; they rule your life.'

'You can say that again,' said Cable, coming in with Nicky and the ice tray. 'There's a ton of rump steak for him in the fridge while we're away.'

'It's not his stomach that bothers me,' said Matt, dropping five Alka Seltzers into a glass of water and watching them fizz, 'it's his soul. I think I'll get Father O'Malley to visit him while we're away. Did my proofs arrive?' he added to Cable.

'About an hour ago. They're over there on the table. They said you could telephone any corrections through tonight.'

Matt half-emptied his glass and grimaced. Then he

picked up some long narrow sheets of newsprint from the table and began to examine them.

'Who've you taken apart this week?' said Nicky.

'The medical profession,' said Matt, 'and they're not going to like it.' He picked up a biro, added one word and crossed a couple out.

Suddenly Imogen twigged. 'You're not *the* Matthew O'Connor?'

Matt looked up. 'I'm not entirely sure today.'

'But you're marvellous,' stammered Imogen. 'I loved your book on Parnell. There's still a waiting list at the library. And I always read your pieces in the paper. We all do – even my father thinks you're funny.'

'And that really is saying something,' said Nicky. 'Not given much to giggling is our vicar.'

'Well, that is nice,' said Cable with a slight edge to her voice. 'You've got a fan at last, Matt. Aren't you lucky?'

'Very,' said Matt, seeing Imogen flush and giving her a reassuring smile. 'It's manna to my ears, darling.'

'I suppose you two'll be rabbiting on about Proust all the way to Provence,' said Cable.

'It'd make a nice change,' said Matt.

Imogen couldn't believe it. Nicky and Matthew O'Connor in the same party as her. Any moment she expected Jackie Kennedy or Mick Jagger to pop out of the grandfather clock.

'What time do we leave tomorrow?' asked Nicky.

'The boat sails at eleven. We ought to leave the house by eight,' said Matt.

For a while they discussed arrangements; then Imogen's stomach gave a great rumble and Nicky said that he was hungry.

'I could cook something,' said Cable, as though it were a rare occurrence.

'I'm not having you slaving over a hot tin opener all night,' said Matt, who had picked up the evening paper. He gave an exclamation of pleasure.

'The little darling – she won by three lengths, romped all the way home like a child off to a party. Come on, my angels, on the strength of that, I'll buy you all dinner.'

They piled into a large, incredibly dirty, white Mercedes.

'You might have had it cleaned before we left,' grumbled Cable. Imogen found she was sitting on a bridle. They ate in a little Italian restaurant and drank a good deal of wine. Nicky talked about his tennis exploits, grumbling how political the game was getting these days. Matt asked the questions; he had a journalist's ability to get an incredible amount of information out of people without their realising it. Every place Nicky had played at, Cable seemed to have been there too, filming or modelling, which produced the inevitable questions about 'Did you meet the so-and-so's?' and 'Have they split up yet?'

Imogen didn't say much; she was too busy taking it all in. But there was a bad moment when Nicky suddenly put his hand on her thigh and she jumped so much that her fork fell on to the floor, taking most of her spaghetti with it. Nicky was insane with irritation, but Matt just laughed and ordered her some more. He was very funny throughout dinner and Imogen found herself liking him more and more.

Cable she was less sure of – sitting there picking at her food, examining her reflection in her spoon, looking at Nicky with those sly green eyes.

'Sophia Loren was in here last week,' she said, 'just sitting over there, wearing the most incredible plunging neckline.'

'I went to the gents fifteen times during dinner, just so I could look down it,' said Matt. 'I'll get the bill,' he said, seeing Imogen was nearly falling off her chair with exhaustion.

'It's only midnight,' said Cable. 'Can't we have some brandy?'

'Some of us who do a decent week's work get tired on Friday.'

'I work,' snapped Cable. 'I went to two cattle markets yesterday.'

'Any good?' asked Nicky.

'Second one might be. They're launching a new chewing gum. The bread's terrific. My agent's going to ring me in France and let me know.'

Matt handed the waiter what seemed an inordinate number of notes. 'A cattle market is a model's audition,' he explained to Imogen. 'Very appropriate, too, when you see some of the cows that turn up. Come on, let's go.'

There was another bad moment when they got back to the flat. Cable had opened the door of one of the bedrooms, and said, 'You and Nicky are in here.'

Oh, my goodness, thought Imogen, her mind racing like a weasel in a trap. Did Matt see her expression of dismay? Five minutes before he had been yawning his head off; now he suddenly asked Nicky and Cable if they wanted a night-cap.

'I wouldn't mind,' said Nicky. He ruffled Imogen's hair. 'Go to bed, love. I'll be with you in a minute.'

But an hour and a bottle of brandy later, when he went to bed, he found Imogen fast asleep with the light on, *Tristram Shandy* still open on the pillow and Basil sprawled beside her.

'Bloody dog,' he said, trying to push Basil off. The dog gave an ominous growl.

'Foiled again,' said Matt sympathetically. 'You'll never shift him now he's pitted down for the night. I'll give you an eiderdown and you can kip on the sofa.'

Chapter Six

A gale was lashing the rain against the windows when they woke next morning. Nicky was moaning about his hangover and the rotten night he'd spent. Matt and Cable were having a row.

'Next time you shave your legs with my razor for God's sake wash it out. Now for the fourth time, may I take the cases down to the car?'

'I'm not ready,' snapped Cable, putting on a second layer of mascara.

'Look, baby, it's ten past eight. I'm leaving in five minutes, with or without you!'

'Oh, don't go on,' said Cable, her voice rising. 'Have you hidden my jewellery?'

'Yes – in the window box.'

'Well, take these three cases down – at least it'll give you something to do.'

The front door slammed.

'Nickee!' called Cable.

'Yes, love?'

'I can't shut my suitcase.'

Imogen, who had been sitting about feeling spare for the last half hour, wandered along to

105

Cable's bedroom to see if she could help.

Nicky and Cable, who was wearing the most ravishing pink suede suit, were sitting side by side on the suitcase.

'That's it,' said Nicky, leaning across Cable and clicking the second flap down.

Imogen froze in the doorway as she saw Cable put her hand over Nicky's. Nicky looked up at Cable and smiled. 'You'd better lock it,' he said slowly. 'I wouldn't like you to lose anything valuable – to anyone else!'

'I'm so glad you're coming with us,' purred Cable. 'It makes everything so much more – well – exciting.'

Imogen didn't know which of them jumped the most when Matt's voice behind her said, 'A quick worker, isn't she? She'll have you tied in knots if you're not careful, Nicky.'

For a minute Cable glared at Matt, and then, to Imogen's amazement, she burst out laughing.

'Darling Sloblomov,' she said, wrinkling her nose at him. 'You don't let me get away with a thing, do you?'

In that pink suit, thought Imogen wistfully, she was so lovely she could get away with murder. Matt grinned reluctantly, picked up the long khaki scarf that was lying on the bed and wound it round Cable's neck, pulling it tight and pretending to throttle her. 'So sweet were ne'er so fatal,' he said. 'Come on, Circe, let's go.'

'Bloody English weather,' grumbled Nicky.

'At least it might wash the car,' said Matt.

They had only been driving ten minutes when Cable gave a shriek.

'My night cream. It's still in the fridge!'

'Well, I expect Basil will be having it on his strawberries,' said Matt calmly.

'Don't be bloody silly,' snapped Cable. 'We must go back.'

'Look, baby, you've kept us hanging about for twenty minutes already.'

'But my skin will dry up.'

'Why don't you dry up?'

Imogen gazed in trepidation at Cable's rigid profile. Was Nicky really keen on her, or just flattered by her attentions? As if in answer Nicky put an arm round Imogen's shoulders. 'All right, sweetheart? Excited?'

When he looked at her like that, she was incapable of answering. She just nodded and snuggled against him.

'Who are the couple we're joining at Dover?' he asked Matt.

'Cable's chums,' said Matt. 'I disclaim all responsibility.'

'Very funny,' said Cable, darting a venomous glance at him. 'Actually, they're an awfully sweet couple.'

'Which puts the kiss of death on them,' said Matt.

'Will you shut up! They're called Edgworth, James and Yvonne Edgworth. James is very straight and does something with shares in the City. She's a very well known model. You'll recognise her face.'

Oh God, sighed Imogen, another model. I hope she doesn't run after Nicky too.

The weather grew worse and worse. The traffic was appalling too. They nearly missed the ferry and were the last to drive into the vast cellar at the bottom of the boat which housed all the cars.

'Why are you looking so sour, Matt?' asked Cable petulantly.

'As we were last on we shall be last off. And as we're booked into an hotel a hundred miles south of Paris, you're unlikely to get any dinner tonight.'

A sailor advanced on him waving a chamois leather.

'No, I don't want my car washed,' he said and stalked upstairs. Cable grinned at Nicky. 'We're meeting James and Yvonne in the bar,' she said. Unable to see in her dark glasses she stumbled over a step. Nicky caught her elbow, stopping her falling, and leaving his hand on her arm far too long for Imogen's liking.

'God, the English dress badly,' he said, as they walked along the deck. Imogen pulled her sweater further down over her ill-fitting trousers.

'Cable, darling!' shrieked a voice, as they went into the bar.

'Yvonne, angel!'

'We thought you'd missed the boat!'

'We nearly did!'

'Terrific hat!'

'Fantastic shoes!'

'Stunning suit!'

'You've changed your hair!'

After screeching at each other for some minutes like a couple of parakeets, they remembered the rest of the party. Yvonne, Imogen decided with relief, wasn't half as dangerous as Cable. It must be the inspired ordinariness of her features – china blue eyes, curly red hair and dimples – that made her such a success as a model. She would automatically have the creamiest margarine, the whitest wash and the steaming hot milk drink ever on the boil for the homecoming husband. She was wearing a grey trouser suit and a spotless white blouse, with an embroidered '30s couple tangoing over her bosom.

'You must be Matt,' she said, flashing her teeth at Nicky. 'Cable's told me so much about you, but she never said how good-looking you were.'

Cable looked put out. 'This is Nicky Beresford,' she said sharply.

'Of course,' giggled Yvonne. 'How silly of me. I've seen you playing at Wimbledon.'

'This is Matt,' said Cable.

'Oh,' said Yvonne, looking up at Matt rather dubiously. 'Awfully pleased to meet you. This is my Jumbo.'

James Edgworth had the rosy complexion, puffed out cheeks and curly hair of cherubs that blow the wind at the corner of old maps. He was small, plump, and wore a yachting cap and a look of eager expectancy.

'Let's have a drink,' said Nicky.

'Tomato juice for me,' said Yvonne.

'Pity to waste it when it's duty free,' said Nicky, giving her one of his hard, sexy looks.

'Oh, well, if you twist my arm I'll have a Babycham,' said Yvonne.

Everyone else had double brandies.

'This is jolly, just like going on an away match,' said James Edgworth.

'How many bikinis did you bring, Cable?' asked Yvonne.

Nicky was busy converting English money into francs on the back of a sick bag.

'You're going to need that bag,' said Matt, 'when you realise how low the rate of exchange is.'

Two giggling teenagers sidled up to Nicky. 'Could we possibly have your autograph?'

Everyone was gaping at them. Not surprising, thought Imogen, they were easily the noisiest, most glamorous group on the boat. She hoped she wasn't letting the side down.

'I say,' said James happily, 'it's beginning to get choppy.'

The boat, having left the harbour, was bucking like a bronco. Every few minutes the windows were entirely covered by angry grey water. Imogen's stomach began to heave. All the chairs in the bar, she noticed, were chained to the floor. On her right, James, Cable and Nicky were talking about people she didn't know, so she idly listened to Yvonne attempting to chat up Matt.

'You write for the papers, don't you? Rather fun, I should think. I was rather good at English at school. They all said I should take up writing.'

Matt looked at her. 'It would have been tragic to deprive the modelling world,' he said drily.

Imogen suppressed a smile.

'That's what I thought,' said Yvonne. 'Now I just write Jumbo's speeches.'

'His speeches?'

'Didn't you know?' She bared her teeth like the wolf in Red Riding Hood. 'James is prospective candidate for Cockfosters. He's awfully busy at the moment, but if you ask him nicely, I'm sure he'd spare the time to give you an interview for your paper.'

'I'll remember that,' said Matt.

'Mind you,' said Yvonne, 'I do think the articles you write are rather – well – exaggerated.'

'In what way?' said Matt, his eyes narrowing.

'Well that piece last week on Northern Ireland. I mean I didn't finish it, and I know all journalists sensationalise things for the sake of circulation . . .'

'Go on,' said Matt, an ominous note creeping into his voice.

'Well I do think it's rather disloyal to write things like that.'

'Disloyal to whom? Those men had been tortured. One young boy committed suicide rather than take any more.'

'These things happen,' said Yvonne. 'But surely it's better not to make too much fuss? It only stirs

111

up hatred and makes things difficult for the poor soldiers. To be quite honest, I can't stand the way you Irish come over here and take our jobs and use our Health service, and then say beastly things about us.'

'Whenever I come across atrocities I write "beastly things" about them,' snapped Matt.

'Now, you mustn't get uptight,' said Yvonne reprovingly. 'I bet you didn't have any breakfast. Why not have a matchstick?' she added, producing a polythene bag of cut up carrots from her hold-all. 'Veggies don't put on an ounce of weight. Do have one.'

Imogen didn't stay to hear Matt's reply.

'I must get some air,' she gasped, staggering across the bar. It was better outside. She clung to the rails and the spray lashed her face. Down below, the sea was writhing and foaming. Two minutes later Matt joined her. His face was olive green.

'God! Cable does pick them,' he groaned.

'She thought she was bringing you out.'

'In a nervous rash most likely.'

'I'm sure she's awfully good as a model.'

'Forces grey in, you mean. The only thing she could sell is packaged nausea.'

'Are you all right?' asked Imogen anxiously. The olive green was now tinged with grey.

'I'll manage. Be back in a second,' and he practically hurled himself over the edge of the boat.

'Oh, poor, poor thing,' she said, when he came back.

He grinned weakly. 'There goes yesterday's dinner and tea. At least I've ruined their rotten boat.'

Imogen was amazed at his stoicism, particularly when he added a moment later, 'You mustn't let Cable upset you.'

Imogen flushed. 'I wasn't! I mean, I like her very much.'

'She's only flirting with Nicky to annoy me,' he said. 'She does it with any attractive man who comes along.'

'But whatever for?'

'She's trying to pressure me to marry her.'

'Don't you want to?'

He shrugged his shoulders. 'I'm a Catholic, if somewhat lapsed. I'm supposed to try to marry for good. I can put up with a free range mistress, but not a free range wife.'

'She'd probably settle down once you married her,' said Imogen.

'Perhaps. Oh, my God,' he muttered, turning green again. 'Here goes yesterday's breakfast.'

She had never known anyone could be so seasick. Each time he returned, more white and shaking, to her side. In the middle Cable had the gall to saunter up and put a proprietorial hand over his: 'We're going to have some lunch, darling. See you later. Isn't Yvonne nice?'

'Adorable,' said Matt. 'I'm just wondering how I'm going to kill her.'

At last they sighted Boulogne, hanging in a mist of

seagulls, its cranes jabbing the sky. They were now joined by the rest of the party, bumptious from duty-free drink, and clutching their packets of duty-free cigarettes.

'Hullo,' said Cable. 'You do look peaky, darling. Do you like my new scent?' and she thrust her wrist under Matt's nose.

The skies were overcast as the boat drew in and it was still raining. A few fat Frenchmen in blue overalls and berets were waiting on the quay. Goodness, they look very English, thought Imogen, and the weather's just like Yorkshire.

'Shall I drive?' asked Nicky as they got back into the car.

Matt shook his head. 'It'll take my mind off my stomach.'

'Imogen looks rather grey. She'd better go in the front,' said Cable, nipping into the back beside Nicky.

The Mercedes was soon eating up the miles. So this is France, thought Imogen. Great avenues of poplars, cornfields stretching to infinity, incredibly ugly towns with their peeling Dubonnet posters and gaudy gardens like seed packets. There was no one in the streets. Perhaps they were all making fantastic French love behind those closed shutters.

'The First World War was fought all over here,' Matt told her. 'Most of the old houses were razed to the ground. That's why the villages are so new and hideous. Have you read *Goodbye to All That*?'

Imogen shook her head.

'Marvellous book. I've got a copy in my case. I'll lend it to you.'

'I couldn't get beyond the first page,' said Cable.

'Too many long words for you,' said Matt, 'and no pictures.'

'Oh, don't be so effing superior,' snapped Cable.

'There are still plenty of unexploded bombs in the fields,' said Matt, ignoring her.

And plenty inside the car too, thought Imogen. Nicky and Cable chattered away, the names dropping like autumn leaves. But finally even they fell quiet. Glancing round, Imogen saw that Cable was asleep, her head on Nicky's shoulder. She looked away quickly, trying desperately not to mind. If Matt saw anything through the driving mirror he took no notice.

The rain had stopped and a few stars were trying to peer through the veil of cloud as they reached their hotel. It stood on the edge of a river, festooned with bright pink geraniums and creepers trailing down into the water. The attractive mademoiselle behind the desk seemed delighted to see Matt again. But she looked aghast when James and Yvonne came through the door. There was much hand-waving and shoulder-shrugging, and Matt came over looking rueful.

'Sorry, loves, my crazy secretary's only booked two double rooms instead of three.'

'That's OK,' said Cable. 'We're all whacked. Yvonne and Imogen and I can shack down in one double bed. You three can have the other.'

Matt looked relieved. 'If that's all right with every-one else?'

Imogen nodded. Another day's reprieve – she wasn't up to a sexual marathon with Nicky tonight.

'Rather a lark,' said James Edgworth. 'Just like the dorm at school.'

Yvonne's face, however, was working like milk coming up to the boil.

'But that's absurd. Jumbo and I are married.'

'We all know that, baby,' said Matt.

'Don't call me "baby"!' Yvonne stamped her foot. 'I've had an exhausting day. I don't see why I should suffer merely because you've made a hash of things.'

Her eyes brimmed with tears. James patted her shoulder gingerly. 'Don't cry, dear. Matt, would you mind awfully if we had one double room?'

Matt looked at Nicky, who nodded.

'Right you are, James; anything to oblige. Nicky and I can kip in the car. Dinner in quarter of an hour then.'

'I'm not going to change if I've got to use these clothes as pyjamas,' said Nicky.

Up in the bedroom Cable got out her heated rollers.

'I don't think Matt and Yvonne are going to hit it off,' she said happily. 'Do you know, she's filled a whole suitcase with packets of All-Bran to keep James regular?'

116

Chapter Seven

Imogen felt absolutely knackered. She longed to soak in a hot bath, and spend ages tarting up and putting on something sensational. But she had nothing sensational to put on, and she felt far too fat and cumbersome to undress and change in front of Cable. With all Cable's suitcases and bottles of make-up, there wasn't really room enough for them both anyway. Besides, if she got down early she might snatch a few moments alone with Nicky, so she contented herself with a quick wash and brush-up.

'If Matt's belly-aching, tell him I won't be long,' said Cable who was now wandering about the bedroom totally naked, except for a green silk scarf holding her rollers in.

Imogen averted her eyes and fled. Was modesty perhaps a question of fatness, she wondered. If she looked as marvellous as that, perhaps she'd wander around with no clothes on. On the landing she found Yvonne, wearing a pink plastic cape round her shoulders to protect her clothes from make-up, and brandishing a hairdryer at a nervous looking maid.

'You speak English, don't you?'

'Oui, Madame.'

'Then why don't you speak it, instead of standing there talking in a foreign language? I want the plug on this dryer exchanged at once.'

Imogen slunk past them. No one was about in the hall. She looked at the menu in the glass case, her mouth watering. The kitchen was wafting beguiling smells of garlic, wine and herbs from its warm interior. She went into the lounge and sat down with *Tristram Shandy*. An English family nearby whispered as though they were at a funeral, and gloomily lifted the brass hats on their *café filtrés*. On her table a vase of mauve and salmon pink gladioli clashed horribly with each other and even worse with the tartan table cloth. Odd that the French, who were supposed to be so chic, should have so little colour sense.

She tried to read. It was really awful the way her concentration had gone to the wind since she met Nicky. She gazed out of the window where an orange street lamp lit up the poster of a forthcoming circus.

We're a bit like a travelling circus, she thought. James is one of those eager perky little dogs that jumps through hoops, and Yvonne is a trapeze artist, tough but dainty, tripping around with her feet turned out, and Nicky and Cable were like sleek beautiful wild animals, panthers or tigers, who kept escaping from their cages and disrupting the local community, and she was a small fat shaggy pony trying desperately to keep up with everyone. She was just trying to work out what Matt was, something large and friendly, when she jumped as she heard his voice saying, 'You'll never get yourself a drink that way, sweetheart. We're in the bar. What are you reading?' He picked up her book. 'Oh, that, never managed to get through it myself.'

They found Nicky sitting on a bar stool.

'Hullo, pet, what d'you want?' Matt and I are drinking Pernods.'

'That'd be lovely,' said Imogen, not having a clue what it was, some kind of alcoholic pear juice perhaps.

Matt ordered another round and dropped a packet of crisps into her lap.

'You must be starving.'

'You looked bushed too,' said Nicky, pouring water into the Pernod so it went cloudy like Dettol. 'Probably a good thing you're going to get a decent night's sleep tonight, but there'll be no holding me tomorrow,' he added, lowering his voice.

Imogen went pink, took a great slug of her drink, and nearly spat it out. It was unbelievably disgusting, like distilled liquorice allsorts. And she needed a drink so badly. She took another cautious sip and almost threw up.

Matt picked up a copy of *Le Figaro* that was lying on the bar.

'I say,' said Nicky, 'have you heard the one about the Irishman who tried to swim the channel?'

'No,' said Matt, not looking up.

'He tried to swim it "lenktways".'

Imogen giggled. Nicky put a warm hand over hers. 'At least someone thinks I'm funny.'

'Jesus,' said Matt. 'Braganzi's in Marseilles only a few miles from where we're staying.'

'With the Duchess?' asked Nicky.

'So it says here.'

'Never understand that,' said Nicky, peering at the paper. 'Beautiful classy bird throwing everything up to run off with a little wop runt like Braganzi.'

'Hush,' said Matt looking round in mock alarm. 'The Mafia are everywhere. Anyway he's probably more enterprising in bed. According to Fleet Street, the old Duke was a bit of a stately homo, one pretty valet after another.'

'Every valet shall be exalted,' said Nicky.

'Didn't the Duchess have Braganzi's baby?' asked Imogen.

'Yeah,' said Matt. 'Must be 18 months now. They've been together nearly three years. Perhaps she enjoys living with a hood. Women are always turned on by power, and Braganzi's got the whole of the Midi sewn up.'

Nicky squinted at his reflection in the smoked looking-glass behind the bar. 'All the same he is an oily little runt.'

Matt grinned. 'Once she hears you're in the area, Nicky baby, she'll promptly abandon Braganzi.'

'I've never had a Duchess,' mused Nicky, as though it was a matter of surprise to him. 'Can't you imagine her gliding downstairs in one of those red robes lined with ermine, and nothing on underneath, saying, "Would you prefer the West Wing or the East Wing, Mr Beresford?"'

'Then she'd probably hand you over to the National Trust,' said Matt, catching sight of Imogen's stricken face. 'Anyway, you'd just be getting down to business when the door'd be flung open and you'd have some guide showing a coachload of large ladies on a Mothers' Union mystery tour all over you.'

'I'd like that,' said Nicky. 'I'm turned on by crowds.'

Imogen, who was feeling quite sick at the thought of Nicky and the Duchess, took another slug at her drink, and felt even sicker, and had to have three potato crisps to take the taste away.

'Hullo, you chaps, what's anyone going to drink?' said a jolly voice. It was James, wearing a pale blue corduroy coat, his light brown curls smoothed flat to his head. Perhaps Yvonne insisted on 100 brushes a day – like Nanny.

'It's my round,' said Nicky.

'I'll have whisky then, a large White Horse please, *un grand cheval blanc*,' said James and giggled, looking furtively round. 'You'd better make it snappy. Yvonne doesn't approve of spirits.'

'Make it two,' said Matt, and, picking up Imogen's Pernod, emptied it into his own glass. 'You're not enjoying that much, are you, sweetheart?'

'Oh thank you,' stammered Imogen, touched that he'd noticed.

'D'you know the story of the white horse going

into a pub and sitting down on the bar stool and ordering a large whisky?' said James.

'No,' said Nicky, who didn't like other people telling jokes.

'The barman gave the horse his drink, and said "Did you know there's a whisky named after you?" "Really," said the white horse, "I didn't know there was a whisky called Eric."'

James laughed so hard that in the end everyone joined in. He's really rather nice, thought Imogen, taking a thankful gulp of her whisky.

The head waiter was hovering with a menu, chat *du jour* at the ready.

'Were Cable or your wife looking within a million years of being ready?' asked Matt. 'They're getting a bit restless in the kitchen.'

'No,' said James cheerfully.

Imogen's stomach gave a thunderous rumble.

'Hear, hear,' said Matt, 'I'll keel over if I don't eat soon.'

'You chaps didn't have any lunch, did you?' said James sympathetically.

'Jesus,' said Nicky, looking at the bill for the round of drinks. 'It's even gone up since I was here in May.'

'Exactly,' said Matt. 'That's why we're not staying in four star hotels. We'll have to put Imogen on the streets as it is.'

'They say vicars' daughters are always the worst,' said James.

The whisky was making Imogen perk up. It was

nice being just her and the three men. The conversation moved on to Northern Ireland. Imogen ate her crisps and let the world flow over her. Nicky held her hand and occasionally stroked her hair. James was caught red-handed buying another round of large drinks by the arrival of Yvonne.

'I'm not late, am I?'

'Yes,' said Matt. 'What d'you want to drink?'

'Tomato juice, please,' said Yvonne. 'No thanks, Imogen, I won't have any of your crisps. They're *so* fattening and it's more than my life's worth to exceed my calorie count.'

She looked rather disapprovingly at Imogen's thighs splayed out on the bar stool. Imogen blushed, let the large crisp already in her mouth melt like a communion wafer, and gazed at Yvonne in admiration. There wasn't a chip of varnish off the long coral nails, nor a newly curled red hair out of place, and the white silk blouse with the couple tangoing over the bosom was still spotless from that morning.

Having got her way over the room, Yvonne was also prepared to be conciliatory. The vibes sizzling between Nicky and Cable had not been lost on her. Cable mustn't be the only one with a holiday admirer. Yvonne decided to charm Matt.

'Are you feeling better?' she asked. 'Mind you, I always suspect seasickness is psychosomatic.'

'I agree,' said Matt. 'So's bloody-mindedness.'

The irony was quite lost on Yvonne.

'I do envy you coming from Ireland,' she went on.

'I did a butter commercial there once. It was all so green and unspoilt. Where do you live, Matt?'

'In Moone.'

'Is it pretty?'

'Well, it's very good hunting country.'

'I think hunting's rather cruel,' said Yvonne, 'but I suppose people in the country have to occupy their time somehow.'

'Indeed they have,' said Matt. 'The Irish haven't discovered the infinite possibilities of sexual intercourse yet.'

'The men in the Moone always came too soon,' said Nicky.

Matt laughed. Yvonne hastily changed the subject. 'I don't always agree with what you say, but I do admire your ability to do it week in week out.'

'Do what?'

'Write your amusing articles. Where do you think up your ideas?'

'In the bog,' said Matt. 'I'm thinking of doing a piece on bitches next week.'

'Oh, I can help you with that,' said Yvonne enthusiastically. 'One meets so many in the modelling world. It's the price you have to pay for being at the top,' she added, draining her tomato juice. The head waiter was hovering again, looking bootfaced.

'Where is Cable?' said Yvonne disapprovingly. 'You haven't trained her very well, you know.'

'She knows people'll wait for her,' said Matt.

'So inconsiderate to keep the kitchen staff waiting. I must say I am looking forward to my meal.

You can't beat French cuisine,' Yvonne retorted.

At that moment Cable sauntered in, looking quite unrepentant in khaki jeans, and a tight olive green T-shirt with 'I'm Still A Virgin' printed in large letters across the front. The colour gave a warm dusky glow to her brown face and neck, and intensified the greenness of her eyes. The barman nearly dropped the glass he was cleaning, the head waiter stopped in mid-grumble. Nicky's hand slid out of Imogen's and his presence seemed to slip away from her too, as he examined the lettering on Cable's bosom.

'Matt's just been telling us the Irish haven't discovered sex yet. Here we have the proof,' he said.

'You'll get clobbered under the trade descriptions act,' said Matt.

'I'd better give it to Imogen, then,' said Cable. 'She's the only one entitled to wear it.'

Everyone glanced at Imogen, who blushed crimson and looked down at her hands, speechless with embarrassment. Nicky *must* have told Cable. How *could* he?

'Sorry,' said Cable. 'That *was* below the belt.'

'Your mind's never anywhere else,' said Matt sharply. 'Let's go and eat.'

'Let me have one drink,' said Cable, smiling witchily at the head waiter. 'Surely we've got time?'

The head waiter promptly melted and said there was all the time in the world, and why didn't they have a round of drinks on the house?

'I thought you weren't going to change, Cable,'

said Yvonne. 'No, thank you, *garçon*, I won't have another drink, and you've had enough, Jumbo,' she added to James who was still gaping at Cable. 'You know I hate you drinking spirits.'

'Don't be silly,' said Matt, accepting large glasses of whisky and handing one to James. 'Never look a gift White Horse in the mouth.'

At last they went in to dinner. Most people had reached the coffee stage. After a quick calculation, Imogen posted herself next to where she thought Nicky would be. But at the last moment Cable sat down beyond Matt, and Nicky moved in opposite her, with Yvonne next to him, leaving James and Imogen on the outside.

'We can play footy footy,' said James.

His fat little legs would never reach me, thought Imogen. At least she was next to Matt, which was a comfort. He promptly began to guide her through the menu.

'Have that and that if you're starving,' he said. 'This place really deserves every flicker of its three stars.'

'I'm going to have a large steak,' said Nicky. 'I'd better make some attempt at keeping fit.'

'Oh good, they've got crudities. Can I have mine undressed?' said Yvonne to the waiter.

Undressed crudities! thought Imogen. Perhaps Yvonne was going to whip off her clothes and tango naked on the snow white table cloth. It must be all the whisky, it was beginning to make her feel fuzzy and irresponsible.

Everyone, except Cable and Yvonne, fell on the bread.

'What's *cervelles*?' said James, unpacking a square of butter.

'Brains,' said Matt.

'Ugh,' shuddered Yvonne. 'I can't stand brains.'

'That's patently obvious,' said Matt to Imogen in an undertone.

'Shall we all drink red?' he added, looking round the table.

'I want white,' said Yvonne. 'Much less fattening, don't you agree, Cable?'

'What?' said Cable, who was smouldering at Nicky. 'Oh yes I'm sure.'

Yvonne decided it was high time to break them up. 'I've just been telling Matt how much I love Ireland, Cable, it's so wonderfully primitive.'

'You'd enjoy our hovel then,' said Matt, taking another piece of bread. 'Chickens in the parlour, me granny shacked up with the donkey in the best bedroom, and my mither entertaining gentlemen friends, while the pig waits at table.'

'Now you're teasing me,' said Yvonne, her eyes crinkling. 'I bet your family are charming, aren't they, Cable?'

'I haven't been allowed to meet them,' snapped Cable.

Suddenly the temperature seemed to have dropped below zero.

'I'm frightened she might go off me,' said Matt lightly.

There was an awkward pause, broken fortunately by the arrival of the wine. James, who was oblivious of any undercurrents, started to tell a stock-exchange joke, waving a large radish around as he talked. With his pale blue coat and his puffed out cheeks, he suddenly reminded Imogen of Peter Rabbit.

'Don't crunch, Jumbo,' said Yvonne irritably. 'You know how it gets on my nerves. The service is awfully slow here.'

A moan of greed escaped Imogen at the sight of her first course, a sort of chicken rissole, stuffed with foie gras, and surrounded by bright orange sauce flecked with black. Opposite her James was smacking his lips over smoked salmon and a shiny green sauce. Matt was eating snails. Yvonne was chewing grated carrot 20 bites a mouthful. Nicky and Cable had skipped a first course and were smoking.

The wine, even to Imogen's uneducated palate, was spectacular, thick and sultry with grapes.

'You can almost taste the peasants' feet,' said Matt.

'What are the black bits?' she asked him, as she used her fourth piece of bread to mop up the sauce.

'Truffles,' said Matt. 'Bloody bad luck for pigs, really. They rootle round for days, and the moment they find some marvellous delicacy, it's snatched from under their nose.'

Like Nicky from me, thought Imogen wistfully.

Cable and Yvonne were talking shop.

'They sacked her from a bikini feature because she was too fat,' said Yvonne.

'That pale lipstick makes her mouth look like a rubber tyre,' said Cable.

'It's her own fault. She's in Wedgies or Tramps every night, and after all the client is buying your face, not your ability to drink in the right places till four o'clock in the morning.'

'Who are they talking about?' muttered Imogen.

'Obviously someone extremely successful,' said Matt.

'I got the Weetabix commercial,' said Yvonne patronisingly, starting on strips of green pepper. 'You were after it weren't you, Cable? The producer told me you were too overtly sexy for the part.'

'That's obviously why he tried to take me to bed,' snapped Cable, lighting one cigarette from another.

Nicky suddenly glanced across at Imogen, his eyes swivelling from Cable to Yvonne, then raising them to heaven. Imogen giggled with relief.

'No more bread, Jumbo,' said Yvonne, still chewing everything 20 times. 'You've already had quite enough.'

Everyone else had finished except her. The waiters were hovering to take the plates and putting silver dishes over blue flames.

'I should go on,' Matt told them. 'We can't hang around all night.'

Imogen's second course, boeuf bourgignon, rich, dark, aromatic and pulsating with herbs, was almost better than the first.

'I've never tasted anything so heavenly in my life,' she said to Matt.

'Good,' he said, filling her glass and looking across at Cable, who was picking imaginary bones out of her trout. 'Nice change to have someone around who enjoys eating.'

'These quenelles are very disappointing,' grumbled Yvonne.

'What d'you expect from upmarket fish cakes?' said Nicky.

'I always thought a quenelle was something the dog slept in,' said James, and roared with laughter.

'No more wine for you, Jumbo,' said Yvonne sharply.

'How long have you two been married?' asked Matt.

'Forty-eight weeks exactly,' said Yvonne, with what she thought was an engaging smile. 'We still count our marriage by weeks not months.'

'Weekiversaries,' said Matt drily. 'How touching.'

Cable shot him a warning glance.

James started to tell Imogen a long complicated joke about a parrot, upon which she found it impossible to concentrate because at the same time Yvonne turned to Nicky, saying:

'How did you and Imogen meet?'

'In Yorkshire.'

'Oh, I love Yorkshire, it's so unspoilt.'

'Like Imogen,' said Nicky.

'They tied a handkerchief over the parrot's eyes,' said James.

'Have you been going out long?' said Yvonne.

'No,' said Nicky.

'And another one round its beak,' said James.

'She looks awfully young. I'm surprised her father let her go away with you.'

'So was I.'

'What does she do?'

'Sits and dreams in a library.'

'And then they both got into bed,' said James.

'That's nice,' said Yvonne. 'She and Matt'll be able to have a lot of good talks about books.'

'They already have,' said Cable. She put her hands behind her head and leant back against the wall, her breasts jutting out dramatically. The effect was not lost on a handsome Frenchman drinking brandy with a plain wife at the next table. He and Cable exchanged a long lingering eye-meet. The Frenchman dropped his eyes first, then, after a furtive glance at his wife who was still spooning sugar into her coffee, looked at Cable again. Cable smirked and looked away. Even the cook had come out of the kitchen to have a look at her and was standing open-mouthed in the doorway with a lobster in his hand.

Suddenly Imogen was brought back to reality by James roaring with laughter and saying, 'And the parrot said Kama Sutra is a liar. Get it? Kama Sutra is a liar.'

Imogen, realising he'd reached the punchline, roared with rather forced laughter too. Matt filled up James's glass. Yvonne glared at Matt.

'Please don't. I don't want him to have any more. You won't be jogging every day in France you know, Jumbo.'

'Have some more,' said Matt, ladling more beef and potatoes on to Imogen's plate.

'Oh I shouldn't.'

'You should. Do you good to have a blow out on your first night. No one else will but us,' he went on, emptying the casserole dish on to his own plate.

Yvonne smiled at Imogen brightly.

'I hear you work in a library.'

Oh God, thought Imogen, she's going to bring *me* out now.

'Yes,' she muttered, with her mouth full.

'I used to love reading,' Yvonne went on, 'but I don't get the time now. I have to read a lot of papers from Central Office for James. I've got an aunt who reads though, four novels a day. We all call her the book worm.'

She then proceeded to launch into a long and unutterably boring description of her aunt's reading habits and literary tastes.

'Someone ought to put a green baize cloth over her,' muttered Matt as he leant across to fill Imogen's glass.

Having finally exhausted her aunt, Yvonne said, 'You're so lucky not having a job where you have to watch your figure.'

Imogen blushed and put down the potato she was about to eat.

'I'd be very happy to watch Imogen's figure all the time,' said Matt evenly.

'Me too,' leered James.

The head waiter came up and put his hands on Matt's shoulders.

'Everything all right, Monsieur O'Connor?'

'*Formidable*,' said Matt, breaking into fluent French.

'My trout was simply delicious,' said Cable, who'd left most of hers.

Imogen's waistband was biting into her stomach. She wished she hadn't eaten so much.

The restaurant was empty except for their table. Matt ordered coffee.

'Not for me,' said Yvonne. 'It keeps me awake, and we've got a long drive tomorrow.'

'I'd like an enormous brandy,' said James defiantly.

'Bravo,' said Nicky.

'Mustn't squander all our money at once, Jumbo. Night, night all,' said Yvonne, getting to her feet and dragging the reluctant James off to bed.

'Got to get her ugly sleep,' said Matt.

'God, she's a bitch,' said Nicky.

Matt ordered Marcs all round.

'If you go away in a party,' he said, 'it's essential to have a holiday scapegoat, so that everyone can gang up and work off their spleen bitching about her. Mrs Edgworth fits the bill perfectly.'

After dinner they wandered round the village. The sky glimmered with stars now, and down by the river the air was heavy with the musty scent of meadow-sweet.

Imogen and Nicky dawdled behind the others.

'Lovely moon,' sighed Imogen.

'Seen it before,' said Nicky.

He put a protective arm round her shoulders. She could feel the warmth of his body through her sweater. Suddenly he paused. Perhaps at last he might be going to whisk her off down some side road and the primrose path. She felt weak with abandon. But he was only pausing to read a poster giving details of a forthcoming tennis match.

'They wanted me to play in that,' he said. 'Didn't offer enough bread though, and the L.T.A. get very uptight if one does too many exhibition matches.'

Imogen felt overwhelmed with humility. What right had she got to be here at all with such a star? Ahead of them Matt's blond hair gleamed in a street lamp.

'How are you getting on with Matt?' said Nicky.

'Oh, very well. He's so nice.'

'He is, isn't he? She's a funny girl.'

'In what way?' said Imogen carefully.

'You never know what she'll do next. Unlike you, my angel, who are totally predictable.'

'I do love you,' she murmured, like a child touching wood.

'Well that's nice, except that we seem to be frustrated at every turn. Never mind, we've got a whole fortnight ahead of us.'

He dropped a kiss on top of her head. The night

was really very warm. Imogen tried to suppress the thought that back in June, when he'd been mad to pull her, he'd certainly have whipped her off to some discreet corner of a foreign field, and made passionate love to her, and not given a damn about the others.

'I have observed a faint neglect of late,' she thought sadly, then felt furious with herself. In Yorkshire she'd never stopped panicking and belly-aching because he was trying to pull her, now she was in a state because he wasn't. Her father would be delighted by such circumspection anyway. Perhaps Nicky was playing a waiting game so as not to frighten her.

In front she could see Cable's hips undulating languorously as she walked beside Matt. She wished she hadn't eaten so much. She wished she was as tall and as slim as her shadow.

Outside the hotel, quite without self-consciousness, Matt had taken Cable into his arms and kissed her very thoroughly. Nicky had followed suit with Imogen but when she opened her eyes in the middle, he was gazing over her shoulder at Cable and Matt.

'Sweet dreams, darling,' said Matt, reluctantly, relinquishing her. 'And I'd love to be away by ten – we've got a long drive.'

Up in their room, Imogen undressed quickly and jumped into bed. It was long after midnight, but she'd never known anyone take so long to get into bed as Cable, removing her make-up several times, massaging skin food into her face, brushing her hair, touching up her nail varnish, doing long, complicated exercises and chattering all the time.

'Such a relief not to have Matt beefing at me to hurry up,' she said, rubbing Vaseline into her eyelashes, and because there were no men present giving Imogen the benefit of her enchanting wicked smile. 'In fact it's rather a relief to have a night off sex as well.'

Imogen, snuggling down in the coarse sheets, fought sleep, tried to concentrate on *Tristram Shandy* and not stare at Cable too hard.

'God the bed's hard,' said Cable, finally getting in beside her. 'I hope you're not finding this trip too alarming.'

'No it's lovely,' said Imogen timidly, touched that Cable should be concerned.

Cable, however, immediately got the subject back to herself. 'I remember the first time I came to France on an exchange scheme when I was fifteen. I was absolutely terrified. I travelled by train overnight, 3rd class can you believe it? And there was this repulsive man who had little finger nails longer than the rest, and put on a blue hair net after he got into his couchette. The moment we dimmed the lights, he tried to fiddle with me, and there were two nuns in the bottom couchettes. I bit him so hard, he nearly pulled the communication cord. What d'you think of that?' She laughed to herself.

But before Imogen could think up a suitable answer, she realised Cable had fallen asleep like a cat. Having fought sleep for so long, Imogen now felt wide awake. Thank goodness Yvonne was not sharing the bed too, or she'd be a model sandwich. Every man in the hotel would give a million francs to be in my place, she thought as, petrified she'd touch Cable, she perched on the edge of her side of the bed. She hoped she'd dream of Nicky, but she didn't.

Chapter Eight

Imogen went down to breakfast next morning and found Nicky and Matt dirty and unshaven like a couple of bandits.

Matt smiled at her and asked her if she had slept well.

'Marvellously,' lied Imogen.

'I'm glad someone did,' said Nicky sulkily. 'The Royal Philharmonic of tomcats started caterwauling around five o'clock.'

'We abandoned all hope of sleep and invented tortures for Mrs Edgworth,' said Matt.

At that moment Yvonne bustled in wearing a dress and a pink headscarf.

'Good morning,' she said briskly. Matt and Nicky looked at her stonily.

'I didn't sleep a wink,' she grumbled. 'What with the cats and the clocks striking. Do remember to book rooms at the back in future, Matt. And the beds were awful.'

'Surprised you didn't use James as a mattress,' said Matt.

'Why are you all done up like a dog's dinner?' said Nicky.

Yvonne's lips tightened as she pulled on white gloves. 'I'm off to Mass, where you all should be!' she said.

The next stage of the journey was a disaster. Cable took so long to pack and get ready that she and Matt had another blazing row.

'They ought to hold sheepdog trials for people like me,' said Matt as he finally rounded the three of them up into the car. James and Yvonne had already gone on ahead. Nicky and Imogen sat in the front, Cable and Matt in the back, Matt reading a French Sunday paper, Cable looking stonily out of the window.

Nicky, whose turn it was to drive, was determined to notch up more miles an hour than Matt had yesterday, but Imogen spoilt everything by reading the map all wrong. The countryside they passed through had been so beautiful – old mills covered in reddening Virginia creeper, tender green poplar groves rising out of lush grass, and huge golden chateaux at the end of long shining lakes. Then suddenly she realised to her horror that she'd missed an important turning. As a result Nicky had to spend the next three-quarters of an hour disentangling them from the tentacles of a large industrial town. He got more and more angry, which was not helped by Imogen out of sheer nerves telling him he could overtake three times when he couldn't, directing him slap into oncoming traffic.

Cutting short her stream of apologies, Nicky had

turned on the car wireless. They could still get Radio 3. Patricia Hughes was announcing a performance of Handel's Little Organ Concerto.

'I didn't know Handel had a small prick,' drawled Cable.

Nicky grinned round at her. 'Probably couldn't Handel it,' he said.

They both giggled and started swapping more anecdotes about mutual acquaintances, ostentatiously excluding Matt and Imogen.

Imogen wished she could amuse Nicky like that. But we've only got my family and Homer in common, she thought dolefully, and we can't really talk about them for a fortnight. She noticed that each time they reached the end of a village, its name was signposted with a diagonal red line through it. She had a gloomy vision of Nicky taking a ruler and calmly drawing a red line through her name to signify the affair was over.

Later, tempers were not improved by no one being able to decide on the right picnic place, which at 110 miles an hour on the motorway was admittedly quite hard to find. James, who had been obliged to stop for Yvonne several times, was driving just behind them now. Imogen could see his eager pink face, with Yvonne beside him, wearing dark glasses, her mouth opening and shutting in a constant stream of chat.

Cable meanwhile was driving Matt insane by sitting with a red Michelin Guide in her hand, saying every time they came to a village, 'There's a fabulous restaurant here. It'd be so much nicer to stop here than have a rotten picnic.'

'And five times more expensive,' snapped Matt. 'I'm buggered if I'm going to fork out 100 francs for something you won't eat. I'm fed up with providing expensive left-overs for restaurant cats all over England and France.'

'Oh, shut up,' said Cable.

Eventually they stopped high up in the mountains, with a deep green valley falling away from them, richly dotted with herds of golden cattle, and russet farm houses. Despite the height it was appallingly hot. A heat haze danced above the rocks. Cheese, pâté and garlic sausage were soon sweating and melting in the blazing sun, ham curled and turned brown, the acid red wine was as warm as tea.

Yvonne perched on a rock, still looking as though she'd been wrapped in tissue paper, daintily eating cottage cheese with a pink plastic spoon, and grumbling about the insects.

'Doesn't the silly cow remind you of little Miss Muffet?' said Matt to Imogen. 'Pity a big spider can't roll up and put the frighteners on her for good.'

Nicky, having wolfed a couple of pieces of bread and pâté, had annexed a bottle of wine, and was further punishing Imogen by dancing attendance on Cable. Lying on the grass beside her, he alternately fed her swigs of wine from the same paper cup, or dropped green grapes into her mouth. Occasionally, after shooting a venomous glance in Matt's direction, Cable would whisper something in his ear, sending them both into fits of laughter.

Yvonne looked disapproving, and unpacked yet another polythene bag of carrot matchsticks. Ignoring them both, Matt stretched out and fell asleep among the wild flowers like Ferdinand the Bull. Imogen, incapable of such *sang-froid*, miserably ate her way through five pieces of bread and garlic sausage and then felt sick.

James had positioned himself so he could look up Cable's skirt. As she writhed on the ground with Nicky, her pink dress rode up further and further to reveal black *broderie anglaise* bikini pants, threaded with scarlet ribbon.

Suddenly a car drew up on the road below and three Frenchmen got out, quite unselfconsciously unzipped their flies and relieved themselves against the grass verge.

'How disgusting,' spluttered Yvonne, going scarlet with disapproval.

'How lovely and uninhibited,' said Cable, sitting up and putting a cigarette in her mouth. In a flash James's lighter was out, the flame shooting into the air, nearly singeing Cable's hair and eyelashes.

'Overeager, like its master,' said Nicky pointedly.

James went slightly pink and helped himself and Imogen to more wine.

'That's enough, Jumbo,' snapped Yvonne. 'You know what I feel about drinking and driving.'

She got off the rock and started to tidy up the

picnic, exclaiming over the ants that had already crawled into the pâté, neatly tidying the rubbish into a polythene bag and stacking it in the boot.

'Don't work so hard,' said Cable lazily. 'You're making us feel so guilty.'

'Someone's got to do it,' said Yvonne. 'I, for one, like things ship-shape.'

Imogen got back into the car, wincing as the sun-baked seat burnt her skin.

'Everyone's awfully prickly today,' she said to Matt.

'That's why it's called a holly day,' said Matt.

And now it was late afternoon. Imogen sat in the back feeling car sick, homesick, cooped up and uncertain where life was taking her. After the long hours of travelling, she felt sluggish and weighed down, as though all the pieces of bread she'd eaten in the last twenty-four hours were lying in a leaden lump at the bottom of her stomach.

And now the shadows were lengthening and Matt was driving again, sweat darkening his shirt, an old panama hat pulled over his nose to keep his dark blond mane out of his eyes. All the windows were open; the heat was coming in great waves; the windscreen was coated with dead flies.

The road was curling now through pine woods and burning red rock, the crickets were going like rattles, the air was getting clearer and clearer. Up and up they went, round and round, until it seemed their car would touch the sky. Then, suddenly, like a sheet of metal glinting in the evening sun, sparkled the Mediterranean.

Imogen caught her breath. Cable got out her make-up case. Imogen wished she had some of those little cleansing pads which Cable and Yvonne whipped out on every occsion. Even her flannel was packed in her suitcase in the boot.

'There's Port-les-Pins,' said Matt.

Imogen craned her neck. Down below, the hill was thick with little white villas with red roofs and green shutters. Shops, cafés, casinos and pale pastel houses jostled for position along the sea front. A fleet of fishing boats and yachts tossed in the harbour. Some tiny fishing village, thought Imogen.

Another shock awaited her. She had always believed the French were an ugly race, dumpy with incipient moustaches. But as they drove along the front, she had never seen so many beautiful girls, trailing back from the beach, with their waist-length hair, long limbs and brown faces. No wonder Cable had spent three-quarters of an hour on her face. No wonder Nicky looked like a small boy let loose in a sweet shop.

Their hotel, La Reconnaissance, was at the far end of the front. Drying bathing dresses and towels hung from every balcony. The fat Madame, accompanied by an even fatter poodle, came waddling out gabbling with excitement and kissed Matt on both cheeks. Imogen was relieved to discover that she and Nicky had a room each.

Madame combined respectability with avarice,

Matt explained in English as they climbed the red-tiled staircase. She got more money for two single rooms than a double, but as long as appearances were kept up, she didn't mind who slipped into whose room after lights out.

Imogen's room was extremely small with a large single bed, no soap, no coat-hangers, no drawer space and the tiniest of face towels. A piece of plastic holly was tucked behind the only picture. Five pink, lurex bulrushes stood in a vase beside the bed. If she leaned right out of the window she could just see the sea.

She sat down overwhelmed by another desperate wave of homesickness. Her hair felt stiff with dust, her body ached with the inactivity of the long day's drive. Outside, Yvonne was complaining bitterly that baths cost 10 francs each and Cable was bullying Matt to go downstairs and get the plug changed on her Carmen rollers. I must pull myself together, thought Imogen. She was on holiday, after all, and she must try and enjoy herself. She washed as best she could in stone cold water and put on one of her new voluminous orange kaftans. She wore stockings and high-heeled shoes to make herself look taller and slimmer and took a lot of trouble over her face, before joining the others in the bar on the front.

Immediately she was conscious of wearing quite the wrong clothes. Most people were in trousers and shirts in soft pastel shades. Girls in dresses wore them fitted or tightly belted, with Greek sandals on their bare feet. She was aware of brown faces laughing at her all around.

Nicky looked at the kaftan in ill-concealed disapproval.

'Expecting a baby, darling?' said Cable in her cool, clear voice.

'She looks lovely,' said Matt, who was filling in the brown identification forms.

He patted the chair beside him. 'Come and sit here, baby, and let me take down your particulars. Is your room all right?'

'Oh yes, it's fine,' she said gratefully.

'Ours isn't,' said Yvonne, 'I haven't got a bedside lamp.'

'With all those raw carrots you eat,' said Matt, 'I would have thought you could see in the dark.'

'It is rather a dump,' snapped Yvonne. 'I had expected something a bit better – like that for instance.' She waved in the direction of the huge white Plaza Hotel which, with its red and white umbrellas, dominated the bay.

'You can stay there if you're prepared not to eat or go out in the evening,' said Matt. 'One night at the Plaza'll cost you as much as a fortnight at La Reconnaissance.'

'Well perhaps not the Plaza,' conceded Yvonne, 'but there must be somewhere a little less primitive.'

Matt went on filling in Imogen's form. For her occupation he put *bibliothecaire* which sounded very grand.

'Madame was good to Matt in the old days,' said Cable defensively.

'When I was an undergraduate she let me stay for practically nothing,' said Matt. 'She used to be in the Resistance. I'm sure she'll lend you her revolver if it comes to a shoot out with the cockroaches.'

Imogen gazed at the Prussian blue sea which glittered and sparkled in the sinking sun.

'What's the French for "Model"?' said James trying to bridge an awkward silence and fill in Yvonne's form at the same time.

'*Catin*,' said Matt.

Cable stifled a giggle and James solemnly wrote it down.

A party of Germans sat down at the next table and started banging the table for waitresses.

'This place is awfully touristy,' grumbled Yvonne.

'Well, you're a tourist, aren't you?' said Matt.

A slim brunette went by in a lace shirt with the tails tied under the bosom to reveal a beautiful brown midriff.

'Everyone seems to be wearing those this year,' said Cable. 'I must get one.'

'What does *catin* really mean?' said Imogen to Nicky later, as they strolled along the front.

'Prostitute,' said Nicky.

They had dinner in a restaurant overhung with vines. Below, the sea was a wash of blue shadow, sparked by the lights of the fishing boats putting out for the night's catch. Everyone was hungry and they ate garlicky fish soup and cassoulet. The wine flowed freely. Even Yvonne seemed more cheerful when suddenly she put on her wolf in Red Riding Hood smile and turned to Matt.

'Isn't it time you and Cable named the day?'

Everyone stopped talking. Matt looked at Yvonne steadily and said, 'What day?'

She waved a playful finger at him. 'Now don't be evasive. You and Cable have been going out for nearly two years now. It's only fair to make an honest woman out of her.'

Cable flushed angrily. 'It's none of your damn business, Yvonne.'

'Darling – I was only interested in your welfare.'

Matt took Cable's hand and squeezed it. Then he turned to Yvonne and said softly, 'Let's get three things straight. First, I have Cable's welfare very much at heart; secondly, I agree with her, it's none of your damn business; and thirdly, you've got butter on your chin.'

There was a frozen pause, then everyone burst out laughing, except Yvonne who went as red as her hair with rage.

Nicky yawned. 'God, I'm so tired I could sleep on a clothes line.'

Matt was gently stroking Cable's cheek. 'Early bed, I think, darling, don't you?'

She looked at him and nodded gratefully. He's a nice man, thought Imogen, a really nice man. She was beginning to feel sick. Perhaps that garlic soup hadn't been such a good idea. Nicky was eyeing a sumptuous blonde at the next table.

'Don't forget to sleep on the right side of the bed,' said Cable mockingly to Imogen as she climbed the stairs to her room. She felt sicker and sicker. White-faced, white-bodied, she looked at herself in the mirror. Oh, fat, white woman who nobody loves, she thought sadly, as she put on her nightdress and jumped into bed.

There was a knock on the door. It was Nicky in a violet dressing-gown and nothing underneath. His black curls fell becomingly, the gold medallions jangled on his chest, aftershave lotion fought with the sweet scent of deodorant. Imogen's heart turned over. She had never seen such a beautiful man. If only he weren't going round and round.

'Hullo, darling,' he said huskily, sitting down on the bed. 'Thank God we're alone at last. I couldn't sleep last night for thinking about you.'

Or the tomcats or the clocks, thought Imogen. He was kissing her now and his hands started to rove over her body. He put his tongue in her ear, and Imogen, who couldn't remember whether she'd washed her ears that morning, wriggled away, simulating uncontrollable passion.

Nicky laughed. 'Underneath the surface, you're a hot little thing.'

Great waves of nausea were sweeping over her.

'Come on,' he said. 'Let's have that stupid night-dress off.'

'Nicky, I feel sick,' she said, leaping out of bed and rushing to the bidet.

'You can't be sick here,' said Nicky in horror.

'Can't I?' said Imogen, and was. And all night long, like the Gadarene swine, she thundered down the passage to the black hellhole of a lavatory.

Nicky, foiled yet again, went back to his room in an extremely bad temper.

Chapter Nine

Next morning, feeling pale and sickly, Imogen staggered down to the beach. The sea was blue and sparkling, the sand hot and golden. Umbrellas stretched six deep, edge to edge, for half a mile along the beach. Bodies lay stretched out hundreds to the acre, turning and oiling themselves like chickens on a spit.

Nearly everyone, Imogen realised to her horror, was topless. Cable, as brown as any of them, was wearing the bottom half of the briefest bikini – two saffron triangles, held together by straps of perspex. Her small perfect breasts gleamed with oil. Her hair hung black and shiny over the edge of her lilo. Nicky lounged beside her, slim, lithe and menacing. He totally ignored Imogen when she arrived. Matt lay on his back, his eyes closed, his powerful chest curved in an arch above his flat heavily muscled stomach. Having sallow skin, he was already going brown.

He opened a lazy eye and grinned at Imogen. 'Come and join the oppressed white minority.'

As she struggled into Lady Jacintha's red bathing

dress, she tried to protect herself with a small face towel.

'There's masses of room on my towel if you need it,' said Matt who had been watching her struggles with unashamed amusement. He rolled over and went back to sleep. Imogen lay in silence, bitterly ashamed of her whiteness.

'Christ,' said Nicky, who was reading a copy of yesterday's *Daily Telegraph*, 'Nastase was knocked out in the first round.'

'Damn, damn, damn!' said Matt suddenly. Everyone looked up. 'Here comes Mrs Set-your-teeth-on-Edgworth and the prospective candidate for Cockfosters.'

Yvonne was picking her way daintily across the miles of tangled brown flesh. Behind her staggered James weighed down by towels, lilos, snorkel masks, picnic baskets, a large parasol and Yvonne's make-up case, but still managing to cast excited glances at the naked bosoms around him.

'They look as though they're going on safari,' said Cable. 'There's something rather prehistoric about James's shorts.'

'He looks as though he's crossing the foot hills,' said Nicky.

'What a crowd,' sighed Yvonne. 'You get such lovely deserted beaches in the Bahamas. No, put the lilo there, Jumbo, with the towel spread over it. I don't want to perspire. And put the parasol so it keeps the sun off my face. Can you move just a fraction of an inch, Imogen? Yes, that's lovely.

When you've finished, James, just pop over to the café and get me some orange squash. Such a funny thing's just happened,' she added to Cable. 'A little French girl came up to me and asked me for my autograph. She'd seen one of my commercials when she was staying in England.'

Matt, looking at her with acute dislike, was about to say something, then turned over and went back to sleep.

Although she was pouring with sweat, Imogen was too ashamed of her white body to go and swim until Cable and Nicky were safely in the sea. Then how cool and sympathetically soothing the water felt to her limbs. Below the dark green surface, she could see the slow moving shape of a fish. Then suddenly someone grabbed her ankles and she was falling. She seemed to swallow half the ocean. Choking, she came to the surface to see Nicky shooting away at a flashy crawl. Later he and Cable played very ostentatiously with a yellow beach ball.

'I say, that's rather naughty,' said James, staring fascinated at a girl whose bikini pants had practically no back to them.

'I don't know why she bothers to wear anything at all,' snapped Yvonne.

'Why don't you wear a bikini?' Yvonne asked Imogen. 'I'd lend you one, but I don't think you'd get into it. I really think you ought to do something about your thighs.'

'Exercises are the best thing,' said Cable, flopping

down on the lilo. 'Sally Chetwynde lost five inches by bicycling every night.'

Imogen blushed as red as her bathing dress. If Matt had been there she was sure they would never have been so nasty to her. They shut up as soon as he came back.

She watched him oiling Cable, his hands moving steadily over her slim brown body, big practised hands, as skilful at making love as keeping a large car steady on a winding road at excessive speeds.

Her heart suddenly twisted with loneliness. Her skin was already turning as pink and as freckled as a foxglove. Oh, to be as beautiful as Cable, and to be loved by a man like Matt.

She was also worried that although she'd searched her room high and low she couldn't find her pills. What on earth was Nicky going to say when he discovered she'd lost them? Perhaps she could get some from a chemist. '*Avez-vous la pilule pour arreter les bébés?*' But wasn't France a Catholic country which forbade the pill anyway? If only Yvonne or Cable were more cosy she could have asked them.

'Of course *Vogue* pay peanuts, only twenty-five quid a day,' Yvonne was saying.

'I wouldn't put on my make-up for twenty-five quid a day,' said Cable.

Matt sighed and took refuge in a tattered copy of *Brideshead Revisited*.

*   *   *

When Imogen looked at herself in the glass before dinner, she was scarlet. Her head and her eyes ached; she had obviously overdone it. Her hair was stiff with oil, sand and sea water. Sand also seemed to have got into everything: towel, comb, bag, clothes; the floor of the room was just like the Gobi Desert. She lay on her bed and wondered which would be the worst evil, her baggy trousers or her other kaftan. She decided on trousers, which would at least hide her legs. After she had dressed and had another fruitless search for her pills, she wandered into Cable's room and found her busy combing out newly washed ebony curls.

'Goodness, you're red,' said Cable. 'Good thing you kept yourself well oiled. Try some of my green face powder. Guess what? James Edgworth's just made a pass at me. Serve Yvonne right for being so bitchy last night. I can't think why I liked her in London. And, do you know, she was Purley Carnival Queen when she was 14? James made me promise not to tell anyone!'

In spite of the green face powder, Imogen's face glowed like a furnace as the evening wore on. After dinner they went to a nightclub. She couldn't believe how ravishing the girls were with their smooth expressionless faces, and long, long legs. And how beautifully they danced. It was as though the sun had melted their limbs to liquid. Nicky, having drunk too much, spent most of the evening wrapped round Cable. Matt ignored them both, and gabbled away to the nightclub owner. Every so often he smiled reassuringly at Imogen through the soupy darkness.

But later, back in her room, she wondered if she had ever been more miserable in her life. Here she was on the Riviera with the handsomest man in the world – a real daydream situation come true – and she was loathing every minute of it. She winced from sunburn as she climbed into bed. Oh please, God, make him be nice to me tonight.

Much later Nicky came in wearing not the violet dressing-gown which she'd so nearly been sick over last night, but a pair of black pyjamas. His gleaming beauty, after a day in the sun, was over-whelming. Squinting slightly from so much drink, he looked like a dangerous, hungry Siamese cat. He was obviously not going to put up with any non-sense tonight. Her stomach contracted with fear and expectancy.

'Feeling bridal, darling?' he said silkily, and pulled her towards him, his fingers biting into her arms. 'It's time you stopped playing games.'

His kisses were hard and brutal and gave her no pleasure. She was nearly suffocated by the smell of Cable's scent.

'No, no, Nicky, I don't want to!'

'Well, this time you're going to have to, honey child.'

'But you don't love me,' she gasped. 'Not a bit. You've ignored me since we left England.'

'Rubbish,' said Nicky. 'I tried hard enough last night, didn't I?'

'I couldn't help it. Oh, Nicky please, please don't. I can't find my pills.'

'Your what!' It was like a pistol shot.

'I've looked for them everywhere. I must have left them in that hotel on the way.'

His slit eyes were like dark thread. 'Jesus, can't you do anything right? I don't believe you ever got them in the first place.'

Imogen gave a gasp of horror. 'Oh, I did, I did. I promise.'

'Crap,' said Nicky. 'You just pretended you had. We can't do anything to upset Daddy, can we?'

'I *did* get them,' said Imogen, bursting into tears. 'Oh, why won't you believe me?'

Nicky, mean with drink inside him, rattled her like a cat shaking a mouse, calling her every name he could think of until someone banged on the wall and told them to shut up in German. Nicky swore back in German and pushed Imogen back against the pillow.

'I'm s-s-sorry, Nicky,' she sobbed. 'I do love you.'

'Well, I don't love you,' he snarled. 'Get that straight. Nor do I like prissy little girls who string men along just for the sake of a holiday in the sun.'

And he stormed out of the room, slamming the door behind him.

There were four church clocks in Port-les-Pins, and Imogen counted each one chiming the quarter hours through the night, until the crowing cocks brought the morning sun streaming through the shutters.

*   *   *

As she was going downstairs next morning, dark glasses covering her reddened eyes, Cable popped her head out of the bedroom door. 'I just found these at the bottom of one of my espadrilles,' she said. 'I do hope you weren't looking for them.' And, laughing, she thrust the mauve card holding the pills into Imogen's hand.

Laughter, thought Imogen, is the most insidious sound in the world. Cable and Nicky lay on the beach slightly out of earshot from the rest of the party, heads together, laughing and talking in low caressing voices.

The heat of the sun was as fiery as yesterday's. But a fierce wind was raging. It tore the parasols out of the ground, blew sand in everyone's faces, and ruffled the green feathers of the palm trees along the front.

'It's called a mistral,' Matt told Imogen. 'It makes everyone very bad-tempered. Have you noticed how the nicest people become absolute monsters with too much spare time on their hands?'

Yvonne was moaning at James, who was hiding his pink burnt body under a huge green towel. Cable was as snappy as an elastic band with Matt, and Nicky didn't deign to recognise Imogen's existence.

A black poodle with a red collar came scampering by, scattering sand. James whistled and made clicking noises with his hand.

'Don't talk to strange dogs, Jumbo,' snapped Yvonne. 'They might easily have rabies.'

Cable, in an emerald green bikini with a matching turban to keep the sand out of her hair, had never looked more seductive. Matt retired behind *Paris Match*. Yvonne put on a cardboard beak to protect her nose from the sun, which made her look like some malignant bird. James got out his Box Brownie and went on a photographic spree which consisted mainly of front approaches on large ladies. Nicky went off to hire a pedalo.

Three handsome muscular Frenchmen playing ball edged nearer Cable, then one of them deliberately missed a catch, so the ball landed at her feet. With laughter, and voluble apologies and much show of interest, they all came to retrieve it. Cable gave them a smouldering look. They smiled back in admiration. Next moment another catch was missed and the ball landed on her towel and, with a flurry of '*Pardons*', was retrieved again. Cable smirked. Matt took no notice and went on reading. Imogen suddenly thought how infuriating it must be for Cable that he appeared so unjealous. Maybe it was an elaborate game between them. She picked up a copy of *Elle* that Cable had abandoned which said '*une vrai beauté sauvage*' would be fashionable this autumn. The glamorously dishevelled mane of the model on the front cover bore no resemblance to Imogen's awful mop of hair which was now going in '*toutes directions*'. The heat was awful. Imogen, who was burning, picked up a tube of sun lotion and began plastering it over her face.

Yvonne gave a squeal of rage and snatched it

away from her. 'How dare you use my special lotion!'

Matt lowered *Paris Match*. 'Stop beefing,' he said sharply. 'One oil's the same as another.'

'This one was specially made for me at great expense, because of my sensitive skin,' said Yvonne. 'Because I'm a model, it's absolutely vital I don't peel. This stuff is . . .'

Matt got up and went down to the sea leaving her in mid-sentence.

'He's the rudest man I ever met,' Yvonne said furiously as she re-adjusted her cardboard beak. 'I don't know why you put up with him, Cable.'

Cable rolled over and looked at Yvonne, her green eyes glinting. 'Because, my dear,' she drawled, 'he's a genius in bed.'

'What a disgusting thing to say,' said Yvonne, looking like an enraged beetroot.

'Once you've had Matt,' said Cable, 'you never really want anyone else.'

'Then why are you fooling around with Nicky Beresford?'

Imogen caught her breath.

Cable grinned wickedly. 'Because Nicky's so pretty, and I must keep Matt on his toes or, shall we say, his elbows.'

'You're going about it the wrong way,' said Yvonne. 'You should occasionally sew a button on his shirt or cook more. Modelling's not a very stable career, you know.'

'Neither's marriage,' snapped Cable. 'Your husband made the most *horrendous* pass at me last night.'

And getting up in one lithe movement, she made her way down to the sea to join Nicky on a pedalo.

Yvonne turned on Imogen as the only available target. 'I don't know why you came out here with Nicky and then let him get away with it,' she snapped, and, spluttering with fury, went off to find James.

Imogen got some postcards out of her bag. She had bought them to send home to the family and the office, but what on earth could she say to them? They had all been so excited about her going. How could she tell them the truth?

Dear everyone, she wrote very large. *How are you all? I arrived safely. None of the gardens here are as good as ours.* Suddenly she had a vision of the vicarage and Pikely. Juliet and the boys would be at school now, her mother would probably be getting ready to go down to the shops, flapping about looking for her list while Homer waited for her, impatiently trailing his chain lead around like Marley's ghost. At such a distance even her father seemed less formidable. A great wave of homesickness overwhelmed her.

Matt strolled lazily up from the sea, water dripping from his huge shoulders, heavy-lidded eyes squinting against the sun. There was poor little Imogen in that awful bathing dress, surrounded by other people's possessions. He'd never seen anyone so woebegone. Today she was red-eyed, covered in bruises. Nicky must have put her through hell last night. Those pale-skinned English girls always translated badly to the South of France for the first few days. Her clothes were frightful, her hair a disaster. Once she turned brown, however, she might have possibilities. I could teach her a thing or three, he thought. He lay down beside her and put his arm round her shoulders.

'I declare National Necking Week officially open,' he said.

She turned a woeful face to him and held up an arm covered in bites.

'I don't seem to attract anything but mosquitoes,' she said, her lips trembling.

'Has Yvonne been bullying you? Listen baby, don't let her get you down. I know how she comes on, like she owns this beach personally and everyone has to act like a vicarage tea party, but you've just got to ignore her.'

Poor little thing, he thought, she really is miserable. Something will definitely have to be done about it.

Chapter Ten

'I feel lucky tonight,' said Matt after dinner. 'I'm off to the Casino.'

'To blow all our French bread, I suppose,' said Cable sourly.

As they went into the Roulette Room, Imogen was overwhelmed by the smoke, the glaring lights, and the fever the place itself generated. Gambling was obviously taken very seriously here. Round the table sat women with scarlet nails and obsessive faces. None of the pale, hard-eyed men behind them betrayed a flicker of interest in Cable. Huge sums of money were changing hands.

Matt went off to the Cashier and returned with his big hands full of counters.

'Fifteen for Cable, fifteen for Imogen, and the rest for me because I'm good at it. The others are fending for themselves.'

To Imogen, her fifteen counters suddenly became of crucial importance, and the green baize table a fearsome battleground. If she won, she would get Nicky back; if she lost, then all was lost. She would play number twenty-six, Nicky's age. But twenty-six obstinately refused to come up, and gradually her pile dwindled away, until she had only one counter left. She put it on number nine. It came up. Relief flooded her. She backed it again, and again it came up.

'Good girl,' said Matt, who was steadily amassing chips beside her.

But something compelled her to chance her luck and go on playing, and this time she lost and lost until she only had two counters. In desperation, she put them both on Noir. Rouge came up.

Tears stinging her eyes, she escaped to the ladies.

'Oh God, I look hateful,' she moaned. Her face was still bright scarlet. The mistral had played even worse havoc with her hair, whipping it into a wild mop like a Zulu warrior. She couldn't even get a comb through it.

She didn't recognise the couple locked together in the passage when she came out a few minutes later. But she stiffened as she heard the familiar purr of Nicky's voice.

'Darling, you're so lovely,' he was saying. 'And I can feel your heart going like the Charge of the Light Brigade.'

Cable gave a husky laugh, and wound her arms round his neck.

'Do you believe in love at first sight?' he went on. 'I didn't until I met you. Then – pow! Suddenly it happened, as though I'd been struck by a thunderbolt. I don't know what it is about you – something indefinable, apart from being so beautiful.'

Imogen couldn't believe her ears. He was using exactly the same words he'd used when he'd tried to seduce her that first time on the moor. Words that were irrevocably signed on her heart.

'What about old purple sprouting Brocklehurst?' said Cable softly.

Nicky laughed. 'I knew it was a mistake the moment I met you, but I couldn't let her down. She's not much trouble and anyway it gave me a chance of being near you.'

'I feel a bit mean. Can't we find some arresting Provençal fisherman to bed her down?'

'Never get near her,' said Nicky and started to kiss Cable again.

They were so preoccupied they didn't notice her stumbling past.

She met Matt coming out of the Roulette Room. He was looking pleased with himself.

'I've just won nearly three thousand francs,' he said.

'How much is that?' said Imogen, desperately trying to sound normal.

'About £300. I've been good and cashed it in.' He looked at her closely.

'Hey, what's the matter?'

'Nothing, I'm fine,' she said.

'Cable and Nicky, is it?'

She nodded – impossible to keep anything from him.

He took her arm. 'I think you and I had better have a little talk.'

He led her to a deserted corner of the beach. They sat down on the warm sand. A huge white moon had turned the sea to gunmetal; the waves were idly flapping on the shore.

Matt lit a cigarette. 'All right lovie, what happened?'

Stammering, she told him.

'I don't mind him kissing her so much,' she said finally. 'I mean she's so lovely anyone would want to. But it's just his using the same words.'

'Cliché, cliché, cliché,' said Matt scornfully. 'But then you can't expect someone who hits a white ball across a net year in year out to have a very extensive vocabulary, can you?'

Imogen had a feeling he was laughing at her. 'But Nicky's clever. He speaks five languages,' she said defensively.

'A sign of great stupidity, I always think,' said Matt. 'Hell, I'm not trying to put Nicky down. I've nothing against people with IQs in single figures. I just think you should know some home and away truths about him. I bet I know how he picked you up.'

'We were introduced,' said Imogen stiffly.

'No, before that. Wasn't he playing in a match, and he suddenly picked you out in the crowd, and acted as though he'd been turned to stone? Then, I suppose, he missed a few easy shots, as though he was completely overwhelmed by your beauty, and flashed his pretty teeth at you every time he changed ends.'

'He must have told you,' said Imogen in a stifled voice.

'No such luck, sweetheart. It's standard Beresford pick-up practice in tournaments, all round the country. Quite irresistible, too, when combined with those devastating good looks. He never does it if there's any chance he might lose the match.'

'Then why did he bother to bring me on holiday?'

'For a number of reasons, I should think. Because you're very pretty, because he's got a jaded palate, and you're different from his usual run of scrubbers. Because he couldn't make you in Yorkshire, and he always likes to get his own way and, finally, because he hadn't met Cable then.'

'And what chance have I got against her?' sighed Imogen.

'You still want him, after hearing all that?'

Imogen nodded miserably. 'I'm a constant nymph,' she said.

Matt sighed. 'I was afraid you were. Well, we'll have to get him back for you, won't we?'

Outside her bedroom he took her key and unlocked the door.

'Now baby, lesson one. Don't cry all night. It'll only make you look ugly in the morning. And if you're still smarting about the purple sprouting Brocklehurst bit, remember that Cable's real name is Enid Sugden.'

He smiled, touched her cheek with his hand, and went. Imogen undressed and lay on her bed for a few minutes in the moonlight. Fancy Cable being called Enid. She giggled, then her thoughts turned to Matt.

Was it Jane Austen who said friendship was the finest balm for the pangs of despised love? She got up, locked her door and fell into a deep sleep.

It was after ten o'clock when she woke next morning. She found Matt drinking Pernod on the front, surrounded by newspapers, his long legs up on the table.

'You're going brown. Isn't it a pity one can't have the first drink of the day twice?' he said, ordering her a cup of coffee.

'How is everyone?' she said.

'Grimly determined to enjoy their fortnight's holiday. Yvonne running herself up as usual, Cable in one of her moods – I'm not sure which one. They've all gone water skiing.'

'Didn't you want to go?' said Imogen anxiously. It was bad enough that Nicky should annexe Cable without Matt being left with Nicky's boring girlfriend.

'After my performance on the boat coming over – you must be joking. You and I are going to take a trip along the coast.'

It was a perfect day. The mistral had retired into its cave. The air was soft. And as they drove along the coast road, the smell of petrol mingled with the scent of the pines. She still felt upset about Nicky, but for today she was determined not to brood.

'Where are we going?' asked Imogen.

'St Tropez,' said Matt.

Oh, God, thought Imogen as the wind fretted her hair into an even worse tangle. Everyone will look like Bardot there.

Matt parked the car on the front. In the yachts round the Port, the rich in their Pucci silks were surfacing for the first champagne of the day. Matt steered Imogen through a doorway, up some stairs, into a hairdressing salon.

'To kick off, we're going to do something about your hair,' he said.

Imogen backed away in terror. 'Oh, no!' she said. 'They'll chop it all off.'

'No they won't,' said Matt, explaining to the pretty receptionist exactly what he wanted them to do.

'It'll look great,' he said, smiling at Imogen reassuringly. 'I'll pick you up later.'

'*Il a beaucoup d'allure*,' sighed the pretty receptionist to one of the assistants, who nodded in agreement as she helped Imogen into a pink overall.

When Matt came back, he didn't recognise her. He gave her one of those hard, appraising sexy looks that men only give to very pretty girls. Then he said, 'My God!' and a great smile spread across his face.

Her hair hung in a sleek bronze curtain to her shoulders, parted on one side and falling seductively over one eye.

'Very pretty, little one,' he said, walking round her. 'You don't look like Judge Jeffreys after too much port any more.' But the expression in his

169

heavy-lidded eyes belied the teasing note in his voice.

'Let's go and have some lunch,' he said, tucking his hand underneath her arm.

He led her down a labyrinth of alleys smelling of garlic, abounding in cats and washing, to a tiny dark restaurant, which was full of fishermen. The food was superb.

Imogen watched Matt slowly pulling leaves off his artichoke.

'What does *beaucoup d'allure* mean?' she asked.

Matt looked up. 'Lots of sex appeal. Why?'

Imogen blushed. 'I just heard someone saying it about someone.'

As always he drew confidences out of her, as the sun brings out the flowers. Under that exceptionally friendly gaze, she was soon telling him about the vicarage, and her brothers and sister, and what hell it had been to be fat at school, and how difficult it was to get on with her father. He's a journalist, she kept telling herself, he's trained to ask questions and be a good listener. He'd do the same to anyone. But she found herself noticing that his eyes were more dark green than black, and there was a small scar over his right eyebrow.

'You're not eating up,' he said, stripping one of her langoustine, dipping it into the mayonnaise and popping it into her mouth.

'I was wondering what the others were doing,' she lied.

'Bitching I should think. Yvonne told me this

morning that it takes all sorts to make a world. Really someone should write all her sayings down in a book so they're not forgotten.'

He ordered another bottle of wine. Two of the fishermen were staring fixedly at Imogen now. She wondered if she'd got lipstick on her teeth, and surreptitiously got out her mirror.

Matt grinned at her. 'They're staring at you because you look beautiful,' he said.

The musky treacherous fires of the wine were stealing down inside her. She was beginning to feel wonderful. Matt asked for the bill. Imogen got out her purse.

'Let me pay, please let me.'

Matt shook his head. 'This is on me.'

As they went out into the fiery sunshine, she swayed slightly, and Matt took her arm.

'Come on, baby, we've got things to do.'

Imogen kept catching reassuring glimpses of her sleek reflection in shop windows. The rich in their yachts and their Pucci silks held no terrors for her now. She was walking on air.

'I think I'm a bit tight,' she said.

'Good,' said Matt, turning briskly into a boutique.

In a daze, she watched him rifling through a tray of bikinis.

'If it's for Cable,' she said, 'that red one would look lovely.'

'Not for Cable,' he said, piloting her into one of the changing rooms, 'for you.'

'Oh I couldn't! I'm too fat.'

'I'm the best judge of that,' said Matt handing her a pale blue bikini and drawing the curtain on her.

'Oh, what the hell,' thought Imogen, hiccupping gently.

She put on the bikini, and then stood gaping at herself. Except for her midriff which was still pale, there, smiling back at her in the mirror, was one of those beautiful shapely blondes who paraded up and down the beach at Port-les-Pins. Could it really be her? She gave a squeal of delight.

Matt pulled back the curtain and gave a low whistle.

'That's not bad for a start,' he said.

'But I'm practically falling out of it,' she said.

'Disgusting.' He ran a leisurely hand over her midriff. 'You'll have to put in some overtime here. Try these on.'

Everything he handed her – dresses, trousers, shirts, beach shifts – was in pale greens, blues and pinks, calculated to take the last tinge of red out of her suntan.

The record player was pounding out old pop tunes.

'You're just too good to be true,

Can't take my eyes off you . . .' sang Andy Williams.

'Took the words out of my mouth,' said Matt. Still the same teasing note in his voice. But in his eyes, once again, she read approval and something else which made her heart beat faster.

As she struggled into an apple green dress

covered in white daisies, wondering how he should so instinctively know what suited her, she suddenly heard a commotion outside.

'*Matthieu, mon vieux!*'

'*Antoine, mon brave!*' followed by a torrent of excited French.

Imogen put her head round the curtain to find Matt talking nineteen to the dozen to the wickedest-looking Frenchman she had ever seen. He was wearing an immaculately tailored suit in brilliant yellow pinstripe, with a grey shirt and a green carnation in his button hole. Rings flashed from his fingers, gold rings in his ears. He reeked of scent and was smoking a large cigar, and although he had a young dark gipsy face, his hair was already quite grey.

Suddenly his black eyes lighted on Imogen.

'She come with you, Matthieu? What a beautiful girl.'

'This is Imogen,' said Matt.

'Beautiful,' murmured Antoine, fingering the green dress. 'You look like a meadow, Mademoiselle. May I come and roll in you some time?'

'Imogen, baby,' sighed Matt, 'I'm afraid this is Antoine de la Tour, playboy of the Western world. In between bouts of debauchery, he makes films.'

'We are old friends,' said Antoine. 'We were at Ox-fawd together.' He spoke English fluently with a strong Yorkshire accent.

'My Nanny come from Yorkshire,' he explained to Imogen. 'She taught me English, and much else besides. Ever since Nanny, I've a *tendresse* for York-shire girls.'

'Keep your hands off her,' said Matt. 'She's not mine to lend. I only borrowed her for the day. Tell me, do you know anything about Braganzi?'

'I've seen him in Marseilles once,' said Antoine. 'And the Duchess, what a beautiful woman.'

'How do I get to see him?' asked Matt.

'You don't,' said Antoine. ''is house is like a fortress.'

At that moment a redhead came undulating across the room with a pile of silk shirts over her arm. She was of such massive proportions, she made Imogen feel like Twiggy.

'This is Mimi,' said Antoine. 'Good girl, but spik no English.'

He handed her his wallet and, after smiling ravishingly at him, she undulated to the cash desk.

'Look at those 'ips,' sighed Antoine, 'but then I always prefer quantity to quality. Her father is biggest bidet manufacturer in France. 'E finance my next film.'

'What is it?' asked Imogen, wondering where Matt had disappeared to.

'I mek story of 'annibal and the Halps. We import one hondred elephants from Africa. Mimi will 'ave small part as 'annibal's slave girl.'

'She'll be splendid,' said Imogen.

Matt appeared and handed her a bulging carrier bag. She peered inside, aghast. 'But Matt, I can't. I thought we were just fooling about. All these things must have cost a fortune. You can't give them to me!'

'All in a good cause,' said Matt. 'Consider that they come with the compliments of Port-les-Pins Casino. Let's go and see Antoine off,' he added before she could argue any more.

Outside, deep in onlookers, was a huge pale mauve Rolls-Royce with smoked glass windows. Mimi, two Great Danes and a goat were watching television in the back.

A tall sleek Negro in a white suit and dark glasses was opening the door for Antoine.

'This is Rebel,' said Antoine. 'My bodyguard and friend. I want him to play Caesar in my film. But he say it against Black Power principles to play white dictator. We'll come over to Port-les-Pins this evening. *Au revoir, mes petites*,' and he joined Mimi and the menagerie in the back.

'He certainly has great style,' said Imogen, still giggling as she and Matt stretched out on the beach later. 'I mean that grey hair with that young face.'

'It's dyed,' said Matt. 'You may laugh, but he's absolutely lethal where women are concerned. You should have seen him at Oxford, bowling them over with his Cartier watches and his dinner jacket with green facings. Any girl worth her salt in those days claimed to be educated at Roedean, Lady Margaret Hall, and Antoine de la Tour. So watch it, mate.'

Although everyone else on the beach was sun-bathing topless, Imogen jumped out of her skin as she felt Matt's fingers undoing the clasp of her bikini.

'No, I can't,' she gasped.

'Don't be silly,' said Matt. 'Turn over. I'll oil you.'

Imogen shut her eyes and turned over. The hot sun beat red through her lids. Hastily she covered her breasts with her folded arms.

'Come on,' said Matt. 'I want to look at you.'

'Oh please don't,' muttered Imogen. 'I'm so awful.'

'Shut up,' he said, gently pulling down her arms.

'You've been hiding your finest asset for far too long. Nicky was absolutely right about your tits.'

As his hands began to move luxuriously over her stomach, she felt her throat tighten and her mouth go dry. She opened her eyes to find him smiling lazily down at her, the heavy olive lids almost shutting out the dark green eyes. Her heart was going bump-bump like an overloaded spin dryer. Suddenly the beach had become a tiny room.

'I'll oil the rest of me,' she stammered, snatching the tube of *Ambre Solaire* from him and hastily smothering her tits.

Matt laughed. 'Fear no more the heat of the sun,' he said.

'It's not the heat of the sun I'm scared of at the moment,' muttered Imogen, frantically reaching for her bikini top. 'I'm going for a swim.'

'Uh, uh,' he held her down. 'Not when I've just oiled you. Concentrate on getting brown.'

He picked up the evening paper. 'Bugger,' he said.

'Braganzi and the Duchess went to the theatre in Marseilles last night. Jesus, if only I could get in there.'

If he's totally unmoved by my lying beside him half naked, perhaps it's all right, thought Imogen, looking timidly around. A few yards away a handsome German was lasciviously rubbing oil into his companion's enormous breasts. Goodness, I am seeing life, she thought as gradually the tension seeped out of her.

Much later, when Imogen's bosom and the sea were turning a deep rosy gold, Matt glanced at his watch. 'Christ it's late. We'd better get back.'

They drove back in a manic mood. The wireless was roaring out the Fifth symphony. Matt was waltzing the car round the hairpin bends. He was wearing that battered Panama hat to keep the sun out of his eyes. His thick tawny hair was now extravagantly bleached and streaked by the sun, his teeth gleamed white in his brown face.

God, he's divine. How could I ever have thought he was ugly? she wondered.

'Such a lovely day,' she said, stretching luxuriously. 'And all my heavenly clothes. You are good to me, Matt.'

He looked round and smiled approvingly.

'Nicky won't be able to keep his hands off you now.'

Nicky! That brought her up with a jerk. How awful, she hadn't given him a thought for hours.

177

Chapter Eleven

Sulky faces greeted them as they drove up to the hotel.

'Where the hell have you been?' snapped Cable.

'Exciting each other on the beach at St Trop,' said Matt.

Nicky and James were gaping at Imogen, who had got out of the car and was standing in the street in her bikini, her hair streaming down her back.

'Gosh,' said James in awe. 'You look like one of the girls at the Motor Show.'

'Matt seems to have been playing Pygmalion,' said Cable frostily.

'Rather successfully, don't you think?' said Matt, looking at Imogen.

'She looks tremendous,' said James. 'Have a drink?'

'We bumped into Antoine de la Tour, mad as ever. He's coming over this evening. How was the water skiing, darling?' said Matt to Cable. He bent over to give her a peck on the cheek, but she jerked her head away and spat a remark at him which only he heard.

He straightened up and looked at her.

'It's those loving things you do that make me grow so close to you,' he said in an undertone.

'Yvonne's ill,' said Nicky, who was still staring at Imogen. 'She's been stung by a jellyfish.'

'Oh dear,' said Matt in concern. 'Is the poor jellyfish expected to live?'

James tried, but failed, to look affronted.

'She wants me to sit by her bedside all night,' he said plaintively. 'I'd get her some pills to ease the pain, but I can't make the beastly chemist understand.'

'I'll get her something,' said Matt. 'Order us a drink. I'll be right back.'

'First she says I stink of garlic, and then I mustn't touch her because of her sunburn, and now this. What a holiday.' James looked as though he was going to cry.

Nicky turned to Imogen. 'You look sensational,' he said, and began to tell her about the water skiing, his eyes wandering over her body as of old. Cable looked so thunderous, Imogen was glad when Matt came back.

'Here you are,' he said, handing James a phial of green pills. 'But tell Yvonne not to take too many. They're absolute knockouts.'

'Thanks awfully,' said James, bolting into the hotel. He came back five minutes later, his face wreathed in smiles.

'What on earth were they?' he asked. 'She went out like a light.'

'Smarties,' said Matt. 'I got them from the sweet shop round the corner. We extracted the green ones.'

Cable was the only person not to join in the shouts of laughter.

'I'm going to change,' she said.

'So am I,' said Matt grimly.

Imogen, at a discreet distance behind them, saw Matt follow Cable into their room.

'When are you going to stop buggering up every one else's holiday?' she heard him say.

'Male chauvinist Pygmalion,' thought Imogen.

Dinner was decidedly stormy. The collision of wills in the bedroom had obviously escalated into a major row. Cable was in a murderous mood, her jaw set, her green eyes glittering. She kept ordering the most expensive things on the menu, and then sending them back untouched.

She was drinking heavily. And although Nicky was listening to her feverish chatter, every so often he cast discreet glances in Imogen's direction.

Imogen was feeling beautiful in one of the dresses Matt had bought her. She had noticed the way men's heads had turned and looked at her and stayed looking, as she came into the restaurant. It was a completely new experience. Even Cable couldn't destroy her mood of euphoria. James, delirious to be off the matrimonial lead, was getting thoroughly overexcited. Matt appeared outwardly unruffled, but he was lighting one cigarette from another.

No one was sorry when Antoine and Mimi arrived and bore them all off to a disco outside the town.

On the way they passed a large turreted house, strewn with creeper, set back from the road behind high walls and huge iron gates.

'That's one of Braganzi's 'ide outs,' said Antoine. 'It go straight down to a private beach.'

Above the burglar alarm trill of the cicadas, they could hear the faint baying of guard-dogs.

'I 'ave made the enquiries, Matthieu,' Antoine went on. 'If you go along to Le Bar de le Marine tomorrow lunchtime and ask for a Monsieur Roche, 'e might be able to help.'

The disco was called Verdi's Requiem. Imogen was almost knocked sideways by the brush-fire smell of pot, Alice Cooper thundering out of the stereo and a mass of writhing bodies. Antoine promptly ordered champagne all round and installed them at the best table.

Immediately Nicky asked Imogen to dance.

'You look simply terrific,' he said as soon as they were out of earshot of the others. 'I hardly recognised you when Matt brought you back this evening. I'm afraid I've been a bit offish lately. But when you kept hustling me out of the bedroom and then losing your pills.'

'It seemed as though I was deliberately rejecting you?'

'A deliberate rejection was exactly what it semed.'

'I'm sorry, Nicky. I didn't mean it.'

'I'm sorry too. No hard feelings?'

They smiled at each other. His eyes are like velvet, thought Imogen, but was shocked to find

181

herself adding that his forehead was too low, and his smile like a toothpaste commercial. He laid his smooth brown cheek against her hair and drew her closer to him, but her heart didn't thump in the usual way; she even felt very strong at the knees.

'Did you have a nice day with Matt?' he said.

'Yes, thank you. Did you have a nice day with Cable?'

'It's rather like looking after a two year old,' said Nicky. 'You have to keep her amused all the time and she's into everything, particularly boutiques. I can't think how Matt can afford her. She needs a play pen.'

The moment they got back to the table James swept her on to the floor. It was as though he had hitherto proceeded gingerly through life like a sports car towing a huge cumbersome trailer. But now suddenly the trailer had been detached (or rather stung by a jellyfish) and the sports car was careering off joyfully into the unknown.

'Jolly handsome chap, Antoine,' he said as his hands roved eagerly over Imogen's body. 'I wonder if I could get away with wearing earrings.'

'Would it be quite the thing for a Tory candidate?' shouted Imogen above the din of the music. 'You'd have to have your ears pierced.'

'My ears are pierced every day by the voice of my dear wife,' said James petulantly.

Imogen giggled. She realised she'd had a great deal too much to drink. Oblivious that James was breathing down the front of her dress, and caressing her back, she tried to unravel her confused emotions. Whatever had happened to that undying love she had sworn to Nicky last night?

She looked across the room at him, talking earnestly to Cable, as though he was placating her for dancing so long with Imogen. She was alarmed that she felt no pang of jealousy. What price the constant nymph now?

'*Many a tear has to fall but it's all in the game,*' sang the record player.

'That Mimi's a bit of all right, isn't she?' said James, squeezing Imogen ever tighter. 'How do you say, "Do you bop?" in French?'

A few minutes later James and Mimi had taken the floor.

James, just about coming up to Mimi's shoulder, happily buried his pink face in her magnificent bosom.

Imogen meanwhile was having a long dance with Antoine, who divided his time between flirting outrageously and telling her how awful he thought Cable was. 'She is a nighthorse,' he said finally.

'Nightmare,' giggled Imogen. But she was surprised.

She had thought Antoine and Cable would get on. Perhaps they were both too fond of the limelight.

'This is a very nice place,' she said.

'I own it,' said Antoine simply, looking like the devil himself, swaying in front of her, all in black with his diamonds flashing gaudily, and his white teeth gleaming tigerish in his dark gipsy face. Any moment she expected him to disappear through a trapdoor in a puff of smoke.

'Oim jolly well pleased to see you,' he said.

'Mimi goes to Paris at the week-end. I come over and see you. I have villa just behind the village. We might go riding or sailing together. I have been sailing in England, at Calves.'

'Calves?' said Imogen, puzzled.

'Yes, in the Island of Wight.'

'Oh, Cowes!' She went off into peals of laughter. She found it impossible to take him seriously.

'I love England, but I think your countrymen behave atrocious abroad.'

He was looking at James, who, with Mimi's help was energetically lowering his country's prestige on the other side of the floor.

'Mimi make the distress signals,' he said. 'I must salvage her. *A bientôt, ma cherie*,' and kissing Imogen fondly on both cheeks, he delivered her back to the table.

James asked her to dance, and then Nicky again and then James. Cable, refusing to leave the table and the champagne, was looking absolutely thunderous, and didn't even cheer up when Nicky made the disc jockey play one of her favourite tunes.

Fate is conspiring against me, thought Cable bitterly. For the first few days of the holiday, everything had gone so well; she had succeeded in enslaving Nicky and James, irritating Yvonne, utterly overshadowing stupid naïve Imogen, and finally most important of all continually keeping Matt on the jump. She knew how upset he had been beneath that apparent imperturbability. She had felt the whole time as though she'd been driving a coach and five with complete success. But tonight, suddenly, she felt the reins slipping out of her hands. Matt had obviously enjoyed his day with Imogen and brought her back looking quite passable – at least Nicky and James and Antoine obviously thought so and were all over her. Men always went for anything new. Cable was further irritated that Antoine hadn't reacted to her charms.

She'd always heard what a wolf he was and he wasn't even flickering in her direction. As for that blousy overweight Mimi, even in the gloom of the disco everyone was turning their heads and staring at her in admiration.

In the same way, Cable supposed people would stare at an elephant if it came through the door. And then Nicky wasn't being as tractable as usual. That very afternoon she'd caught him exchanging surreptitious but no less smouldering glances with a blonde nymphette at the water-skiing club. She'd have to give him some concessions soon. She drained her glass of champagne and banged it imperiously on the table.

'Get another bottle,' she ordered Matt.

Totally ignoring her, Matt turned towards Imogen, who was coming off the floor with James. Her hair was tumbled from dancing, her cheeks flushed, her breasts rising and almost falling out of the low cut dress.

'My turn I think,' he said, getting to his feet.

'Beautiful, beautiful girl,' said Antoine. 'How I love Yorkshire girls.'

Nicky was about to agree with him, and claim responsibility for discovering her, then, glancing at Cable's face, thought better of it.

'Isn't that Bianca Jagger over there?' said James, peering through the gloom. 'I'm going to ask her to dance.'

Imogen had been waiting to dance with Matt all evening. There was a thrill of excitement in the pit of her stomach, as, loose-jointed, he swayed in front of her, his lazy triangular eyes amused yet approving.

'You're having a good evening, darling. They've been after you like wasps round a water melon.'

'It's entirely due to you,' she said. She looked across the room at Nicky and Cable who were deep in conversation. Nicky was holding Cable's hand and apparently trying to calm her down.

'I'm sorry it didn't work – getting Nicky off Cable, I mean.'

Matt shrugged his shoulders. 'I'm not losing any sleep,' he said. The music accelerated, the colours were shifting like a kaleidoscope. The floor was filling up and they were constantly thrown together. Matt put his hands on her shoulders to protect her. She was finding it difficult to breathe.

Suddenly, he buried his face in her neck. Her body turned to liquid.

'You've been pinching Cable's scent,' he said.

'Oh, goodness, I'm sorry,' said Imogen, blushing crimson in confusion.

'I don't mind. Pinch away. It doesn't suit you, that's all. Too clinging.' Imogen was about to say she *felt* clinging when Nicky came over.

'Antoine's off, James is about to be duffed up by the husband of a girl he's convinced is Bianca Jagger, and Cable says she's bored.'

'And I'm in absolutely no hurry. Cable can do the waiting for a change,' said Matt.

Imogen didn't dare look in Cable's direction, and tried not to feel elated, as they danced on for another two records by which time the table had emptied.

Outside they found Rebel, the black chauffeur, bearing a heavily embracing Antoine and Mimi away in the huge Rolls-Royce. Cable was crouched over the wheel of the Mercedes with Nicky beside her, an arm along the back of the seat.

'Where the hell have you been?' said Cable, furiously revving up the car.

'Keeping you waiting,' snapped Matt.

'You and your darling protégée have been doing that all day.'

'I should write to *The Times* about it if I were you,' said Matt.

'Stop sending me up,' howled Cable. 'You can both bloody well walk home,' and, jamming her foot down on the accelerator, she thundered off down the coast road.

'Oh dear,' said Imogen in horror.

'Silly bitch,' said Matt totally unmoved. 'Shall we walk? It's only a mile or two. If you're too knackered I'll go back and ring for a taxi.'

'Oh, no, I'd love to,' said Imogen, unable to believe her luck.

'Suits me,' said Matt, taking her arm. 'I want to have a closer butcher's at Braganzi's house on the way.'

After the day's relentless heat, the night was warm and sultry. Compared with the stuffiness of the disco the air was sweet and smelt faintly of dew, wild thyme and the sea. The cicadas were cawing in the trees like frogs. Port-les-Pins glittered in its cove ahead of them, and every few seconds its northern jut of rock was bathed in a white beam from the lighthouse. Far above them everything in the sky, stars, planets, Milky Way, moon seemed to be out and twinkling eons away in their own heavens. And I'm so lit up they can probably see me twinkling away down here on earth too, thought Imogen. She was swaying slightly from drink and euphoria, but Matt steadied her, holding her above the elbow, gently stroking the inside of her arm with his thumb. He's probably so used to caressing Cable, he does it automatically, she thought.

'You're too good to be true, can't take my eyes off you,' hummed Matt abstractedly.

They could see Braganzi's house ghostly in the moonlight, its turrets thickly hung with creeper and silhouetted against the sky.

'Is it really necessary to get to see him?' said

Imogen nervously. 'Oughtn't you to be relaxing on your holidays?'

'All journalists are the same. Once they've got on to a scent they can't let it alone, like dogs with a bitch on heat.'

They were only a hundred yards away now. There were two lights on upstairs with bars like lift gates over the windows. Perhaps one was the Duchess's bedroom. Imogen imagined her brushing out her long dark hair with silver brushes with coronets on. She longed to open all the shutters like an Advent calendar and perhaps find the little baby asleep in one room or Braganzi plotting some dastardly crime in a black shirt and a white tie in another.

Outside the main gates, they could see a figure walking up and down with an Alsatian on a lead. The dog growled, the man stubbed out his cigarette and looked around. Imogen started to tremble.

'Let's have a look round the back,' whispered Matt.

Fifteen foot high walls with another three feet of iron spikes, and rolled barbed wire on top of that, went almost all the way round the house, then divided at the back, running down to the sea and protecting Braganzi's stretch of private beach.

'The only way into the house is from the sea,' whispered Matt, 'and I bet that's guarded night and day. He's not taking any chances, is he? It's worse than Colditz.' He looked at the burglar alarms that clung like limpets to the walls of the house.

The brightness of the moonlight and the sweet

heavy smell of tobacco plants and night-scented stocks made it all the more sinister.

'Do let's go,' pleaded Imogen. She was sure the guard dogs could hear the frantic hammering of her heart. They were creeping close to the wall now. Suddenly she heard a tinny sound, as her foot hit something metallic.

'Bugger,' said Matt, bending down to look. 'That's probably an alarm.'

Next moment there was a frantic barking of dogs, and sounds of a door clanging.

'They've rumbled us,' gasped Imogen.

'Come here,' said Matt, and the next moment he'd pushed her down on the ground and was kissing her, tugging down the top of her dress, baring her shoulders. She could feel the rough scrub against her back, and taste the salt and brandy on his lips.

The growling grew closer and more ferocious.

Imogen wriggled in terror.

'Lie still,' muttered Matt, putting his full weight on her. 'It's a lovely way to go.'

Next moment the area was flooded with light. The dogs charged forward. It seemed they must rip them to pieces, and then suddenly the ferocious growling stopped not six inches away. Imogen's French was not particularly fluent, but she could just make out Matt furiously asking what the bloody hell the guards thought they were doing as he pulled Imogen's dress up over her shoulders.

The guards dragged the dogs off and made her and Matt get to their feet. Matt explained that they were holidaymakers who'd got separated from the rest of the party and decided to walk home, that they were staying at La Reconnaissance in Port-les-Pins. Then the guards frisked Matt and had a look at his wallet and his traveller's cheques. Imogen nearly fainted when she saw that all four men had guns. They certainly took their time searching her, rough hands wandering into the most embarrassing places until Matt shouted at them to leave her alone.

Finally the guards conferred among themselves for a minute and then told them to be on their way, shouting something after them with a coarse laugh that Imogen didn't understand. She could feel their eyes following her and Matt like eight prongs sticking into their backs.

'Keep walking! Don't look round,' hissed Matt. 'Thank Christ I didn't have my passport on me, or they'd have rumbled us.'

After what seemed an eternity they rounded the corner, out of sight, with Port-les-Pins's friendly lights winking just below them.

Imogen started to tremble violently.

Matt put his arms round her. 'Darling, I'm terribly sorry. Are you all right?'

'I'm not sure,' she said. 'I thought our last moment had come.'

He held her close to him and stroked her hair and her bare arms until the reassuring warmth of his body made her calmer.

'But your reactions were like lightning,' she stammered. 'Pushing me on to the ground like that, then acting dumb and outraged like any old tourist caught in the act.'

Matt laughed and got a packet of cigarettes out of his pocket.

'I always turn into a bumpkin at midnight. Anyway I've talked myself out of much worse trouble spots than that. All the same, I'm really sorry, I shouldn't have put you through it.'

'What did they say as we were leaving?'

'Next time I brought a bird up on to the cliffs for a quick poke to choose somewhere else.'

'So they really believed you?'

Matt shrugged his shoulders. 'They won't tomorrow when they check up with the hotel.'

He was walking along with an arm round her shoulders now, and suddenly she felt choked with happiness almost to the point of tears, as it dawned on her how much, in spite of the danger, she'd enjoyed being kissed by him, and feeling the muscular weight of his body on top of her. She was still trembling, but not from fear.

'He must be terrified of something to wire a place up like that.'

'Losing the Duchess, I guess,' said Matt.

They had dropped down into the port now. Lights from the boats shivered in the black water like fallen earrings; the forest of masts swayed gently against the stars. In the distance they could hear the faint splash of the sea as it rolled over and over on the white sand.

They came to an all-night café along the front. A

few fishermen were drinking morosely at the bar; a tired-looking waitress had kicked off her shoes and was polishing glasses as though in her sleep.

'What we need is immediate first aid,' said Matt, and as he was ordering black coffee and triple brandies for them both, he suddenly turned round and smiled at her. The effect of him that close was so mind-blowing that her knees gave way. She had to fumble for a bar stool and clamber on to it.

'Will you bother to go and see Antoine's contact tomorrow?' she asked, as they got their drinks.

'If that doesn't lead to anything, I'll scrub the whole thing and preserve my energies for squabbling with Mrs Edgworth.' He took her hand and she hoped he couldn't feel the tremor that shot through her. 'Look, angel, I'm really sorry you were frightened. When one's had scraps with Provos, and white Rhodesians, and even Amin's henchmen, as I have in my time, Braganzi's hoods seem pretty small fry, but I know how terrifying it was for you.'

'Honestly, I'm fine now.' She could hardly tell him she'd never felt so happy in her life, and she thought he was the nicest man she'd ever met, and if he'd taken her in his arms, and thrown her down on the heath again, she wouldn't have minded if the entire criminal world formed a shrieking witch's coven round them. So instead she said, 'What were Amin's henchmen like?'

Then he told her about some of the trouble spots he'd been to and they had several more brandies by which time the stars were fading and the horizon was lightening to a pale turquoise. They walked back past the Bar de la Marine and the Plaza Hotel, with its striped umbrellas folded and its dozing doorman. They passed a few elderly homosexuals looking for comfort, and guitarists from the night-clubs sleepily twanging their way home.

'You're too good to be true, can't take my eyes off you,' hummed Matt.

At the reception area of La Reconnaissance with its one naked light bulb, he took down her key and extracted a dripping purple aster from the vase on the desk. Imogen ran upstairs pressing the lights and racing to catch the next switch before it went out and plunged them into darkness.

Outside her room, he stopped. 'Good-night little accomplice,' he said softly, handing her the dripping purple aster.

He's going to kiss me, she thought in rapture. But as he bent his head and touched her lips a door flew open, and out charged a fat woman in a hair net, who barged past them and rushed down the passage to the lavatory. Next minute they heard the sound of terrible retching, and both collapsed with silent laughter.

Then suddenly another door opened and there was Cable wrapped in a dark green towel, a cigarette hanging from her scarlet lips.

'And about bloody time too,' she said.

Inside her room Imogen wandered around in a daze. Matt had kissed her. She knew how casual kisses could be, and they'd both been drinking all day. But she didn't think Matt was a casual person. Port-les-Pins was teeming with beautiful girls but, unlike Nicky and James, beyond a cursory approving glance, he'd never shown much interest in any of them.

She looked in the mirror, and touched her lips where he'd kissed off all her lipstick, then ran her hands over her body with a shiver of excitement – a genius in bed Cable had said. But it wasn't just the bed she wanted.

Wipe that silly grin off your face, she kept telling herself, you're banking on too much. She lay down on the bed, but the room swung round and round, so she got up, and tried on all her new clothes, standing swaying on the bed to see them full length. Tomorrow she'd wear the pale green sundress, or perhaps the duck-egg blue shirt with most of the buttons undone like Cable did. She imagined Matt at this moment having a blazing row with Cable, saying it's all over between us, I love Imogen.

You mustn't hope, she told herself sternly, he loves Cable, he only gave you those clothes to get Nicky off her back, but the words made no sense to her.

I love him, I love him, she said, pressing her burning face in the pillow. Then she carefully put the purple aster between the pages of her diary, which wouldn't shut now because of the yellow centre bit, and lay for a long time watching the sky lighten, listening to cocks crowing and cars starting up, and children shouting, before she fell asleep.

Chapter Twelve

She was woken by the sun on her body, the same delicious feeling of happiness spreading through her like a rosy glow. She put on the new pale blue sundress and went downstairs to find the rest of the party in various stages of disintegration, having breakfast on the front and reading the papers.

Yvonne was displaying a black and blue foot on a chair for everyone to see. Having had no dinner last night, she had insisted on James ordering a boiled egg for her.

'This egg is as hard as a bullet, Jumbo,' she was screeching as she tried to force a buckling toast soldier into it.

'I asked for *quatorze* minutes,' said James defensively.

'That's fourteen, not four,' shrieked Yvonne. 'Why do you drink so much when you know you can't hold it, Jumbo? You know how idiotic it makes you next morning.'

James, desperately trying to disguise his hangover, was lifting his cup of coffee with both hands. He looked terrible. Matt didn't look much better.

He smiled rather guardedly when he saw Imogen, and didn't quite meet her eyes as he ordered her some coffee.

Nicky, looking healthy as ever, was reading the sports page of *The Times*.

'Christ,' he said, 'Connors got knocked out in the third round.'

Imogen watched him surreptitiously move his foot forward, and rub it gently against Cable's ankle. Cable returned the pressure, then stretched her beautiful brown legs out in front of her. She was wearing a Jean Machine rugger shirt and sitting on one of Matt's knees, reading the *Daily Mail* horoscopes.

'I do hate not getting the horoscopes till the day after. Evidently I should have had a disastrous day for romance yesterday, which simply wasn't true, was it, darling?' She coiled an arm round Matt's neck, and kissed him lingeringly.

Imogen picked pieces of skin out of her coffee with a spoon, and felt happiness slowly oozing out of her like air out of a badly tied balloon.

Madame waddled out with a telegram for Matt.

'It's from Larry Gilmore,' he said, when he'd opened the orange envelope. '"Arriving Plaza 8 p.m.,"' he read.

'Oh, that's great,' said Cable.

'Is that Larry Gilmore, the photographer?' said Yvonne. 'I thought he was supposed to be a monster.'

'He's fine as long as you don't burst into tears every time he calls you a stupid cow, and Bambi, his wife, is lovely,' answered Cable defensively.

'Bambi and Jumbo,' said Nicky. 'It's getting more like the zoo every minute.'

Everyone brightened at the prospect of new blood, it would perhaps get them off each other's backs, except Imogen who merely expected it would mean more talk about models.

'What d'you want to do today, Jumbo?' said Yvonne petulantly.

'Anything you like, darling.'

'Oh, don't be awkward. Anyway I've got to go into Marseilles to show this foot to a decent doctor.' She turned steely forget-me-not eyes on the rest of the company. 'They shoot horses you know, when they're in this kind of pain.'

'I'd like to go to the Isle of Levant and bathe nude,' said Cable. 'Have you any idea how lovely water feels on your naked body?'

'Yes, every day in the bath,' said Matt.

Nicky yawned and stretched out his legs, once again rubbing his foot against Cable's.

'I feel bloody unfit,' he said. 'I'm going to find some courts in Marseilles and have a workout. Will you be all right on the beach, darling?' he added to Imogen, who nodded with relief.

'I'm going into Marseilles too then,' said Cable, shooting a spiteful glance at Imogen. 'I think it's *my* turn to buy a few new clothes today. Are you coming too, darling?' she added to Matt, slipping a hand inside his shirt and stroking his chest.

'Can't, really. I've got to see this chap at the Bar de la Marine at twelve.'

Imogen's face lit up. Perhaps he was staying behind to be with her.

'Jesus, can't you ever stop working?' snapped Cable.

She glanced at Imogen, who was stirring her coffee and crumbling her croissant with a trembling hand, not looking at Matt and avoiding Cable's eye. She's got a schoolgirl's crush on Matt, thought Cable. It had happened before fairly often, with women friends of hers Matt had been particularly kind to, or girls who worked on the paper who came round for drinks, all tarted up, then looked at Cable with dismay, realising the competition. It was all Matt's fault for paying Imogen so much attention yesterday, as if he honestly believed that by buying her a few clothes he'd get Nicky back for her. She was a drip and Nicky didn't like drips, and a few sophisticated clothes wouldn't change that. Cable wasn't in the least jealous of Imogen. The blazing row she'd had with Matt last night had been followed by the most passionate rapturous love-making. But she didn't like him singling anyone out for attention. He never bothered with Yvonne like he did with Imogen.

As she and Matt went upstairs to get her some money, she said quite gently,

'Darling, you must stop leading Imogen on. She's got a terrible crush on you. She hasn't taken her eyes off you all morning.'

*   *   *

199

Matt sat on the beach beside Imogen, reading the same page over and over again. Ever since he'd woken up he'd been kicking himself, and going round saying damn, damn, damn, damn, like Professor Higgins. Admittedly he'd been smashed out of his mind last night, or he'd never have risked casing Braganzi's house and putting himself and Imogen in such danger, but he never should have given her that aster, or kissed her good-night. If they hadn't been interrupted by that fat woman rushing down to the lavatory, heaven knows how far he might have gone. He had his hands full with Cable. He liked Imogen far too muuch to hurt her.

It was a soft day. The breathing of the sea was remote and gentle; the sky arched a perfect corn-flower blue over their heads. But yesterday's easy camaraderie had vanished. Imogen didn't seem to be getting on much better with *Tristram Shandy* either. Matt shut his book.

'Let's go for a walk,' he said.

He bought her a Coke and a can of beer for himself, and they wandered along the beach, Imogen gathering shells and popping seaweed. As she popped away he could see her mouth moving – he loves me, he loves me not – and the look of desolation on her face when it came out, he loves me not.

They examined a dead jellyfish (like a striped red blister), overturned rocks so that little crabs scurried out, and when they walked over the dark wet saffron masses of seaweed covering the rocks, her hand slid into his as trustingly as a child to stop herself slipping. Oh Christ, why had he led her on? He had only meant to be kind.

They reached the end of the beach, and sat down to cool off under the indigo shadow cast by a huge red rock. He looked at her round innocent face longing to be kissed.

'Imogen, darling?'

'Yes,' she said, her eyes lighting up.

'How old are you?'

'Nearly 20.'

'And how many affairs have you had?'

'None really,' she blushed. 'Not bed anyway. I expect I would have with Nicky, but I lost my pills. But I found them again. I took three yesterday,' she added quickly.

'Well, don't tell him,' said Matt, deliberately misreading her offer. 'Nicky's no good for you. He's only interested in conquest, servicing totally *compris* in fact. He treats birds like French letters, throwing them away as soon as he's used them.'

He picked up a handful of sand, letting it drift through his fingers.

'Do you know what you should do after this holiday? Get away from your father and the family and Yorkshire and get a job in London. The paper's got a terrific library; they sometimes have a vacancy. Would you like me to see if I could get you a job?'

'Oh, yes, please,' she gasped. 'Oh, yes.' To have a chance to see him every day, to cut out his stories every week and file them under 'O'Connor, Matt', to do telling research for him whenever he needed help with a story.

'But I don't really know anyone in London,' she stammered.

Matt smiled. 'You know me and Basil – and Cable.'

Her fingers, which seemed to be sleepwalking towards his hand, suddenly stopped at the mention of Cable. She took a hasty swig from her tin, leaving a moustache of Coke on her upper lip.

'You should live a little,' he said very gently. 'Get more experience. Play the field. Break a few hearts, and have fun. You'll soon grow out of men like Nicky.'

'I don't want to play the field,' she said dolefully.

'Cable and I have been together a long time. We understand each other.'

He was trying to tell her something, however gently, and she didn't want to hear it. Keep out of Ireland. Hands off O'Connor. In the heat, he had pushed his damp blond hair back from his sweating forehead, showing the thick horizontal wrinkles, and the laughter lines round his eyes, which were bloodshot from drinking and lack of sleep, the heavy lids swollen. He looked thoroughly seedy and hung over, and every bit of his thirty-two years. But gazing at the battered sexy face she wondered how she could ever have loved anyone else in her life.

Matt sighed. He wasn't finding this at all easy. 'Look, sweetheart,' he said, 'I shouldn't have kissed you last night. I was extremely drunk and I enjoyed it, but I shouldn't have done it. You've had enough flak from Nicky without my putting the boot in.'

Imogen watched a speedboat shooting by, rearing up thirty degrees out of the water. The noontide sky was the same colour as the sea now; you could hardly distinguish the horizon.

She leapt to her feet.

'If you're trying to pretend last night meant any-thing more to me than a friendly good-night kiss,' she said, 'you're very much mistaken.'

And, turning away, she ran back down the beach towards the hotel.

'Hell, hell, hell and damnation,' said Matt.

A huge pair of dark glasses over her reddened eyes had got her through lunch. She could hardly eat anything, picking away like Cable. She avoided looking at Matt, who wasn't eating much either. He announced he was going into Marseilles by him-self that afternoon, to follow up a tip-off Antoine's contact had given him at the Bar de la Marine.

'I've had quite enough of Marseilles for one day,' said Cable, who'd had a successful shopping ex-pedition. 'I'm going to sleep for a few hours. Such an exhausting night, darling,' she added, running a caressing hand inside Matt's shirt. Imogen gritted her teeth. Yvonne, looking smug and well bandaged after a trip to the doctor, said the sun was too hot for her foot, and she would like James to drive her to look over a nearby château.

'And Imogen shall come with us,' insisted James, terrified of being left on his own with Yvonne.

'That's a good idea, darling,' said Nicky, running a lazy finger down Imogen's cheek. 'I've found some passable courts about five miles from here, so I'll have a workout this afternoon. You go with James and Yvonne. You'll enjoy it.'

He was wearing a navy blue T-shirt and white shorts, and Imogen could see the muscles rippling on his thighs and his shoulders, and suddenly she was shot through with sadness, because she had adored him so much and she remembered the ecstatic admiration she had felt when she'd first watched him playing tennis. And now, although she could still appreciate his beauty, he meant nothing to her. Maybe one day she'd feel as indifferently towards Matt.

'I'm cured of Nicky,' she thought dolefully. 'Now I've got to start again and get over the cure.'

In the end, when Cable had gone up to bed and Nicky and Matt had set out, she suddenly felt she couldn't face Yvonne bitching all afternoon at James and told them she felt like a walk on her own.

It was very hot. She wandered out of the town up a hill path which began with shallow steps between red and white holiday villas, then became a rough track leading on to wilder heath above the cliffs, not unlike the moors at home. The sea sparkled below and the air had a marvellous sweetness from wild lavender and thyme mingling with the sharper tang of the sea. If only Matt were here all would be perfect, but she mustn't think of him.

The path forked. She followed a track leading steeply down. She was pouring with sweat by the time she reached the sea's edge, picking her way across the jagged red rock, feeling its heat and sharpness even through the soles of her espadrilles. She took off her dress and shoes and dropped in her bikini into the cool green water, hoping it might bring her some relief. She swam out to sea, wondering in a brief despairing moment whether to swim on and on. But they always said you saw your past life again if you drowned, and the past four months had been far too traumatic for her to want a replay.

She floated for a bit, then swam round into the next cove, climbing back on to the rocks, regaining her breath. Suddenly she could hear the sound of voices and edged her way round the cove, until she could see a beautiful stretch of beach deserted except for one family. She sat down to watch them. A dark-haired, dark-eyed child in a pink sun hat was aimlessly banging a red spade on the ground, and watching his pretty mother and father build him a huge elaborate sandcastle. The girl was wearing a red bikini, the man a shirt and black trousers. He must be baking in this heat.

Tears filled Imogen's eyes. They looked so united and happy. She had a sudden fleeting picture of herself and Matt laughing together, building a castle for their own suntanned blond baby.

The child got unsteadily to its feet and waddled off, clambering on to the rocks, about twenty yards from her. He was so beautiful and fat and brown, she longed to call to him. The parents hadn't noticed his departure, they were so intent on building their castle. The man was kneeling down tunnelling a moat round the castle, forging a hole under a bridge, keeping the sand firm with his other hand. The girl was laughing and very close to him, bending over to look. The man suddenly turned round, looked at her for a second, and then kissed her, taking her by surprise. For a second she struggled then lay still in his arms, kissing him back. Imogen looked away. The world was like Noah's ark, everyone in twos, in love with each other, except her. She looked back at the child, then gave a strangled cry of horror. He was teetering on the edge of the rocks now, looking down into the deep water, where more sharp wicked rocks lay beneath the weed below. The next minute he had overbalanced and fallen in.

Imogen gave a scream.

'He's fallen in!' she yelled to the couple, who looked round at her uncomprehendingly. 'Vite vite!' she went on in her schoolgirl French, 'Il a tombé.'

Frozen with horror, neither of them moved. The only thing to do was to plunge into the water herself, swimming round the rocks to where she could see the little pink sunhat bobbing on top of the water. The current was suddenly terrifyingly strong, tugging her in every direction. When she dived under, frantically searching around, all she could feel was thick weed, and sharp rocks jagging her legs. She surfaced gasping, to find the man swimming in her direction, followed by the hysterically screaming mother.

'Ici,' she called to them shaking her hair out of her eyes. 'He's down here.' And she plunged down under the surface again. Next time she came up for air, choking and spluttering, the father had reached her, his face ashen, the mother followed him, frantically dog-paddling, still yelling hysterically.

Over and over again, they all dived down. He can't be still alive, thought Imogen despairingly, then suddenly between two rocks, she felt something soft, she tugged and tugged, but the object seemed wedged by the weed. She surfaced once more, her ears drumming.

'I think he's down here,' she spluttered. 'I can't shift him.'

Taking a huge breath, she plunged under once more and this time managed to catch the child's hair, and then one arm, and just as she thought her lungs would explode, she dislodged him, and lugged him to the surface. His eyes were shut, his mouth open.

The mother redoubled her sobs.

'Help me,' gasped Imogen, taking great shuddering gulps of air.

She was so exhausted now, the child felt like lead in her arms.

The father took the weight from her, and together they towed him to the shore, with the mother screaming behind them. They laid the child on the sand, and the man started pummelling and pumping at his chest.

'Let me do it,' said Imogen, frantically trying to remember her first aid classes. First you had to jerk

back their heads to see if the wind pipe was blocked.
It didn't seem to be. Then bending down, she put
her lips to the slack little mouth, and slowly started
breathing into it. He felt so cold and lifeless. She had
a terrible feeling they were too late. She was so worn
out by diving, it was almost impossible to keep her
breathing even. She tried to ignore the hysterical
ranting of the mother.

It seemed for an eternity she laboured, but it was
obviously hopeless, not a flicker of response, there
was no point in going on. She willed herself to
continue, she could feel the sun burning into her
back, then suddenly, miraculously, there was a faint
flutter in the child's chest, and slowly she could feel
his lungs expanding like a bellows, and gradually
with agonising slowness he took up the breathing of
his own accord.

Imogen knelt back on her heels, feeling dizzy, the
next minute the child opened bloodshot eyes, gave a
sob, and was violently sick.

'He's going to be all right,' said Imogen.

The mother's hysterics incomprehensibly increased. Imogen noticed a trickle of blood on her
left leg where she had jagged it on the rocks.

'*Ferme ta gueule*,' snarled the father, still looking
grey with fear. A fat lot of help they're being,
thought Imogen. She reached for a towel, cleaned
the child's face, and gently began to dry him.

'He'll be OK honestly,' she said, wrapping another
towel round him. They still seemed incapable of
movement.

'You must get him home at once,' she urged them as though speaking to children, 'and keep him warm and very quiet, and call the doctor immediately.' The man began to gibber his thanks.

'Honestly, it's nothing,' she said. 'You're probably suffering from shock too,' she added to the snivelling mother. 'But he's all right, *really* he is.'

'But how did you come to be here?' said the father in very broken English. 'Didn't you know the beach was private?'

'Oh, goodness. No I didn't. I'm so sorry. But look, the important thing now is to get him home.'

'Where are you staying?' asked the father slowly.

'In Port-les-Pins.' She picked up the shivering child in his towel and handed him to the father. 'At once, go home. C'est très important.'

Only after she'd got dressed and begun the long walk home did she realise how much the incident had shaken her. She must go back to the hotel and tell someone. Her thoughts veered towards Matt and then away. Matt was out of bounds and belonged to Cable. Perhaps Madame was in; she was always good for a gossip. But when she reached the hotel, she heard the ricochet of bullets and the thunder of horses' hooves coming from Madame's room behind the reception desk – the family must be stuck into some television Western. Then she saw Nicky's key was missing from its hook; he must be back.

She ran upstairs and knocked gently on his door;

there was no answer. She knocked again. Perhaps he was asleep. She tried the handle and the door opened. The shower was going. He couldn't have heard her. Then she saw Cable lying naked on the bed, her beautiful breasts poking up in the air. She was smoking a cigarette and laughing and saying something to Nicky, who was obviously in the shower, because he shouted back something Imogen couldn't hear and Cable laughed even more.

Imogen shut the door and ran down the corridor. Her legs felt completely weak. Her body was one burning blush. Oh, poor, poor Matt; he loved Cable, and she could do this to him. And Nicky, allegedly his great friend, pretending he was going off to practise tennis. What on earth would happen if he came back from Marseilles and caught them at it?

In a state of complete shock she wandered round and round the town, then went and sat trembling on the beach. A sailing boat was putting out. She noticed how pretty its red sails looked against the darkening blue of the sea, and the soft ochre of the sand. She wished she were on that boat escaping from all the turmoil and cross-currents and the misery.

Chapter Thirteen

She was suddenly aware of a clock striking seven and, turning round, saw that the tables at the bars along the front were filling up. It was part of the Port-les-Pins ritual. Every night you sat and drank and commented on the beautiful people drifting along the street on foot or driving slowly by in open cars. Often they merely paraded to one end of the beach, turned round and walked back again, over and over again, so everyone could admire them. Reluctantly she decided she had better be getting back.

The rock that overhung the bay was turning rose red in the sunset; the cypress trees reared up stiff as cats' tails against the glowing sky; the sea was veiled in an amethyst haze.

To her horror the first people she saw were Nicky and Cable drinking vodka and tonics under a Coca-Cola umbrella which gave a faint red glow to their sunburnt faces. Cable was wearing a white lace top tied under her breasts, with matching lace Bermudas which would have made anyone else look fat. Her long expanse of midriff was as smooth and brown as mahogany. Nicky was wearing white trousers and a grey cashmere sweater, his black curls still hanging in wet tendrils from the shower. They both looked superbly indolent, replete and handsome, like two panthers after feeding time.

Blushing crimson, aware of her tousled hair and unkempt appearance, Imogen tried to creep past them, but Nicky saw her and called out:

'Where have you been? I've been looking everywhere for you. Come over here and tell us all about the château and the embattled Edgworths.'

'I didn't go in the end,' she stammered.

For a second Nicky looked wary.

'I walked along the beach,' she added quickly, 'and sunbathed and wrote postcards instead. I must go and change.'

'Have a drink first,' said Nicky, steering her firmly into an empty seat beside him. 'You look bushed.'

Fortunately at that moment Yvonne and James arrived, both washed and changed and looking incredibly well laundered.

'The château was quite lovely. You *did* miss a treat, Imogen. The owner happened to be in residence, and took quite a fancy to me,' said Yvonne, patting her hair, 'and showed us everything. They had a wine-tasting on too, and gave us free glasses of wine. No, I'll only have a pineapple juice thank you, Nicky, and James doesn't need anything stronger.'

Nicky ordered the drinks in his rapid French, and went on eating his way through a packet of crisps.

'It's a pity you don't take more interest in culture,

Cable,' said Yvonne, looking disapprovingly at Cable's stretch of midriff. 'I'm sure you and Matt would find a lot more to talk about in the evenings if you did.'

'Matt and I have got more exciting things to do in the evenings than talk,' snapped Cable.

A seagull that had been circling overhead looking for titbits suddenly swooped on one of Nicky's crisps that had dropped on the floor.

'Bugger off,' said Nicky, swiping at it with his foot.

'Bet you say that to all the gulls,' said Cable.

Nicky grinned. 'I don't want it to dump on me.'

'Supposed to be lucky,' said James.

'One dumped on me when I was playing in Rome. I promptly dropped the set.'

'How did the workout go?' asked James. 'Find someone good enough to play with?'

Nicky laughed. 'Surprisingly, yes. For once I was really stretched,' and in the diversion caused by the drinks arriving Imogen saw him stretch a hand out and gently stroke the underneath of Cable's thigh. She wriggled luxuriously and smiled at him.

James took an unenthusiastic gulp of his pineapple juice and nearly choked.

'Must have gone down the wrong way,' he said, his eyes streaming, as Imogen thumped him on the back.

'I didn't think your hair would stay like that, Imogen, once it got wet,' said Yvonne smugly.

I hate her, thought Imogen. I'd like to take her beastly clean neck between my fingers and throttle her. Then she saw Matt coming towards the table, and her stomach dropped with love and she felt as though she was hurtling downwards in a very fast lift. He looked bug-eyed and exhausted, and collapsed into a chair next to Cable.

'Darling,' she said with unnatural enthusiasm, 'how was the tip-off?'

'Disastrous, complete bum steer. I give up. It's obviously impossible to reach Braganzi.'

'Can't say I'm sorry,' said Cable, running her hand sexily over his thigh. 'We might have the pleasure of your company for a change.'

How can she? thought Imogen, appalled. She's just got out of bed with Nicky, and in front of him she's fawning all over Matt.

Matt threw a bulging airmail envelope down on the table.

'Braganzi's cuttings. I asked the paper to send them out,' he said ruefully. 'Arrived by second post. Won't be needing them now, so I might as well get drunk tonight.'

'You did that last night, remember?' said Cable, with a slight edge in her voice. She pointedly removed her hand from his thigh.

Another large round of drinks was ordered. Imogen hadn't even finished her first. She wondered how on earth she was going to get through the evening. There seemed to be so many people in the party whose eyes she couldn't meet any more. It was as though Matt had read her thoughts.

'Gilmore'll be here any minute,' he said to the

table in general, but more in her direction. 'You'll like him. He and Bambi are one of the few happily married couples I know.'

'She actually *likes* staying home and being a mother and baking bread and polishing furniture,' said Cable.

'How nice,' said Yvonne. 'How old is she?'

'About forty.'

'I love older women,' said James, taking a hefty belt at his pineapple juice and looking very excited.

'She's happily married, Jumbo,' snapped Yvonne.

'I don't think Gilmore's ever strayed either,' said Matt.

Cable smirked as though she knew better.

'Oh, he may have pinched your bottom at the odd press party,' admitted Matt, 'but it's all show.'

'I must say it will be nice to have another wife to talk to. Once one gets married one does find single girls rather limited,' said Yvonne, getting to her feet. 'I must just pop over to the newsagents and get some more postcards. I haven't sent one to your mother yet, Jumbo.'

'Bitch,' said Cable, sticking her tongue out at Yvonne's trim departing back.

'What *did* you ask them to put in these pineapple juices, Nicky?' said James.

'Vodka,' said Nicky. 'I thought it was the least obvious. Probably disgusting.'

'At least it's alcohol,' said James. 'Thanks awfully. Let me get another round quickly while the old girl's buying postcards.'

'You're very quiet, Imogen,' said Cable. 'Are you all right?'

'The heat's probably been too much for her,' said Nicky. 'We should have taken better care of you, and not left you alone.'

They were all looking at her now. Imogen thought her face would crack with trying to smile.

'I think I'll go and change,' she said.

Upstairs she listlessly flipped through her wardrobe. In the end she put on the green dress with the white daisies, though it seemed far too frivolous for her mood of black gloom. The low-cut neck showed her shoulders and breasts, beautifully tanned now. During a day of such traumas it seemed odd that she should have turned so brown. Her hair, despite Yvonne's acid comments, fell into perfect shape when she combed it. She fiddled around a long time getting ready. She didn't want to go down; she couldn't bear to face the faces. A knock on the door made her jump. Matt, she thought with longing. But it was Cable.

'Hullo, that's nice,' she said, not looking Imogen in the eyes. 'Did Matt get it for you yesterday?'

Imogen nodded.

'He really ought to be on the women's page. We were worried about you, you took so long.'

You can talk, thought Imogen.

'I'm so pleased Larry and Bambi are arriving tonight,' said Cable as they went downstairs. 'Bambi'll be such a relief after Yvonne. She's sliding into middle age in such a happy leisurely sort of way.

216

Makes one think getting old might not be so desperate after all. You'll love her.'

Bambi was obviously no competition, thought Imogen. From Cable's Mona Lisa smirkings earlier, Larry Gilmore was obviously an old flame of hers. With Nicky as a current admirer, James ever ready to pounce and Matt in attendance, no wonder she was in such a good temper.

When they got to the table, James wolf-whistled at Imogen and Nicky told her she was looking beautiful. Imogen went and sat next to him, as far away from Matt as possible. I've got dinner to get through, and then I'm going straight to bed, she thought. A girl a few tables down was petting a panting golden retriever. It reminded her of Homer. Suddenly she felt so homesick she could hardly see straight. She mustn't cry. She stared down at her clenched fists, fighting back the tears.

'The Blaker-Harrises are supposed to be arriving at St Syriac tonight,' said Cable. 'We must call them tomorrow.'

Conversation fortunately moved on to the rocky state of the Blaker-Harrises' marriage, and Imogen was able to recover herself. Glancing up, she saw Matt was watching her. She flushed and looked quickly away. I'm an embarrassment to him now, she thought miserably.

Then, to her relief, Cable said, 'Look, there's Gilmore.'

'Over here,' yelled Matt, waving his arms at a very suntanned man of medium height with a thin hawk-like face. He was wearing a beautifully cut cream boiler suit, slashed to the waist and tucked into black boots. He was screwing his eyes up and looking round.

'He can't see a thing without his glasses,' said Cable. 'Christ, what has he done to himself?'

The suntanned man finally located them and, stopping to gawp at a sensational brunette as he crossed the road, nearly got run over by a couple of stunning blondes in a pink convertible.

'What a lovely way to go,' he drawled. 'Hullo, everyone.' He clapped Matt on the shoulder, kissed Cable and collapsed into a chair. 'Jesus, I need some first aid. Order me a quadruple whisky.' No one moved.

'What *have* you done to yourself?' asked Matt.

'You've changed your hair,' said Cable.

'It's the Mark Antony look.' Gilmore pulled the black tendrils over his forehead.

'*And* you've been at the Grecian 2000. You're as brown as a berry.'

'It's been a very good summer in Islington,' said Gilmore, and roared with laughter.

'You've had your ear pierced. And *where* did you get that white suit from?'

'I decided my image was getting a bit dreary, I ought to jazz myself up a little.'

'A *little*,' said Cable. 'Christ Almighty, Gilmore!'

Matt started to laugh.

'Oh, shut up,' said Gilmore. 'It jolly well works anyway. How are you, Nicky? You look disgustingly healthy.'

'No more than you,' said Nicky, and introduced Imogen and James.

Matt ordered Gilmore a drink and another round for the rest of them.

'Any luck with Braganzi?' said Gilmore.

Matt shook his head. 'Not a squeak. I've tried everything; *and* he machine-guns doorsteppers.'

'Well, if you can't get in there no one can,' said Gilmore.

'They were bloody good, those beauty queen pictures of yours,' said Matt.

'Took a hell of a lot of re-touching, both beauty queens and pix.'

'How's the paper?' asked Matt.

'Much the same when I left it.' Gilmore drained half his whisky in one gulp. 'Bruce Winter gave in his notice again; wrote a 17-page letter of resignation which no one could be bothered to read. So he's staying on after all. Our man in Jerusalem was wounded in the foot in a riot. H.E. sent his love. All he can think about at the moment is the All-Woman Everest Expedition.'

'Are we going to sponsor it?'

'Not if the finance boys have their way.'

'I picked up a good story this afternoon,' said Matt. 'All the kids have been cheating in their *Baccalaureate*. Some child got hold of the papers in advance and gave the answers to all and sundry. The authorities are completely flummoxed. They can't fail the whole lot of them.'

'Wish that would happen in London,' sighed

Gilmore. 'It's the only way my children would ever get their A levels. Are you going to file any copy?'

'I might,' said Matt, 'if I can summon up the energy.'

'There's trouble blowing up in Peru,' said Gilmore. 'If it gets any worse H.E. did say you might have to cut short your lotus-eating and fly out there.'

'What sort of trouble?' said Matt.

He's happy, thought Imogen wistfully. He must have been bored out of his mind this week with the rest of us.

It was Cable who broke them up.

'Must you two talk shop all day? Where's Bambi? In the bath?'

'Er, no,' said Gilmore, wincing as he gingerly turned the ring in his ear. 'God, these things hurt! She's in Islington.'

'She's *what*?' said Cable.

'In Islington.'

'You've come on your own, then?'

'In a word, no,' said Gilmore.

'You haven't brought someone else?' said Cable suspiciously.

'In a word, yes,' said Gilmore.

The stunned silence was interrupted by a gasp of amazement from James. An incredible blonde in silver platform heels, a silver space suit, with long blonde hair was causing considerable excitement as she wended her way along the front.

'There she is,' said Gilmore, going slightly pink under his suntan. 'Over here, my cherub.'

'She looks just like Bardot. She isn't, is she?' said James in excited tones.

'Not quite,' said Gilmore. 'I call her Brigitte Barmaid actually.'

'Jesus, look at those tits,' said Nicky, smoothing his hair.

Matt was torn between laughter and disapproval.

'Where on earth did you find her?' he said.

'She came to us as a temporary,' said Larry. 'I kept bumping into her in the lift.'

'There was room for you both in the lift?' asked Matt.

'I thought she'd have a nice soothing influence on Cable,' said Gilmore. 'I know how she likes as many pretty girls around her as possible.'

Cable was looking like the inevitable thundercloud.

'This is Tracey,' went on Gilmore, as the blonde sat down between him and Imogen, with a flurry of 'pleased-to-meet-yous'. 'And she never drinks anything else but sweet Cinzano, because she's hung up on sweet sin, aren't you, my precious?'

'Do you mind?' said Tracey. 'You're lovely and brown,' she added, beaming at Imogen. 'I always think a tan does more for a blonde than anyone else. Thank God I brown very quickly.'

'Don't you burn?' said Imogen, looking at the platinum hair.

'Never,' said Tracey. 'This colour's out of a bottle. Normally it's dark brown.'

Imogen blinked, unused to such frankness. 'Larry's a wonderful colour already,' she said.

'Oh, that's Man Tan,' said Tracey. 'It didn't work on his legs. They're all striped like a tiger.'

Imogen giggled, and suddenly felt more cheerful.

At that moment Yvonne arrived, weighed down with paper bags and postcards.

'I got this for our Daily,' she said, producing a lady in a crinoline made entirely of shells. 'Isn't it original? Oh hullo,' she added to Gilmore. 'You must be Larry. We've never met, but I so admire your work. And you must be Bambi?' she said turning to Tracey. 'I've heard so much about you. May I call you Bambi?'

'Well I keep doing it all the time,' said Gilmore in his lazy drawl, 'but she doesn't like it very much.'

Yvonne sat down between James and Matt.

'Where are you staying?' she asked.

'At the Plaza,' said Tracey. 'The rooms are awfully pokey.'

Yvonne looked put out. 'You should see our little hell-holes,' she said, glaring at Matt.

Tracey turned back to Imogen. 'Isn't it awful? Every time you turn on the bath in an hotel you get absolutely drenched from the shower. I got soaked tonight.'

She can't be much older than I am, thought Imogen. Cable and Yvonne were both glaring at her as though she was a particularly nasty maggot who'd appeared in their salad. Looking at her more closely, Imogen realised that underneath the heavy make-up she had a round face, huge brown eyes and a very sweet smile.

'Ta very much,' she said, taking her Cinzano from Matt. 'Who belongs to who round here?' she added to Imogen. 'Who's the little one with the pink face who looks like Ronnie Corbett?'

'That's James. He's married to Yvonne, the one with red hair. She's a model.'

'And the lovely brown one next to you? Goodness, he's handsome. He must be a coastguard or a swimming instructor or something.'

Imogen stifled a giggle. 'He's called Nicky Beresford.'

At the mention of his name Nicky looked up. 'I was just wondering what you do for a living,' said Tracey, smiling at him with luscious simplicity.

'He plays tennis,' snapped Cable, then after a pause, 'extremely successfully.'

'Oh, how lovely! I love tennis. Perhaps we could have a game tomorrow.'

'Perhaps we could,' said Nicky, smiling into her eyes. 'It doesn't have to be tennis.'

'*Encore de whisky*,' shouted Gilmore, glancing round at the girls sitting at nearby tables and walking along the front. 'Christ, the standard of talent is fantastic here. Just like the King's Road used to be on a Saturday afternoon. Can't think why I brought you, Tracey darling. Rather like carrying electric logs to Newcastle.'

'You'd have to speak French to them, I shouldn't wonder,' said Tracey placidly, 'and you know how that tires you. I'm hungry. I hope the food's better than it was in Paris. We went to Maxim's last night.

223

It was disgusting. I wanted a steak, and they gave me this charred rectangle of beef; when you put your fork in all the blood ran out. I love a nice scampi and chips.'

'I expect it can be arranged,' said Gilmore.

Yvonne was looking at Tracey in a puzzled way. 'I can't believe you're forty,' she said.

'She is round the bust,' said Cable spitefully.

'That's clever,' said Tracey, quite oblivious of either girl's animosity. 'How did you guess? I hear you're a model,' she added to Yvonne. 'I do a bit too in my spare time.'

'What kind?' said Yvonne coldly.

'Oh, nude stuff mostly. I was Penthouse Pet of the Month last July.'

'Were you indeed?' said Nicky, shamelessly undressing her with his eyes.

'They told the most terrible lies,' said Tracey. 'They photographed me cycling against a backdrop of some old university, with some pictures in these lovely silk undies and some in nothing at all.'

'Really,' said James, his eyes out on stalks.

'Then they wrote all this stuff in the paper about me being an intellectual and my father being a don. But they let me keep the undies, and they paid very well.'

'Is your father a don?' said Yvonne.

'No, he's an undertaker,' said Tracey.

Yvonne looked taken aback. 'Well, I suppose they do fill a need.'

'And an awful lot of holes,' said Matt drily.

'Do you do any nude work?' Tracey asked Yvonne.

'I couldn't do that sort of thing,' said Yvonne in a shocked voice.

'Oh, I wouldn't be discouraged,' said Tracey kindly. 'I used to be as flat as a board like you too. Then my manager said, "Tracey, why don't you get some decent tits?" He's got this doctor friend who can give you boobs like Sophia Loren. So I went and saw him. The operation was a bit of a drag, but the after-effect was terrific. These are just silicone,' she said, patting her jutting bosom fondly. 'But I've never looked back since. I'll give you the address of the doctor if you like. Pity not to be able to take your clothes off when it's so lucrative.'

For once Yvonne was completely at a loss for words.

Glancing across, Imogen saw that Matt was crying with laughter.

'Where did you really find her?' he said to Gilmore, wiping his eyes.

'Came to me as a temp. Types 30 words a minute and spells Laurence with a W all the time, but any girl with a body like that deserves to make it in life.'

'Can't think what she's doing with you.'

'She obviously wants to marry her grandfather.'

Yvonne leant across to Cable. 'I don't think that girl's married to Larry Gilmore at all,' she hissed.

'We ought to eat soon,' said Larry, lifting up one of Tracey's silver breasts which was hanging over his watch. 'It's nearly half past nine.'

'I'll get the bill,' said Matt, tipping back his chair

and waving to a waitress. Then suddenly – Imogen could never remember exactly how it happened – the bustling, noisy street went absolutely quiet. Waiters stopped in their tracks with trays held aloft, a man carrying a basket of fish up from the quay dropped it with a crash on the ground and stood motionless as though hypnotised, conversations all along the front slithered to a halt, a poodle barked and was angrily hushed, a child cried and was clouted. Everyone had turned towards the end of the street. Somehow the fear and anticipation had infected even the rowdiest holidaymaker. The only sound was the swish of the waves, and faint complaining of the seagulls. It was like *High Noon*. And then Imogen saw him, strolling lazily down the street towards them chewing on a cigar, a little bald man wearing dark glasses, a black shirt and ill-fitting white trousers, and apparently in no hurry. But even in his leisureliness there was tension.

'Braganzi,' hissed Matt.

'Christ, I wish I had a camera,' muttered Larry.

He was only a couple of tables away now, everyone smiling sycophantically. The same poodle growled and was kicked again.

'He's making for this table,' said Cable, shaking back her hair and licking her lips in anticipation. 'Perhaps he's coming to say you can do a piece on him.'

'More likely to warn us off,' said Matt.

Imogen watched him, mesmerised. It wasn't often you saw a legend that close.

He reached their table now, and paused, taking them all in. Then he took out his cigar and ground it into the pavement.

'Good evening,' he said in a very strong Italian accent. 'I look for Mees Brocklehurst.'

Imogen gasped in terror and threw a supplicating glance in Matt's direction.

'What d'you want her for,' said Matt sharply.

'May I present myself,' said the little man softly. My name is Enrico Braganzi.'

'We know that,' said Matt.

'I would simply like to talk to Miss Brocklehurst.' He smiled, showing several gold stoppings.

Nicky put a protecting hand on Imogen's arm.

'This is her,' he said.

Braganzi removed his dark glasses. His eyes were hooded, watchful, very, very dark. 'Mademoiselle,' he asked, 'were you by any chance swimming round the rocks to the Petite Plage today?'

Imogen gazed down, hoping the ground might swallow her up.

'Were you, lovie?' said Matt gently.

She knew the whole beach was watching her.

'Yes,' she stammered. 'I'm terribly sorry. It was so pretty. I just wanted to be on my own for a bit. I didn't realise it was private.'

'Please, Mademoiselle.' Braganzi held up a beautifully manicured hand, heavy with gold rings. 'I have only come to thank you from the bottom of my heart. You saved my little boy's life.'

'I what?' said Imogen, bewildered.

'You saved him from drowning, and then bring him back to life.'

'He was *your* child?' whispered Imogen. 'But I thought he belonged to that couple.'

'That couple,' said Braganzi in a voice that sent shivers down Imogen's spine, 'were the child's nanny and one of my guards.'

So that was why the girl was sobbing so hysterically, even after the child was revived – from terror of Braganzi.

'The girl came back to the house and tried to pretend nothing had happened. Fortunately another of my men had seen everything through binoculars from the house. You were too far away for him to help. When he arrived you had gone. He said you display amazing courage and presence of mind for one so young.'

'Oh gosh, it was nothing,' muttered Imogen. 'Anyone would have done it.'

'But they did not,' he went on. 'The child would have died if it had not been for you, Mademoiselle. I owe you an eternal debt of gratitude.'

'It was nothing,' she muttered once again, scuffing the ground with her foot. 'Is he all right now?'

'Yes, thank God. The doctor's been, and a specialist. The Duchess was frantic, but they reassured her that all was well. Ricky is sleeping now. The Duchess is naturally still very shaken, but she would very much like to meet you.'

'Oh, really, she doesn't have to. I mean . . .' Imogen stammered, terrified at the prospect.

'Please, Mademoiselle. It will mean so much to her. She wishes to thank you personally. I have my car here. May I drive you up to the house?'

Imogen looked at Matt beseechingly, but he was shaking with laughter.

'You are a dark horse, darling.'

'Why didn't you tell us?' said Nicky.

'We probably didn't ask her,' said Matt.

Imogen turned to Braganzi. 'All right, I'd like to come.'

'Wonderful.' Braganzi turned and raised a hand. It was the first time Imogen had noticed the tattoos on his thick, muscular arms. Next moment a black car that seemed as long as the beach glided up to them.

A chauffeur got out and opened the door for them. As she climbed inside Imogen felt like Jonah being swallowed by the whale. She wondered if she'd ever see the others again.

'Where did you learn your first aid?' asked Braganzi as the car climbed the hill. 'Are you nurse?'

Imogen told him about working in a library, and someone having to do a first aid course. 'I grumbled like mad at the time, and I was awfully bored, but I'm very glad I did now.'

'So indeed are we, Mademoiselle. Can I please tell you something, now we are alone a few minutes? You know perhaps a little about the Duchess and me?'

Imogen nodded.

'When she leave England to come to me, she had to leave her children too. I am not considered suitable stepfather, you understand. Nor are the children allowed to visit us, although we are fighting court battle. Camilla misses the children, although she doesn't show it, so all her love has gone into little Ricky. She had him late in life. We both did. He is – how you say it? – an autumn crocus. She is forty-three now. When she had Ricky she nearly died and the doctors later insisted on a hysterectomy; so it's no more children for either of us. Now you can appreciate how important Ricky is to both of us, and what you have done by saving his life.'

Imogen glanced up and saw that his dark eyes were full of tears, and knew that she was no longer afraid of him.

'How did you track me down?'

'I have, how you say, impeccable spy system.'

Imogen was very nervous about meeting the Duchess. But one glance at that lovely ravished face, with its brilliant grey eyes which were still red from crying, and all her fears vanished.

The Duchess walked forward quickly and took both Imogen's hands, and then kissed her on both cheeks, saying in a choked voice,

'I can never begin to thank you. I really don't know how to start.' But she was so friendly and natural and incredibly grateful that, after a few minutes, armed with a large glass of whisky, Imogen began to feel she really had done something rather good after all. They sat on the terrace, chatting twenty to the dozen together, and breathing in the heavy scent of the tobacco plants and the night-scented stock and later they went up and looked at little Ricky asleep in his cot in his pale blue bedroom, a Basil Brush on the pillow beside him. His cheeks were pinker now, his black hair flopped over his forehead. The Duchess moved round the room on tiptoe, straightening his bedclothes, adjusting the pillow, arranging toys, and checking the heat of his forehead with her hand.

'He looks much better,' said Imogen.

'He does, doesn't he?' The doctor says there's nothing to worry about, but I have to keep checking.'

As they went downstairs Imogen noticed a Picasso, a Modigliani and a Matisse on the wall. Braganzi was waiting for them.

'All right, darling?' he said, taking the Duchess's hand. He must have been three or four inches smaller than her, but somehow his width of shoulder and force of personality made it seem as though he was protecting some infinitely fragile object.

'Miss Brocklehurst must be hungry. Shall we eat now?'

'Yes, of course. How awful of me.' The Duchess turned, smiling, to Imogen. 'You will stay, won't you? We see so few people here, and there are so many things I want to ask you about your holiday and about England.'

'But you must be far too exhausted after such a

terrible shock,' stammered Imogen, terrified her table manners wouldn't be ducal enough. But in the end they persuaded her and she found she was absolutely famished. All her worries about her table manners vanished when she saw Braganzi falling on his food like a starved dingo, elbows on the table, taking great swigs of wine with his mouth full, and picking away at his teeth.

They had some kind of fish mousse, then delicious chicken. If the Duchess and Braganzi both picked their bones, Imogen supposed it was all right if she did too.

'And who did you come out here with?' asked the Duchess.

'He's called Nicky Beresford.'

'The tennis player? Oh, he's frightfully glamorous. I've admired him at Wimbledon so often.'

'And he thinks you're marvellous too,' said Imogen, her mouth full of fried potatoes.

'How lovely.' The Duchess looked pleased. 'So you're both having a wonderful holiday?'

'Yes, I suppose so,' said Imogen.

'You don't sound very enthusiastic,' said Braganzi. 'What was Mr Beresford doing leaving you alone on a hot summer afternoon?'

'He – er he – it's really very boring,' faltered Imogen, but she was so longing to tell someone.

'Go on,' said the Duchess. 'Enrico and I have so little excitement.'

And then the whole awful story came pouring out. 'We came in a party,' said Imogen, 'but it was quite obvious even before we left London that Nicky had fallen for one of the other girls.'

'Did she come with a boyfriend?'

'Yes. He's called Matthew O'Connor.'

'He's a journalist, isn't he, a very good one?' said the Duchess. 'When I can face the English Sundays I always read him.'

'He's terribly nice,' said Imogen, flushing.

'Then why don't you do a swap?' said the Duchess.

'He loves Cable, this other girl. He just ignores her and waits for her to come back. Occasionally they have terrible rows, but he realises she's only doing it, well, to make him keener on her.'

'How very complicated,' said the Duchess.

'O'Connor seemed quite keen on you the other night outside,' said Braganzi drily.

Imogen went crimson.

'How do you know?' she stammered.

'Enrico knows everything,' said the Duchess with pride.

Goodness, thought Imogen, darting a startled glance at Braganzi, so he knew Matt and I were casing his house all the time.

They had their coffee on the terrace. The night was black now, sprinkled with huge stars. The fire-flies darted above the tobacco plants and the Duchess bombarded Imogen with more questions, about her holiday, about her home in Yorkshire and then about England in general. Imogen suddenly realised it was very late.

'I must go.'

'Not yet. Enrico will take you back. Darling, go upstairs and just check if Ricky is all right.'

When he had gone, Imogen turned shyly to the Duchess.

'What a sweet man he is,' she said. 'I never dreamt he'd be so kind.'

The Duchess's face lit up. 'You think so? I'm so pleased. People in England find it quite incomprehensible that I threw up everything to run off with him.'

'I understand it perfectly,' said Imogen stoutly. She was suddenly aware she was more than a little drunk.

'I'd give anything to go home for a few weeks,' said the Duchess, 'but Enrico would be arrested the moment he set foot in England.' Suddenly she looked very tired and shadowed under the eyes. 'I miss the children horribly. Alexander, my ex-husband, won't let me near them in case they are corrupted by Enrico. Corrupted, indeed! If the courts knew what an immoral creature Alexander was!'

'I'm so sorry,' said Imogen.

'Oh, that's enough about me,' said the Duchess lightly. 'Let's talk about you. What can we possibly do to repay you? You have some days left of your holiday. We go back to Paris on Saturday. Why not leave the coast and Mr Beresford – it's too hot anyway – and come back with us? We would love to show you round Paris.'

'Oh no, really not,' cried Imogen. Suddenly the thought of being whisked away from Matt, however little he felt about her, was more than she could bear. 'It's terribly kind,' she added to soften her outburst. 'Honestly, rescuing him was enough, knowing you're pleased.'

'There must be something you'd like.'

Suddenly Imogen's heart beat faster. 'There is just one thing,' she said. 'Matt – more than anything else in the world he wants an interview with your husband. He's been trying to get one ever since we came out here. He's really a very responsible journalist. He wouldn't . . .' Her words faltered. She was about to say 'bitch him up', then thought it seemed rude.

The Duchess looked dubious. But at that moment Braganzi returned. 'The little one is fine,' he said.

For a moment they chattered to each other in Italian, the Duchess still looking worried.

'I'm sorry,' muttered Imogen. 'I shouldn't have asked. It was horribly presumptuous.'

'It is difficult in Enrico's position,' explained the Duchess. 'He is worried that anything Mr O'Connor says about him will prejudice my chances of seeing the children again.'

'Oh well, of course. I should have thought,' stammered Imogen.

Braganzi went over to the window and threw out his cigar into the garden. Then he turned round and smiled at Imogen.

'It is a very little thing, in return for what you have

done for us. Tell him to come at ten o'clock. But he *must* let me see what he is going to print. That is the only condition. He is an honourable man?'

'Oh yes, yes, of course he is. He is very honourable,' she said joyfully, thinking how pleased Matt would be. 'I can't thank you enough. I really must go now.' She couldn't wait to get back to Port-les-Pins and break the news to him.

The Duchess kissed her very affectionately, saying, 'Write to us in Paris and let me know how the holiday progresses.'

Braganzi rode back with her in the car.

'It's been a wonderful evening,' she found herself saying, 'and the Duchess is so wonderful. I think she's one of the nicest people I've ever met.'

'She is,' said Braganzi. 'She likes you too. She is very isolated now, you understand. She gave up so much when she left England for me.'

'But she gained so much.'

Braganzi sighed. 'I hope so. But you will come and stay with us perhaps next year, and we see that you have a better holiday.'

He took her address in Yorkshire. What would her father say if he could see her now, thought Imogen with a giggle, hob-nobbing with one of the most notorious criminals in France.

The chauffeur was driving along the front now. Although it was long after midnight, people were still drinking in the cafés.

Imogen wondered where the others were; probably smashed out of their minds in some nightclub, or perhaps they were at the Casino. It would be awful if they'd gone to bed. It was almost as though Braganzi had read her thoughts:

'There's your friend Mr O'Connor keeping an eye out for you,' he said, as the car drew to a halt, and he leaned across and opened the door for her. Then he smiled as he saw how Imogen's face had lit up. 'That pleases you, doesn't it?'

'D'you want to meet him now?' said Imogen, as she saw Matt get to his feet and walk towards them.

Braganzi shook his head. 'Tomorrow will do, and tell him to bring Larry Gilmore with him. He can take some pictures of Camilla and Ricky.'

'But I didn't even tell you Larry was here,' said Imogen in amazement. 'You really know everything, don't you?'

'I do my rich best,' said Braganzi modestly. 'Goodbye and once again thank you for everything,' and, taking her hand, he kissed it, and Imogen could see exactly why the Duchess had given up everything for him.

She waved as the car moved away. The next moment Matt was beside her.

'What was that hood doing mauling you like that?' he said sharply.

'Just saying good-bye.'

'Was that all he did?' His face was in shadow, so she couldn't read its expression, but his fingers were hard and painful on her arm.

'Of course it was. I had the most wonderful time.'

'You were away so long we were about to send out a search party.'

'You didn't have to. They were lovely to me.'

'Bloody well should have been, after all you did for them. What was she like?' He let go of her arm.

'Oh sweet, beautiful and well – sort of vulnerable. Where are the others?'

'Inside the bar. Gilmore's pissed out of his mind. Come and have a drink.' He put an arm round her shoulders and hugged her for a second. 'Sorry I snapped, darling. I was worried about you.'

A great surge of happiness welled up inside her; then she said 'Down, boy' to herself as she remembered Matt's 'trespassers-will-be-prosecuted' lecture on the beach that morning. He'd have been worried about anyone in the party who'd been closeted in Braganzi's fortress as long as she had.

Inside the bar Larry and Tracey were dancing round to the juke box.

'I'm Larry the Limpet,' cried Larry, shoving his hand down Tracey's dress.

'I do wish you'd stop doing rude things,' she said placidly, pulling his hand out.

They danced past the ladies which said 'Little Girls' on the door.

'I want seven,' said Larry, banging on the door, 'and I want them now.'

Nicky and Cable sat watching them. Nicky was roaring with laughter, Cable wasn't. James and Yvonne appeared to have gone to bed.

'Darling,' cried Nicky, jumping up when he saw her, 'are you all right?'

Tracey and Larry immediately stopped dancing and came over and showered her with questions.

'It was wonderful,' Imogen kept saying, embarrassed yet happy to be the centre of attention. 'The house is beautiful inside and the pictures are amazing.'

'Probably got half the Uffizi and the Louvre in there,' said Larry.

'Weren't you terrified?' said Tracey.

'No, not at all; not even by the Duchess. She was so friendly and – well – un-grand.'

'Why on earth should she be?' snapped Cable. 'She was only some two-bit actress before she married the Duke. She's really as common as muck.'

'Rubbish,' said Nicky. 'She comes from a perfectly respectable family. Did they seem keen on each other?'

'Oh yes, and Braganzi's amazing. He knows everything. He knew all about . . .' She was about to say 'last night', but she didn't know how much Matt had told Cable about their skirmish with the guards. 'He seems to know who we all are,' she added lamely. Matt came over, warming a large glass of brandy with his hands.

'Have a breath of that, sweetheart, and tell me all about it.'

'I'd like one too,' said Larry.

Imogen took the glass from Matt. 'Thanks awfully,' she stammered. 'And, oh Matt, Braganzi's promised to give you an interview.'

'I've just bought you three,' Matt was saying to Larry. Then he double-took. 'He *what*?' he said, his voice like a pistol shot.

'He's agreed to give you an interview. You're to go up there tomorrow at ten o'clock.'

'You're having me on,' he said incredulously.

'No, truly I'm not; and Larry can go too and take some pictures.'

'Holy Mother, you're a genius. How the hell did you swing that?'

'I asked him. The only condition is he wants to see copy.'

'That's all right. So should I, if I were in his shoes. Baby, you really are a beautiful, beautiful thing,' and he leant forward and kissed her on both cheeks. And this time she didn't even bother to say 'Down, boy' to the surge of happiness. She just revelled in how delighted and overwhelmed he was by the news.

'Can't I come and take pictures instead of Gilmore?' said Nicky. 'I'd love a crack at the Duchess.'

Imogen giggled. 'She thinks you're beautiful too.'

'She's heard of me?' said Nicky in surprise.

'Yes. They are capable occasionally of watching television, the Upper Classes. Some of the brighter ones can even read. Now, who's going to buy me a drink?' said Larry.

'No one,' said Matt firmly. 'You're having some coffee to sober you up, or your hand'll be shaking far too much to hold a camera straight.'

'I shall be caught with my Nikkons down yet

again,' said Larry. 'Just a small brandy wouldn't hurt.'

Cable got to her feet. 'Now that she's finally deigned to show up,' she said, shooting a venomous glance in Imogen's direction, 'can we please move on to somewhere slightly more exciting?'

Matt got the envelope of cuttings out of his back pocket and threw them on the table. 'You can if you want. I've got to read this lot. Now sit yourself down, Imogen my darling girl,' he patted the seat beside him, 'and if you're not too tired, would you tell me from the rescue onwards exactly what happened?'

Chapter Fourteen

Imogen woke late the next morning to another blazing hot day. Through the open window she could see a few little white clouds ermining the serene morning-glory blue of the sky. She lay for a minute reflecting on the extraordinary events of the past forty-eight hours; first Matt transforming her in St Tropez, then meeting Antoine, who was pretty bizarre by any standards, then being threatened by Braganzi's guards, Matt kissing her good-night and warning her off next morning, then her rescuing little Ricky, finding Nicky and Cable in bed and finally meeting Braganzi and the Duchess. Live a little, get some experience, Matt had said. Well, she'd certainly made a start. Yet, as she gazed at her smooth brown face in the mirror, she looked as young and as round-eyed as ever. She looked at the purple aster wilting in the diary and sighed.

She'd just got dressed and was wondering how Matt and Larry were getting on with Braganzi when there was a knock on the door. It was Tracey, wondering if she was ready to come down to the beach.

'It's awfully hot,' she said, as they wandered along the front. 'Even a T-shirt feels like a fur coat.'

'Did Larry get off all right this morning?'

'Yes, but he was feeling very poorly. I've never known a guy knock it back like he does. That Cable's a crosspatch, isn't she?'

'Yes,' sighed Imogen.

'I dreamt all my teeth fell out last night,' said Tracey. 'Isn't it supposed to mean something?'

'Probably that you're worried about all your teeth falling out,' said Imogen.

She noticed that even the brownest and most blasé Frenchmen sat up, pulled in their stomachs and took notice as Tracey undulated past, her silver waterfall of hair glinting in the sun. This was going to make Cable even crosser.

They found Yvonne and James parked in the middle of the beach. Yvonne was grumbling away under the cardboard nose shield, looking like a malignant goose.

'Hullo. Did you sleep well? I certainly didn't. Far too hot. I couldn't sleep a wink, and what's more I had this terrible nightmare about a jellyfish, and when I woke up I found this huge mosquito bite, and then the water in the shower was cold this morning.'

'How did you get on last night, Imogen?' said James, who'd brightened perceptibly at the sight of them. 'I was worried Braganzi might have turned you into a Pattie Hearst.'

'It was all frightfully exciting,' said Tracey, laying out a large green towel. 'Go on, tell them, Imogen.'

Imogen's account of the events of last night, however, was slightly overshadowed by the counter-attraction of Tracey stripping down to the bottom half of a leopardskin bikini.

James, who was oiling Yvonne's back, stopped in mid-stroke, his eyes falling out with excitement. Every Frenchman within 200 yards appeared similarly affected.

'Get *on* James,' said Yvonne, chattering with disapproval. 'And do lie down, Tracey, and don't draw attention to yourself. Go on, Imogen. How had the Duchess done up the lounge?'

'Oh, in pale blue silk,' said Imogen, still not feeling her audience was really captive, particularly as Tracey started to oil herself all over.

'That'll keep out the ultra-violent rays,' she said.

Twenty minutes later, by which time every man on the beach seemed to have made a detour past their little group to walk down to bathe, and then return flexing his muscles and dripping water all over them, Yvonne could bear it no longer. 'You'll burn, you know, Tracey. You really ought to cover yourself up, and those – er – bits burn much the worst.'

'Maybe you're right,' said Tracey, getting to her feet. 'I think I'll go and swim.'

'Well, on your head be it,' snapped Yvonne.

'It's not my 'ead it'll be on,' giggled Tracey, and she tripped off down to the sea, followed at a very indiscreet interval by a tidal wave of Frenchmen.

'I'm going to swim too,' said James and, before

Yvonne could stop him, bounded off down the beach.

'It's disgusting the way she flaunts her bosoms,' spluttered Yvonne.

'Well, they rather flaunt themselves,' said Imogen.

'Such a bad example for James, particularly Larry turning up with her. I wondered if she knows he's married.'

Imogen buried her face in the Bodley Head Scott Fitzgerald. She had given up *Tristram Shandy*.

'She's bound to burn,' grumbled Yvonne, adjusting her cardboard beak. 'People simply don't realise you have to take it slowly in this heat. That's why I never burn.' On she moaned, until Imogen was quite glad to see Cable and Nicky walking towards them. She supposed, with Matt gone off to see Braganzi, they'd taken the opportunity to spend a couple of hours in bed – and both got out of the wrong side of it, judging by the set sullen expressions on their faces.

'Good morning,' said Yvonne, cheering up at the sight of Cable's sulkiness.

'What's good about it?' snapped Cable, throwing her flattened lilo down on the ground. 'Will you blow it up for me, Nicky?'

He shot her a look which plainly said – Blow the bloody thing up yourself – then thought better of it and crouched down by the lilo, muttering under his breath.

'I hear Matt's gone to see Braganzi,' said Yvonne to Cable. 'You must be delighted for him.'

'I am *not*! A fine holiday I'm having, with him wasting his time running after silly stories. He'd gone by nine o'clock this morning, and that'll be the last I'll see of him today most likely. He's bound to be up half the night writing the beastly thing. He even asked me to find him a typewriter. I ask you, in a god-forsaken place like this. It's getting more and more like Margate,' she added, glaring round the beach. Then, turning to Nicky, who'd nearly finished blowing up the lilo, 'Why don't we push off to St Trop for the day?'

'No,' said Nicky, suddenly catching sight of Tracey frolicking around in the shallows with James, 'we haven't got a car.'

'Well, let's hire one,' said Cable imperiously, following Nicky's glance.

'Too much hassle,' snapped Nicky, corking up the lilo and laying it at Cable's feet. 'And it's far too hot to drive.' Cable's green eyes flashed.

It was getting too hot right here, thought Imogen. 'I'm going to swim,' she announced, setting off towards the sea.

'So am I,' said Nicky, hastily following her. 'You're looking very choice today, my darling. Let's get out of the line of fire.'

'We're over here,' Tracey called to them, waving frantically, her long blonde hair trailing in the green water like a mermaid's. 'It's lovely. And how are you this morning, Nicky?'

'Admiring you breasting the waves,' said Nicky, 'or rather waving the breasts.'

They all laughed, and splashed around. Then Nicky did his spectacular flashy crawl out to the raft and back.

'Oh, I wish I could swim like that,' said Tracey.

'I'll teach you,' said Nicky. 'Just rest your stomach on my hands, now move one arm like this, and put your head down.'

Tracey emerged giggling and spluttering. 'I wouldn't call that my tummy,' she said.

'Oh well, give or take a few inches,' said Nicky, smiling down at her. Suddenly they stopped laughing and just gazed at each other. Oh my goodness, thought Imogen, nervous but pleased as well, what will Cable say?

'Come on, Imogen,' said James with a jolly laugh. 'I'll give you a swimming lesson too. Ouch,' he squeaked as he stepped forward, 'I feel a prick.'

'Again,' said Nicky.

And they all collapsed into giggles again, which was all in all not the sort of behaviour to improve either Cable's or Yvonne's tempers.

When they finally came out of the water, Yvonne promptly sent James off to the café to get her some lemonade.

'Can you get me a vodka and tonic with ice and lemon?' said Cable.

'I'll come and help you,' said Nicky. 'I could do with a snifter myself.'

'Don't forget to make the tonic Slimline,' Cable called after him.

Yvonne turned her attention to Tracey, who was

sitting up combing the tangles out of her hair.

'My dear, have you known Larry long?'

'Not very.'

'Well, there's something about him I feel you really ought to know. May I be frank with you? He *is* married.'

'Oh, is he?' said Tracey, quite unmoved. 'Is she nice?'

'Very, evidently,' said Yvonne. 'And they've been happily married for seventeen years.'

'Well, I expect he needs a holiday from her then,' said Tracey. 'Then he'll go home all the keener.'

'But put yourself in his wife's place,' said Yvonne. 'How d'you think she feels at this moment, abandoned in Islington with the children, while you sun yourself on the Côte d'Azure at her husband's expense?'

A shadow fell over Imogen's book. She looked up and jumped as she saw Larry, a camera hanging from his neck. He put his finger to his lips.

'My dear,' said Yvonne, warming to her subject, 'don't you realise how physical men are? It's so easy for them to be led astray by the sight of a pretty face. If I encouraged them, I could have hundreds of men and husbands running after me, but it wouldn't be fair. Men are so animal. It's up to us girls to take a stand.'

Larry had crept round to Yvonne, and the next moment he was growling furiously into her ear, making her jump so much she fell off her lilo.

'How dare you?' she screamed.

'Bow wow,' growled Larry. 'Bow wow. I'm an animal being led astray by a pretty face. Bow wow. That nose does suit you, I can't think why you ever take it off,' and picking up his camera he took a succession of quick snaps of her.

'Put that thing away,' squealed Yvonne, furiously tearing off her nose.

'Well, stop brain-washing Tracey then. Not that there's a lot of brain to wash.'

Hullo Larry,' said Nicky, returning with James, a trayful of drinks and a cornet with two strawberry spheres of ice cream spilling out of the top. 'How did you get on?'

'Fantastic,' said Larry, seizing Cable's vodka and tonic and draining half of it in one gulp. 'What a pad they've got up there! It's a tragedy we couldn't use colour.'

'How was the Duchess?' said James.

'Sensational! Christ, what a beautiful woman. I've just been to Marseilles airport and put four rolls of film on a plane to London.'

'Where's Matt?' said Cable.

'Still up there, getting on like a château on fire. Braganzi's being amazingly free and frank.'

'He can afford to be if he's going to see copy,' snapped Cable. 'You might leave me some of my drink, Gilmore.'

'Oh, sorry, darling,' said Larry, finishing it. 'I'll get us both another one in a minute.'

'Ugh,' said Yvonne. 'You're dripping ice cream all over me. Who's it for?'

'Tracey,' said Nicky, handing it to her. 'Somehow its structure reminded me of her.'

'Do you mind?' giggled Tracey. 'Ta awfully, Nicky.'

'I'm going to swim,' said Cable, tucking her black hair into a yellow turban. 'Are you coming, Nicky?'

For a minute they glared at each other, then he laughed and said all right, and, putting an arm round her shoulders, walked down to the beach with her.

'I'm going too,' said Yvonne, still obviously put out by Larry's presence.

Larry took off his shirt and trousers. Underneath he was wearing black bathing trunks. He had a muscular well-shaped body, already very brown. The Man-Tan, as Tracey had pointed out, had striped his legs. He laughed when he caught Imogen staring at him.

'It's terribly difficult to put on over hairy legs,' he said, sitting down beside her. 'It's a great story you got Matt, you know, and you certainly made a hit with Braganzi and the Duchess. They've been singing your praises all morning. Weren't your ears burning?'

'No, but my boobs are,' interrupted Tracey, rolling over on her front and picking up Imogen's book.

Larry looked out to sea at Cable and Nicky who had reached the raft, clambered on to it and were plainly having some kind of argument.

'Cable's being poisonous to that nice tennis player,' he said in his slow voice. 'He must be her latest.'

'Oh, they've been flirting a bit,' said James. 'Jolly pretty girl, but a bit of a handful. Suppose I'm one of the lucky ones,' he said, blowing bubbles into his drink with a straw. 'Old Yvonne's never really looked at another man.'

'I'm one of the lucky ones too,' drawled Gilmore. 'Another man's never looked at old Bambi.'

That's not right, thought Imogen quickly; both Matt and Cable said she was very attractive.

Larry drained Cable's drink. 'Who's for a refill?' he said. 'What are you having, James?'

'Vodka and pineapple,' said James. 'I'm getting quite addicted to it. But for God's sake don't tell Yvonne.'

'And what about you, Tracey?'

'I'm all right for a bit,' said Tracey, licking her ice cream, and still engrossed in Imogen's Scott Fitzgerald. She glanced at the jacket. 'She writes rather well, this Bodley Head. Has she written lots of other books?'

'I'm starving,' said Nicky as the beach emptied for lunch. 'Let's find a nice cool restaurant and have something to eat.'

'And something to drink,' said Larry.

On the way they called in the hotel, where Cable found a note for Matt.

'Hooray,' she said, opening it. 'It's from the Blaker-Harrises. There's a big party on tonight. We're all invited.'

'Will it be smart?' said Yvonne.

'Pretty,' said Cable. 'Lots of Jet Set.'

'Oh, dear,' said Larry. 'I'm getting quite pixillated by high life. The Duchess this morning, the Blaker-Harrises tonight. I must go down to the Sieffs again.'

'What does everyone want to eat?' said James, as they sat down in a little restaurant hung with fishing nets and overlooking the sea. 'Hands up for Salade Niçoise.'

'I'd like an advocado pear,' said Tracey.

'I'd like an enormous vodka,' said Larry.

He's deliberately setting out to get drunk again, thought Imogen. A waiter shot past them bearing a plate of pink langoustines to a corner table, and she suddenly felt a stab of misery, remembering last time she'd eaten them with Matt in St Tropez. She wondered for the hundredth time how he was getting on.

They'd reached the coffee stage by the time he arrived. Cable and Yvonne were discussing what to wear that evening, Nicky was making discreet eyes at Tracey and talking to James about Forest Hills at the same time, Larry was ordering another bottle, when she saw him standing in the doorway watching them.

I can't help it, she thought in misery, every time I see him, I want to bound forward like a dog and wag my tail and jump all over him.

'Matt,' shouted Larry, 'bon journ main sewer. Qu-est-que ce going on up at Château Braganzi?'

Matt pulled up a chair and sat down between him and Cable.

'Jesus, what a story,' he said. 'It's so hot it frightens me.'

'Well, have a drink, and then it won't any more,' said Larry.

Matt shook his head. 'I'd better stay sober. Going to need all the wits I've got. I'll have some coffee. Are you all right, darling?' he said to Cable, then not giving her time to answer, turned to Imogen. 'They both sent their love. They gave me a present for you, but I left it behind. I'll bring it back when I go up this evening and show them the copy – if I ever get it together, that is.'

'You'd better get it written this afternoon,' said Cable. 'The Blaker-Harrises are giving a party tonight.'

'Well, they'll manage without me,' said Matt.

'That's ridiculous,' snapped Cable. 'It can't take you that long. You're not writing a novel.'

'Bloody nearly. I've just talked to the paper. They're going to hold the review front for it. You can't churn that out in a couple of hours.'

'There'll be a lot of talent at the Blaker-Harrises,' said Cable tauntingly. 'Rod Stewart's going to be there.'

'Well, you won't need me either.' As soon as he finished the cup of coffee he got to his feet. 'I'd better get started. Did you find me a typewriter?'

'No,' said Cable.

'Christ,' said Matt.

'I did try, but I had a lot of things to do this morning,' she added defensively.

'I've no doubt one of them was human.'

'What d'you mean?' said Cable, momentarily non-plussed.

'You should tidy up after your gentlemen friends. One of them left this on the bed this morning,' said Matt, and there was a slither of gold as he dropped Nicky's medallion on to Cable's lap.

There was an awful pause, then Cable said, 'Oh, that's Nicky's. The hot tap wasn't working in his room, so he used our shower. Perhaps you'd have a word with Madame, seeing she's a friend of yours.'

Matt looked at Nicky reflectively for a minute and then he laughed. 'I would have thought a few cold showers would have done you all the good in the world, Nicky boy,' and he was gone.

There was another long pause.

'I'm going to the hairdresser this afternoon,' said Yvonne.

'So am I,' said Cable.

Nicky turned to Tracey. 'How would you like to come for a ride on a pedalo?'

Larry looked out of the window at the heat haze shimmering on the road out of the village: 'I think it's going to snow. I want another large vodka.'

Larry and Imogen and James went back to the beach and they taught her how to play poker, but before long the heat and the heavy lunch overcame James and he staggered back to the hotel for a siesta. Larry picked up his camera. 'Let's wander along the beach. I'd like to take some pictures of you.'

'Oh, please no,' stammered Imogen. 'I don't take a very good photograph.'

'Don't be silly,' said Larry. 'I'm the one who takes the good photographs.'

And certainly he was so quiet and gentle, and snapped away so unobtrusively, and flattered her so outrageously, that she was soon relaxing and posing in every position he suggested, on the rocks, paddling in the shallows, lounging against a break-water.

'Has anyone told you what a pretty girl you are?' he said.

Imogen gazed at his thick black and grey hair, as he bent over the viewfinder.

'Yes, one or two people,' she said bitterly. 'And then they rush off with other people, telling me I'm too inexperienced.'

He looked up. 'Finding the musical beds confusing, are you? I must say we're a pretty decadent lot for you to stumble on, except perhaps Yvonne, and she's enough to put one off respectability for life, the frigid bitch. Turn your head slightly towards the sea, darling, but leave your eyes in the same place.'

'But Matt doesn't seem like that.' The temptation to talk about him was too strong.

'Matt's different,' said Larry, changing the film.

'In what way?' said Imogen, letting her hair fall over her face so Larry couldn't see she was blushing. 'I mean, when he gave Cable that medallion he must have known what she'd been up to with Nicky, but he didn't seem in the least put out. He was far more annoyed with her not getting the typewriter.'

'He completely switches off when he's working. Until he's got that piece finished, and it's going to be a bugger – turn your head slightly to the left, darling – he won't notice if Cable's being laid end to end by all the frogs in Port-les-Pins.'

'It must be awfully irritating for her. She's so beautiful.'

'She's nothing special. Just a spoilt little bitch who doesn't know what she wants.'

'She wants Matt,' said Imogen.

'Et alia. But I've got a feeling each time she cheats on him, it worries him less – head up a bit, darling – and if he allows her enough rope, she'll hang herself.'

Imogen giggled, and felt a bit better, and allowed herself a tiny dream about getting a job in the library on Matt's newspaper and his taking her on a story, and then getting snowed up.

'That's enough work for one afternoon,' said Larry. 'Let's go and have a drink.' He screwed his eyes up to look out to sea. 'Where's that pedalo? I hope Nicky hasn't sunk without Tracey.'

'She *is* nice,' said Imogen. 'In fact it's been so much better all round since you and she arrived last night. Will it be frightfully grand this evening?'

'It'll be ludicrous,' said Larry, tucking his arm through hers. 'But we might get a few laughs.'

They turned into the first bar on the front, and sat

idly drinking and watching the people coming back from the beach.

'That girl oughtn't to wear a bikini,' said Larry, as a fat brunette wobbled past them, 'she ought to wear an overcoat.'

'You should have seen the sensation Tracey caused on the beach this morning,' said Imogen. 'It was a bit like the Pied Piper drawing all the rats into the water when she went down to bathe.'

Larry didn't answer, and, suddenly turning round, Imogen saw he'd gone as white as a sheet and was gazing mesmerised with horror at a beautiful woman with short light brown hair, and very high cheek bones, who was walking hand in hand with a much younger, athletic-looking man down to the sea.

'What's the matter?' said Imogen.

He took a slug of his drink with a shaking hand.

'Please tell me,' she urged. 'I know something's wrong. You seem so – well – cheerful, but underneath I'm sure you're not.'

For a minute he was silent, his thin face dark and bitter, and she could feel the struggle going on inside him. Then he took a deep breath and said:

'That woman. For a minute I thought she was Bambi.'

'But she's in Islington.'

'No she isn't. She's down here somewhere with her lover. She left me about a fortnight ago.'

'Oh,' said Imogen with embarrassment. 'I can't bear it. You poor thing.'

'I didn't want everyone pitying me. It was my

fault. I suppose I neglected her. I've been working so hard the last two years just to survive and pay the school fees. Every night I'd come home and collapse in front of the telly with a double whisky, far too zonked out with my own problems to realise she was unhappy.'

'But when did she start seeing this other man?' asked Imogen.

'Oh, last year sometime. Suddenly she started finding fault with everything I did. If the washing machine had broken it was my fault. Going home at night was like being parachuted into a fucking minefield. In retrospect I realise now she was picking fights with me to justify falling for this other bloke.'

'How did you find out?'

'Silly, really. She used to go out every Wednesday to pottery classes. I used to babysit. She was quite often late back, said she and the rest of the class had been to the pub. Then one day I met her pottery teacher in the High Street, and he said what a pity it was she didn't come to classes any more when she was so talented. I went straight home and she admitted everything. In the old days I suppose I'd have blacked her eye, but I was buggered if I was going to be accused of being a male chauvinist pig, so I just got bombed out of my skull every night.'

'And what about Tracey?'

'She's just window dressing. She's a nice girl, but with me putting back the amount I'm putting back at the moment I'm not much use to her in the sack anyway. Best thing for her is to get off with Nicky. They're well matched intellectually!'

He took her hand. 'Look, I'm really sorry to dump on you like this.'

'I like it,' said Imogen. 'I've felt so useless this holiday. But aren't you likely to bump into Bambi any minute?'

He shrugged. 'I know she and loverboy are staying somewhere on the Riviera. He's frightfully rich, so it's bound to be expensive.'

'Does Matt know?'

'Of course,' said Larry. 'He rumbled it last night.'

Back at the hotel they found Cable and Yvonne both with sleek newly washed hair drinking lemon tea with Nicky and James.

'I suppose I'd better ring the paper to see if that film's arrived,' said Larry.

'What time have we got to be on parade?' asked Imogen.

'Well it starts at eight, but I don't think we need roll up much before nine or nine-thirty,' said Yvonne.

'Must make an entrance,' muttered Nicky.

James looked at his watch. 'Five o'clock. I've just got time to ring the office to see if everything's OK.'

After that Nicky decided he ought to go and ring his agent, and Cable and Yvonne suddenly came to the conclusion they ought to ring theirs as well.

Imogen wondered if she ought to keep her end up by ringing the library, but what could she ask them?

Had the Mayor returned *The Hite Report* at last?
Was Lady Jacintha still clinging on to Dick Francis?
She decided to go upstairs and wash her hair.

She met Cable coming downstairs looking bootfaced. 'Matt's lost his sense of humour. He simply
can't get his dreary piece together. He's just bitten
my head off simply because I asked for some change
to telephone. I'll have to borrow from Gilmore.'

Imogen turned around and went out to a nearby
café and bought six cans of iced beer and a couple of
large sandwiches made of French bread and garlic
sausage. She could see Cable safely squawking in the
telephone box as she went through reception, so she
went upstairs and knocked timidly on Matt's door.

There was no answer.

She knocked again.

'Come in,' shouted a voice. 'What the bloody hell
do you want this time?'

Inside she found him sitting on a chair that was
too small, bashing away at a typewriter on a tiny
table that shuddered and trembled under the
pressure. His blue denim shirt was drenched with
sweat; he looked like a giant trying to ride a Shet-
land pony. His shoulders were rigid with tension and
exasperation; there were scrumpled-up bits of paper
all over the floor.

'Can't you leave me alone for five minutes?' he
said through gritted teeth. Then he looked round,
blinked and realised it was her.

'Oh, it's you,' he said.

'I thought you might need something to eat – and

drink – not now but later,' she said nervously. 'You didn't have any lunch. You ought to eat.'

He looked slightly less bootfaced. 'That was very kind of you, sweetheart.'

'Is it going any better?'

'Nope.' He pushed his damp hair back from his forehead. 'It's going backwards. I've got a total brainfreeze. I can't think how to do it. It'll break soon, it's got to. I've got to show it to Braganzi before midnight. The bugger is him having to see it; it's like having to adapt de Sade for the parish mag.'

His eyes were just hollows in his suntanned face. He flexed his aching back. Suddenly he looked so tired and lost and defeated, she wanted to cradle his head against her and stroke all the tension out of him.

'I wouldn't bother about what they're going to think,' she said. 'I'm sure if you get across how much they adore each other, and what a sacrifice they had to make, and how the relationship does work, and how he's not just a cheap hood, they won't mind what else you say. They're just panicking that someone might write something that might prejudice her chances of seeing the children again . . . but you know all that anyway. I used to get panicky about essays in exams,' she said, tumbling over her words in her shyness.

Matt reached over and opened one of the cans of beer. 'Go on,' he said.

'So I used to pretend I wasn't doing an essay at all,

just writing a letter about the subject home to Juliet, trying to make it as amusing for her as possible.'

Matt grinned for the first time. 'You think I should pretend I'm writing to Basil?'

Imogen giggled. 'Well, maybe something of the sort.'

'Are you going to the Blaker-Harrises?' he said.

She nodded.

'Well, for God's sake wear a chastity belt and a bullet-proof vest. It's bound to turn into an orgy.'

He turned back to his typewriter, dismissing her, but as she went out on to the landing, he thanked her once again.

She was just starting to wash her hair when Larry knocked on the door.

'I'm going back to the hotel to have a bath and change,' he said. 'Tracey and I'll come and pick you up about half eight. We don't want to miss valuable drinking time.'

'What shall I wear?' she asked.

Gilmore went over to her wardrobe. 'The pink trousers and that pale pink top,' he said. 'It'll look stunning now you're brown.'

'Will it be smart enough?' she asked, doubtfully.

'Perfect. I want you to downstage the others. And remember no bra.'

What was the point of dressing up for a ball, she thought listlessly, when there was no chance of Prince Charming showing up?

Chapter Fifteen

'Hey, you look good enough to – ah – well good enough for anything,' said Larry when he collected her. 'You certainly do things for that sweater.'

'You like it?'

'Yes, and what's inside it even better.'

'Isn't it a bit tight?' said Imogen doubtfully. 'And are you sure trousers will be all right?'

'Perfect. Why wear expensive gear to go to a rugger scrum?'

He was wearing a pale grey suit and a black shirt, which matched his black and silver hair.

'You look lovely too,' she said.

As they went downstairs they could hear the relentless pounding of Matt's typewriter.

'That's a relief,' said Gilmore. 'Sounds as though he's getting it together at last.'

It was a stifling hot night. Tracey, James and Nicky, all in high spirits, were having a drink in the bar. Tracey was wearing a black dress, plunging at the front, slit up to her red pants at the back. Madame had presented James with one of her purple asters for his button hole.

'I've never been to a jet set party,' he was saying. 'I do hope Bianca Jagger's there.'

'Who are the Blaker-Harrises anyway?' asked Nicky.

'He made a fortune in dog food,' said Larry. 'I gather they're staying with some rich frogs called Ducharmé who are giving the party. Are Cable and Yvonne anything like ready, do you suppose? I'd much rather drink at Monsieur Ducharmé's expense than my own.'

'Well, I'm ready,' said a gay voice, and Yvonne arrived in a swirl of apple green, with green sandals, and a green ribbon in her red curls.

'You look lovely, my darling,' said James dutifully.

'Like *crème de menthe frappé*,' said Larry under his breath.

'I thought you said it'd be all right to wear trousers,' muttered Imogen.

'And the most wonderful news,' went on Yvonne. 'My agent's just rung back and said I'm short-listed for Jane Bennet in the new BBC *Pride and Prejudice*.'

Everyone gave rather forced exclamations of enthusiasm, and James kissed her, but very gingerly, so as not to disarrange her hair.

'When will you know?' said Nicky.

'In a day or two,' said Yvonne. 'They're starting shooting in three weeks. Isn't it exciting?' Suddenly her beady eyes fell on Imogen. 'Oughtn't you to go and change? We're going to be terribly late.'

'She's already changed,' said Larry. 'Aren't you rather miscast as Jane, Yvonne dear? She was supposed to be such a nice sweet natured girl.'

Yvonne was saved the trouble of thinking up a really crushing reply by the arrival of Cable, looking sensational in a dress entirely made of peacock feathers. It was sleeveless and clung lightly to her figure, stopping just above the knee. Two peacock feathers nestling in her snaking ebony hair and bands of peacock blue shadow painted on her eyelids made her eyes look brilliant flashing turquoise rather than green.

Nicky whistled. James gasped. Yvonne merely glared and shut her lips tighter.

'That's the most beautiful dress I've ever seen,' said Tracey.

'I'm going to change,' muttered Imogen.

'Haven't got time,' said Larry, seizing her wrist. 'I'm surprised you haven't borrowed Yvonne's cardboard beak to complete the picture, Cable darling.'

The sun was falling into the sea as the taxi turned off the coast road.

'I'm glad it's getting dark,' said Tracey, adding another layer of mascara to her false eyelashes. 'Party make-up looks so much better at night.'

In James's spotlessly clean, pale-blue car in front Imogen could see Cable, who'd commandeered the entire back seat to herself so her feathers shouldn't be ruffled, and Yvonne getting out combs and beginning to tease their hair with the pointed ends. She wished Matt were there to look after her. She was sure as soon as they got to the party, Larry would get drunk and disappear. Nicky already had his arm along the back of the seat and was surreptitiously caressing the back of Tracey's neck, so she couldn't expect much support from him either.

The taxi turned and sped up a drive, the gravel spluttering against the wheels. Vineyards and olive groves on either side stretched to infinity. Ahead in the dusk, every window blazing with light, was a huge white house.

'It's a mansion,' said Tracey.

They could see a man in a pink suit, with red and pink hair, get out of a Rolls-Royce and ring the door bell.

'I think that's David Bowie,' said Larry.

'Oh, dear,' said Imogen faintly.

As they walked up the marble steps, a butler opened the door. Then a maid whisked Imogen and Tracey upstairs to a room with walls covered in pink satin. On the floor was a thick fur carpet, the bed was covered in fur coats, which must have been brought by guests just to show off – it was such a stifling hot night.

'Do you take cloth coats too?' said Tracey, taking off her white blazer and handing it to the maid.

Cable and Yvonne were still engaged in teasing their hair in front of the mirror.

'I'm sure I caught a glimpse of Omar Sharif,' said Yvonne.

Out of the window Imogen could see a jungle of

garden, punctuated by lily ponds, aviaries full of coloured birds, two lantern-lit swimming pools and, in the distance, the sea.

Shaking with nerves, she went downstairs to find Larry waiting for her and talking in a low voice to a splendid blonde covered in sequins.

'Imogen darling, this is your hostess, Claudine. Take a good look at her. She may not pass this way again.'

But before he had a chance to say anything else, Claudine had shimmered forward and seized Imogen's hands.

'Mees Brocklehurst, how wonderful to meet you. What a fantastic coincidence that you should be on holiday with Matt and Nicky Beresford,' and the next moment she had drawn Imogen into a huge room, which seemed to be seething with suntanned faces with hard restless eyes, constantly on the look-out for fresh excitement.

'Wait for Larry,' begged Imogen.

'Larry who?' screamed Claudine and, shoving a drink into Imogen's hand, she dragged her from one group to another, crying, 'This is lovely Imogen Brocklehurst' . . . whisper, whisper . . . 'Yes, really. Braganzi's child snatched from the jaws of death.'

Everyone started oohing and aahing as though Claudine was bringing in the Christmas pudding flaming blue with brandy.

'How do you do? How do you do? Hi Imogen, glad to know you. How do you do?' People were thrusting forward to meet her.

Imogen turned to Claudine in horror. 'But what have you told them?'

'Did you really meet the Duchess? What was she like? Did she seem keen on Braganzi?' clamoured the faces.

'Oh stop,' called Imogen after a disappearing Claudine. 'Please don't tell people. Braganzi doesn't want publicity.'

Now everyone was mobbing her and introducing her. She was so breathless with answering questions, she found she'd finished her drink, which was delicious and tasted rather like coke filled with fruit salad. The moment she put her glass down another was thrust into her hand.

'How has she furnished the house?' 'Are the guard dogs as ferocious as everyone makes out?' 'Weren't you terrified to meet Braganzi?' 'Does he keep her chained up there?' 'Has she lost her looks?' 'I hear the Duke . . .'

More people were crowding round her, asking excited questions. Finally somebody introduced her to Larry. 'No, we haven't met,' he said, grabbing her by the arm and pulling her into a side room.

'This place is a lunatic asylum,' she gasped. 'What on earth did you tell Claudine?'

'I gave her a brief run down on your life-saving activities yesterday. You're certainly the star attraction. Have another drink.' He grabbed one from a passing waiter.

'I've had several already,' said Imogen with a giggle. 'It's delicious and so refreshing. What is it?'

'Pimms,' said Larry. 'Practically non-alcoholic.'

A vision in yellow flew out at him. 'Larry darling, where did you get to? I've been looking for you everywhere.' And she hauled him away.

Next moment a stunningly handsome man in a white dinner jacket had crept up and put his arm through Imogen's. 'I hear you know darling Camilla,' he said. 'Do give her my love next time you see her.'

A light flashed. 'Thank you,' said a photographer moving away.

The sounds of revelry grew louder, the heat grew more oppressive by the minute.

'Come and look at the garden,' said the man in the white dinner jacket. Two beautiful young men, in shirts slashed to the waist, met them in the door-way.

'At last we've found you. You must be Morgan Brocklehurst,' they chorused. 'We've been simply dying to meet you all evening.'

'I hear you had dinner with Braganzi last night,' said the first.

'Is he as butch as everyone says he is?' asked the second.

A large woman in crimson with one false eyelash hanging askew like a ladder from her bottom lid charged up to them.

'Does anyone know which Morgan Brocklehurst is?' she said, eagerly. 'I hear she's actually met Braganzi and the Duchess.'

'She's somewhere in there,' said the first young

man, pointing back at the drawing-room, from which a hysterical rush of talk was now issuing.

'Oh dear,' said the woman in crimson, 'I've just fought my way out of there. I want to try and nail her for a beach party I'm having tomorrow.' She dived back in the mêlée.

'I'll get you another drink, Morgan,' said the man in the white dinner jacket.

'Thanks, I'd adore one,' said Imogen, who was beginning to enjoy herself.

One of the beautiful young men took her arm and led her through the gardens, past huge jungle plants with leaves like dark shining shields, and brilliant coloured birds, scarlet, turquoise, dark blue and emerald, all chirruping and fluttering about their aviary, like guests at the party. Round the corner they found two pale pink flamingos standing on one leg in a bright green pond, full of fat golden carp gliding in and out of the water lilies.

In the stifling heat Imogen was quite happy to rest on a cool stone bench with lions' heads rearing up at either end. The two young men sat at her feet, a captive audience. She was soon quite happily recounting the events of yesterday.

Soon quite a crowd was gathered round her. People kept topping up her drink. 'It really is very moreish,' she said to the company at large. She kept looking around for Larry, and hoping Matt would arrive, but after a bit she stopped worrying even about them.

'Can I get you something to eat?' asked the man in the white dinner jacket.

'Oh, no thank you,' said Imogen. She seemed to have consumed far too much fruit salad already.

'Well, come and dance then,' he said, leading her back into the house. 'Claudine brought in 600 bottles of champagne for this party, plus 50 lbs of caviar, and God knows how many gallons of Diorissimo to put in the swimming pool. Of course she'll claim it all on tax.'

It was far too dark to see anyone on the dance floor.

'Morgan, Morgan, you're so fresh and unspoilt,' said the man in the white dinner jacket, drawing her to his bosom.

Oh· dear, she thought, I do hope I don't leave make-up all over him. Another man cut in and danced her off into another room where he tried to kiss her. She wanted to slap his face, but he wasn't very steady on his feet, and she thought she might knock him over. Then a haughty aristocratic beauty drew her aside.

'I'm giving a party in Marbella tomorrow night. Love it if you could make it. We could easily send a plane. Bring anyone you like. Perhaps Camilla'd like an outing? Has she put on any weight since she's been living with Braganzi?'

The band was playing *Smoke Gets In Your Eyes*, the laughter and tinkle of broken glass were getting louder, a crowd was clamouring round her again. Suddenly a hand shot out and grabbed her; it was Larry, waving a full bottle of champagne.

'Doctor Livingstone,' she screamed.

'I've been looking for you everywhere,' he said, dragging her through the french windows out into the garden.

'Where are the others?'

'Well, I've just seen Nicky and Tracey come out of the library, looking rather ruffled. Nicky was wearing lipstick, Tracey wasn't any more. Mrs Edgworth's been dancing the night away with Omar Sharif, and Cable's been dividing her unwrapped attention between Rod Stewart and Warren Beatty.'

'So she's happy?'

'Not entirely. No point in being the Belle of the Ball if the guy who matters isn't here to witness it. Matt hasn't showed up yet. He can't *still* be wrestling with his copy.'

'He's probably having trouble getting Braganzi to OK it,' said Imogen.

'If he does get it through he'll make a bomb on syndication. Bloody well need to, to pay for Cable's peacock feathers.'

Pity someone can't lock her away in the aviary with all those coloured birds, thought Imogen. She held out her glass.

'I'd like another drink, please.'

'That's my girl,' said Larry, filling her long Pimms glass up to the brim with champagne. For a while they danced on the lawn, both slightly supporting one another.

'Christ, I wish I'd brought my camera,' said Larry. 'Half the crowned heads of Europe are frisking nude

in the swimming pool. Evidently Leonard is on hand
with a fleet of minions to blow dry anyone who
wants it when they come out.'

Imogen listened to the shrieks and splashes
from the pool, and wished she felt slim enough to
bathe in the nude. She seemed to have drunk all her
champagne.

'I really must go to the loo.'

'Well, don't be long,' said Larry. 'It's nearly light
up time.'

Imogen realised how drunk she was when she
found herself liberally pouring her hostess's scent
over her bosom in the pink satin bedroom. Breaking
the eighth commandment again. She put the bottle
down hastily. What would her father say, and Matt?
Her face, however, looked rather sparkly-eyed and
pink-cheeked and much better than she'd expected
after so much booze.

'Have you met Morgan Brocklehurst?' she
heard two women saying as she went downstairs.
'Quite ravishing. I must ask her who does her hair.
Evidently Braganzi's leaving her half of Sicily.'

As she reached the bottom step, a large brunette
shot past her shrieking playfully, followed two
seconds later by James, very pink in the face and
emitting Tarzan howls. They both disappeared into
the shrubbery.

'Why aren't you dancing, Morgan?' asked
Claudine, rushing forward.

'I'll take care of that,' said a smooth voice, and
the next moment she felt herself clutched to the

muscular, scented hairy-chested bosom of one of the screen's greatest lovers.

'I took one look at you,' he crooned in her ear, 'That's all I meant to do, And then my heart stood still. How would you like to go to a party in Rome?'

'I'm supposed to be going to one in Marbella tomorrow,' said Imogen.

'Oh, that'll be Effie Strauss's thrash. I'll give you a lift if you like.'

They danced and danced, drank and drank, and although she was slightly missing the forehand drives of conversation he didn't seem to mind at all. Then she remembered she'd left Larry in the garden. She must go and find him. As she reached the end of the lawn, she passed a couple under a fig tree locked in a passionate embrace. The girl's silver blonde hair fell below her waist.

'The moment I saw you yesterday,' the man's voice was saying huskily, 'Pow, suddenly it happened, like being struck down by a thunderbolt. I don't know what it is about you, Tracey darling, but it's something indefinably different.'

'And your pulse, my darling, is going like the Charge of the Light Brigade,' shrieked Imogen loudly, and rushed off howling with laughter as they both jumped out of their skins.

She was still laughing when she found Larry rolling a joint by the flamingo pool. 'It's light up time,' he said again.

'This is the best party I've ever been to,' she said.

'Have a drag of this,' said Larry, 'and it'll seem even better.'

'I don't smoke,' said Imogen.

'Go on. I'm a great believer in first times. There may not be another opportunity.'

He lit the cigarette, inhaled deeply two or three times, then handed it to her. She took a nervous puff and choked, then took another one; then she put the joint in the snarling mouth of the stone lion at the end of the seat, and she and Larry both laughed immoderately. Then she took another drag.

'Nice?' asked Larry.

'Yes,' sighed Imogen. 'It makes the flamingos so pink and the water so green.'

Three-quarters down the cigarette, by which time they were both cackling with laughter over anything, she turned and looked at him. He was really very attractive in a hawk-like ravaged way. And quite old enough to be her father – so that made everything quite safe.

'Larry.'

'Yes, angel.'

'Do you think I'm pretty?'

'Exquisitely so,' and he bent over and kissed her very slowly and with velvet artistry.

'And now you're even prettier.' He took a deep drag on the cigarette, then kissed her again, and this time it took much longer.

Imogen got to her feet and went to the edge of the pool. The flamingos seemed to be floating above the water, the turning beam of the lighthouse revolving most erratically. The huge stars were so near she could have reached up and plucked them.

'Don't go away,' said Larry. 'The way to heaven is paved with bad intentions.'

'I'm not going anywhere.' She could hear the throb of drums and the carnival howls of the party. 'When love comes in and takes you for a spin, Oh la la la, c'est magnifique', played the band.

The night was so warm and beautiful, yet she felt a terrible stab of longing. If only Matt were here. Then suddenly she was filled with passion and resolve and 86 per cent proof courage.

'Larry darling,' she turned to him. 'People keep telling me I've got to grow up and live a little and get some experience with men, and catch up with Cable and Yvonne and Tracey and things. You wouldn't help me, would you, and teach me about sex?'

'Wouldn't I just? What an offer! Christ, if you want experience, I'm your man, sweetheart. *Je suis le professeur.* Now stay here and finish the joint, and I'll go and get another bottle and we'll take it down to the beach.'

Imogen collapsed back on the seat. 'When love comes in and takes you for a spin,' she sang to the flamingos. She was feeling very light-headed.

From where she was sitting, she could see some planes parked in a field. Perhaps one was waiting to whisk the screen's greatest lover off to Rome. Beyond the planes were a row of cars, mostly Rolls-Royces and Bentleys, but standing there, cleaner than any other, was James and Yvonne's pale blue

Cortina. Suddenly Imogen felt an overwhelming urge. She opened her bag, scrabbling inside for a lipstick. She found one that Gloria had given her for her birthday that she'd never used. It was dark maroon and called Plum Dynasty – to make you more sophisticated, Gloria had said.

'Jolly soppy name,' said Imogen, giggling hysterically to herself as she ran through the trees towards the cars. 'Fancy founding a dynasty of plums. Anyway, your hour has come, Plum,' and she repeated 'Come Plum' several times to herself, giggling some more.

And *there* was the pale blue boot door of Yvonne's car, just asking to be scribbled on. She unscrewed the lipstick and wrote 'Yvonne Edgworth' in a large maroon scrawl. Then she added 'is a stroppy cow', then crossed out 'cow' and put 'bitch' and 'hen-pecker'. Then she wrote 'bugger' three times on the top of the car, and 'fuck' twice on the windscreen. Then she rushed round to the other side and wrote 'Yvonne Bismarck – the Iron Duke', but that wasn't quite right, so she crossed out the D and changed Duke to Puke, and laughed immoderately at her own joke. She'd just started to write 'Go Home Carrot Top' when the lipstick broke in half, so she ran shrieking back to Larry, who had returned and was swaying dangerously as he tried to balance along the top of the stone seat with a bottle in one hand and a glass in the other.

He jumped down, spilling some of the champagne, and said, 'I've just seen Yvonne Edgworth asking

Omar Sharif if he'd ever bought a whole flower stall for anyone.'

The path down to the sea was quite steep and they were both very drunk, but somehow they managed to support each other.

'I want to get my organ into Morgan,' chanted Larry, and they both roared with laughter.

'I seem to be going from one bad end to another,' said Imogen. 'I do love you, Larry. Is it possible to love two people at once?'

'I think so,' said Larry, 'but it's rather expensive.'

His drawl was more exaggerated than ever. His hair was all over the place.

They reached the beach. Imogen could feel the sand cool and separating beneath her feet. Somewhere on the way down she'd lost her shoes.

'When love comes in and takes you for a spin,' sang Larry. 'I want to get my organ into Morgan. So do a lot of other guys at the party. I found several men in white dinner jackets looking for you when I went back to the house.'

'There was only one,' said Imogen. 'You must have been seeing quadruple.'

And they both shrieked with laughter again. Pot on a lot of drink makes the stupidest things funny.

The whole beach and the distant lights of Port-les-Pins and the lighthouse seemed to hang in a rosy glow. The waves were hissing like little white snakes on the sand. A half grapefruit moon lay on its back in the dark sky – waiting to submit like me, thought Imogen. She felt weightless like an astronaut.

278

Larry picked up a stick and tried to write with it, but the sand was too dry.

'Tell the sea to come nearer,' he said.

They ran whooping hand in hand down to the water's edge where he wrote Larry Loves Imogen in huge letters in the wet sand. Then he kissed her, and she could feel the warm sea washing over her feet.

'I'll give you a crash course in experience,' he muttered into her hair, 'you lovely warm thing.'

'You do realise I haven't been to bed with anyone before?'

'I said I was a great believer in first times,' said Larry, gently pulling her sweater over her head. 'Shall we swim first? One should always have a bath before sex.'

Perhaps I'm not too fat to bathe in the nude after all, thought Imogen hazily, as she ripped off the trousers and pants and threw them down on the sand. There was no shock as, shrieking with joy, she paddled ecstatically into the waves. It was almost as warm in the water as out.

'It's heavenly,' she shouted to Larry.

Next minute he was chasing after her, and she felt his hands round her waist.

'You're beautiful,' he said looking down at her. 'You look like Venus coming out of the waves.'

'Bottichilly,' giggled Imogen. 'Though actually it's not chilly at all, quite the reverse.'

'That's enough overture,' said Larry. 'Let's get down to Act One.' As he kissed her his lips tasted of salt, and Imogen was glad he was holding her; she doubted she could have stood up alone. She really felt very hazy. She asked Larry if he thought there was any point in having a crash course if she wasn't going to remember the finer points afterwards.

Larry laughed and said two of her finest points were sticking into his chest at the moment and he certainly wasn't going to forget them, and began to kiss her in the hollow of her throat.

In the distance she could still hear the sound of revellers, and shrieks from the swimming pool. Then she heard voices much nearer, angry voices, and she was gradually aware that Larry had stopped kissing her and was gazing over her shoulder.

There was a long pause, then Larry muttered, 'My God, it can't be.'

Then she heard an all too familiar voice saying, 'For Christ's sake, Gilmore.'

Imogen buried her face in Larry's neck, then slowly swivelled round. A man and a woman were standing on the sands only a few yards away from them. Both their faces were in shadow, but she could see the girl had short streaked blonde hair and was very slim, and no one could miss that height and the width of the man's shoulders.

Larry swallowed nervously. 'Hi, Matt,' he said brightly.

'Oh dear,' said Imogen, 'I'd better do a Venus in reverse,' and, giggling frantically, she slid back into the water.

'What the bloody hell have you been up to, Gilmore?' said Matt icily.

'You told me to keep an eye on her,' protested Larry.

'And so he has,' said Imogen's head, just above the water. 'Two eyes most of the time, and a lot of hands. He's been lovely. We've had such a nice time. When love comes in and takes you for a spin, Oh la la la.'

'Jesus,' said Matt. 'What *have* you done to her?'

Larry now seemed to be on shore, futilely trying to tug on Imogen's pink trousers which came no higher than his knee caps.

'Imogen dear,' he said, 'you haven't met Bambi.'

'Bambi,' squeaked Imogen, looking at Matt's companion. 'Oh my goodness, how do you do? I've heard so much about you.'

'Funny,' said Bambi acidly. 'I've heard absolutely nothing about you.'

Matt picked up Gilmore's trousers and threw them at him.

'I know you've been trying to get into Imogen's pants all evening,' he snapped. 'Now try and get into your own for a change.'

'Awfully good party,' said Imogen, flipping water at them.

'Come out of there at once and get dressed. I'm taking you home,' said Matt.

In no time at all, it seemed, she was sitting beside Matt in her dripping clothes, as he belted the Mercedes down Claudine's drive. Somewhere in the distance behind them she could hear Yvonne's voice rising and falling in fury like a fire siren.

'I don't want to go home. I'd like some more champagne,' said Imogen petulantly.

'You've had quite enough.'

Imogen let her head loll back on the seat.

'You're a rotten spoilsport,' she said in a slurred voice. 'I've been having the time of my life. Everyone's been trying to get off with me – Morgan the hero, the intrepid rescuer. Stars of stage and screen have been battling for my favours. I've been smoking pot, and drinking quite a lot, and having a whole load of new experiences. In fact I was just about to embark on my first affair with a married man when you and Bambi came along so inconsiderately and put a spoke in the wheel.'

Matt gazed stonily at the road in front, and jammed his foot down on the accelerator.

'Darling Larry was giving me a crash course in experience.'

'A crash course! Larry ought to be shot.'

'I don't know why you're so cross,' grumbled Imogen. 'You don't want me. You're just being a dog in the manger. Larry was just being kind. I *asked* him to seduce me. I thought if I became a woman of the world like Cable, a few more people might fancy me.'

'Well, you're going about it the wrong way.' Matt ground the gears viciously.

'When love comes in and takes you for a spin,' sang Imogen tunelessly. 'Oh, la la la, it's bloody awful. Do you think Bambi'll excite me as correspondent?'

'Probably.'

'Well, what a stupid time for her to stage a come-back, in the middle of an orgy. She must have known Larry'd be up to someone, if not me.'

Matt ignored her and lit a cigarette.

She was beginning to feel very odd. Everything like Vesuvius seemed to be erupting inside her.

'Oh well, this time next week, I'll be back in my little grey home in the West Riding,' she said fretfully, 'and you can forget all about me.'

Then suddenly out of the corner of her eye she saw he was laughing.

'You're not cross anymore?'

'Absolutely blind with rage.'

'I'm awfully sorry,' she said, her head flopping on to his shoulder, 'but I do love you,' and she passed out cold.

Chapter Sixteen

When she woke next afternoon she thought she was going to die. She'd never known pain like it, as though a nutcracker was slowly crushing her skull in, and a lot of gnomes were hammering from the inside. For a few minutes she lay groaning pitifully, then opened her eyes, whereupon an agonising blaze of sunlight stabbed her like a knife and she hastily shut them again. Wincing, she started to piece together the events of the evening, the crazy lionising, the drinking and pot smoking, and finally the nude bathing. Someone had hung her wet trousers and jersey from the window. She wondered what had happened to her knickers and her shoes. She also had hazy memories of meeting Bambi, and Matt being very cross and bringing her home. But who the hell had undressed her? Sweat broke out, drenching her entire body. She only just made the lavatory in time and was violently sick.

On the way back to her room she passed Madame and a squeegee mop, wanting to hear all about her encounter with Braganzi and the Duchess. Muttering about shellfish poisoning, Imogen apologised and bolted back into her room, where she cleaned her teeth and then crawled miserably into bed. She tried to remember what she'd said to Matt on the way home. Oh, why had she made such an idiot of herself?

There was a knock on the door. It sounded like a clap of thunder. It was Matt wearing jeans and no shirt. He had just washed his hair and was rubbing it dry with a large pink mascara-stained towel. Imogen disappeared hastily under the bedclothes. She felt him sit down on the bed and slowly emerged.

'You're an absolute disgrace,' he said.

'Oh, go away,' she moaned. 'I know I behaved horribly. I'm quite prepared for what's coming to me, and I don't want any flowers or letters please.'

A smile so faint it was almost imperceptible touched his mouth at one corner.

'Rotten France,' she said, burying her face in the pillow. 'One spends one's time being sick for love or just sick. I feel terrible.'

'Serve you right trying to pack ten years' experience into one night, and as for scribbling obscenities in lipstick all over Mrs Edgworth's clean car.'

'Holy smoke!' She sat bolt upright, clutching her head with one hand and the sheet to her breasts with the other. 'Did I really? Does she know it was me?'

'No, thanks to me. I managed to blur the Yvonne Bismarck bits, so she assumes it's some random scribbler who got lit-up at the party.'

'Oh, thank goodness!'

'"Goodness," as Mae West said, "had nothing to

do with it." ' He shook his head. 'I must say the most outrageous *alter ego* emerges when you get stoned. I'm not sure your father would be very pleased by your performance last night. Not that anyone else appears to have behaved particularly well. Nicky hasn't surfaced yet and Jumbo's looking very poorly.'

'W-where's Larry?' she stammered, pleating the sheet with her fingers, unable to meet Matt's eyes.

'Gone. He sent fondest love and a letter. Bambi's taken him off to Antibes.'

'Will they be OK?'

'Probably, after a bit of straight talking. They're both equally to blame.'

'And Tracey?'

'Gone to a thrash in Marbella with some movie star. He wanted you to go too, but I thought you'd had enough excitement to be going on with. By the way I've got a present for you,' and out of his pocket he produced a leather jewel box. For a glorious, lunatic moment Imogen wondered if he was giving her a ring. Then he said, 'It's from the Duchess and Braganzi to say thank you. There's a letter from her, too.'

Imogen opened the box. It was a gold necklace, set with seed pearls and rubies. She gave a gasp of delight.

'Pretty, isn't it? Try it on.'

She bowed her head forward. He put his arms around her to do up the clasp, his broad brown chest was only inches away from her. She ached to reach out and touch it. She trembled as she felt his fingers on her neck. She prayed it was clean enough.

'There.' Matt leaned back. 'It looks terrific. Have a look.' He reached for a hand mirror beside the bed and held it up for her. The necklace was beautiful but the effect was slightly spoiled by a mascara smudge under one eye and a large bit of sleep in the corner of the other. Hastily she rubbed them away.

'It's so kind of them both. It was so little that I did,' she muttered. Then she gave a gasp of horror. 'But I never asked you, I quite forgot. What happened about the piece?'

'They liked it. They hardly changed a thing.'

'Oh, that's wonderful. And your paper?'

'They're pretty pleased too.'

'I'm so glad. So it was worth it after all that struggle.'

'Yes, it nearly always is. I feel sort of Christlike today. It's the best feeling in the world, or almost the best feeling . . .' he smiled . . . 'the day after you've finished something you've really sweated your guts out over.' He squeezed her thigh gently through the blanket. 'And it's all due to you, darling.'

Imogen wriggled with embarrassment. 'It was nothing,' she cast desperately around for a change of subject. 'Look, does Yvonne really not realise it was me?'

'Well, her mind's on other things today. Evidently Jumbo disgraced himself last night, and being

Saturday, the beach is like Oxford Street in the rush hour, but she's forgotten all that. She got a telegram midday confirming her film part.'

'Oh dear,' said Imogen.

'Quite. She's being utterly insufferable, upstaging Cable in particular; so you can imagine Cable is not in the sunniest of tempers.'

His hair was nearly dry now. Blond and silky, it flopped over his tanned forehead. Imogen longed to run her fingers through it. She was driven distracted by his nearness, but it was such heaven having him sitting gossiping on her bed, she'd almost forgotten her hangover.

He got to his feet.

'To celebrate her new starring role, Mrs Edgworth has actually offered to take us all out to dinner. I hope you'll be able to make it. I need a few allies.'

When he had gone she opened her letters. There were several invitations, addressed to Morgan Brocklehurst, asking her to parties in various parts of Europe. Someone even wanted her to open a fête in Marseilles next week.

Larry's letter was scrawled on a piece of flimsy:

'Darling little Imogen, you were very sweet to me last night, when I needed it very badly, and you succeeded in making Bambi wildly jealous, which is all to the good, although I had great difficulty on the evidence of last night in persuading her how miserable I'd been without her. I'll send you those pictures when I get them developed. If you ever want a bed in London, come and stay with us. Je

t'embrasse, Larry. PS I thought your piece on Mrs Edgworth's car was inspired.'

The last letter was from the Duchess.

'My dear Imogen, Thank you again a million times for what you did for Ricky. This little necklace is only a small way of expressing our gratitude. Do come and stay with us next time you have some time off and write and let me know how your holiday works out. I liked your Mr O'Connor and he writes very well too. I wouldn't give up hope if I were you. Love, Camilla.'

But hope would be hope of the wrong thing, sighed Imogen, but allowed herself a daydream of having a flat in London, and giving dinner parties, asking the Duchess and Braganzi to meet Larry and Bambi, with Matt coming early to help with the drinks, and her letting him in in a black satin petticoat, and him starting to kiss her so neither of them were remotely ready when the guests arrived.

Stop it, she told herself firmly, but with the thought that she really would ask him to help her get a job in London, she drifted off to sleep.

When she woke up around eight, she felt a bit shaky, but normal. The rest of the party, gathered in the bar, greeted her like a long lost sister. Within a few minutes she realised that they were in for a decidedly stormy evening. Yvonne, dressed in a cowl-necked sky-blue dress which could easily have been worn by the Virgin Mary, was at her most poisonous, smiling smugly, and queening it over everyone, particularly Cable, whom Imogen would have felt extremely sorry for if she hadn't been in such a filthy temper, biting people's heads off, and casting dark spiteful looks in Imogen's direction. Now Tracey had gone, she had apparently made it up with Nicky, and insisted on sitting next to him at dinner.

They had just finished eating. Cable had only toyed with a few asparagus tips, when the waiter put a shampoo sachet on the side of her plate.

'What's that for?' said Cable. 'Do they want me to wash my hair?'

'Cleaning your fingers,' said Nicky.

'I prefer finger bowls.'

'They'd be quite useful for après-sex,' said Nicky, examining the sachet. 'They should put them in bedrooms.'

'I prefer finger bowls for that too,' said Cable.

'Tinker, tailor, soldier, sailor,' said Imogen idly counting her olive stones.

Cable shot her an uncontrollable look of hatred. 'Pity there isn't a rhyme that includes dissolute Irish journalists. That's what you're really after, isn't it Imogen?'

'Pack it in,' said Matt, icily.

'Well it's true,' said Cable, opening her bag and getting out her lipstick. At the same time a bill fluttered out on to the table. Cable quickly reached out to retrieve it, but Matt's hand closed over it first.

'Give it to me,' hissed Cable.

Matt smoothed out the bill and looked at it for a minute. A muscle started to flicker in his cheek.

'What's this for?' he said quietly.

'A few things I bought in Marseilles.'

'But this is for 4,500 francs!'

That's well over £500, thought Imogen incredulously.

'It must have been your peacock feather dress,' said Yvonne, brightening at the prospect of a showdown. 'I told you it was a rip-off at the time.'

'Particularly as someone ripped it right off you at that party,' said James and roared with laughter, stopping suddenly when he realised no one else was.

'D'you mean to tell me you spent 4,500 francs on one dress?' said Matt slowly.

'I had to have something new. You couldn't turn up in any old rag to that party. Everyone noticed it. That's the way one gets work.'

'Not that kind of work. How the hell d'you think we're going to pay for the rest of the holiday?'

'You'll have to win it back at the Casino. You can always cable the paper. You must have made twice that on your precious Braganzi story already.'

They paused, rigid with animosity, as the waiter cleared away the debris, leaving only clean glasses and ashtrays.

'Anyway,' Cable went on, 'since you decided to buy her' – she glared at Imogen – 'an entire new wardrobe, I thought it was my turn to have a few new clothes. Don't you agree, Nicky?'

Nicky showed his teeth non-committally. He wasn't going to be drawn in.

'Children, children,' cried Yvonne, dimples flashing, highly delighted by the turn of events, 'please don't spoil my party. I've got something to tell you all. This is a very special night for Jumbo and me.'

'So you've already told us,' snarled Cable. She turned to Matt. 'I don't know why you've got so fucking tight with bread recently.'

'Skip it,' said Matt, 'we'll discuss it later.' His face was expressionless but his hand trembled with rage as he folded up the bill and put it in his pocket.

'That's right, kiss and make up,' said Yvonne.

There's going to be one hell of a row later, thought Imogen, as the waiter arrived with an ice bucket and a bottle of champagne.

'What's that for?' said Nicky, as the waiter removed the cork and filled up everyone's glasses.

'Because I want to celebrate my first and last film part for a long time.'

'Your last?' asked Imogen.

'When I went to the doctor about my foot the other day, he was able to confirm that I'm expecting a baby.' Yvonne, her head on one side, looked even more like the Virgin Mary than ever.

There was a long pause. Imogen caught Nicky's eye and for a terrible moment thought she was going to laugh. She could see Matt still gaining control of himself with an effort. Then his natural good nature conquered his fury with Cable.

'That's great news. Congratulations to you both.' He raised his glass in the air. 'To Baby Edgworth.'

'Baby Edgworth,' said Nicky and Imogen dutifully.

'I must say I'm jolly excited,' said James, leaning across and giving Yvonne a great splashy kiss, which she immediately wiped away with her napkin.

Cable said nothing. She was drumming her fingers on the table. Then she got to her feet.

'I'm going to the loo.'

'Aren't you going to congratulate me?' said Yvonne.

'The prospect that there might be another replica of you in the world shortly is too horrible to contemplate,' said Cable and turned on her heel.

There was another long pause.

'How horrid of her,' said Yvonne in a choked voice, then added more brightly, 'Of course she's only jealous. As I told her this morning, she's twenty-six now, her days as a model are numbered. She really ought to think about settling down soon. I know you don't like talking about marriage, Matt, but I'm sure if she had a tiny baby of her own, she'd be a different person.'

'Even worse I should think,' said Nicky, filling up everyone's glasses. 'I can't see Cable changing nappies.'

'Oh, she could always use the nappy service, or disposable nappies, don't you agree, Matt?'

'When's it due?' asked Imogen hastily.

'May the 10th,' said Yvonne. 'I'm awfully glad it'll be a little Taurean, rather than Gemini, so much more placid. Cable's Gemini, isn't she, Matt?'

She knows exactly to the day, thought Imogen. She and James can't sleep together very much.

Yvonne was still rabbiting on about the baby when Cable came back. Imogen could catch an asphyxiating waft of her scent from across the table. She'd drawn even darker lines round her eyes. She looked like a witch. For a moment she stood glaring at them until Nicky and James rose dutifully to their feet. Matt remained seated, his eyes cold, his mouth shut in a hard line.

Cable slipped into her seat.

'Where are we going next?' she said. 'Let's drive over to Antoine de la Tour's place.'

'We're not going anywhere,' snapped Matt. 'We can't afford it.'

'Oh, don't be bloody stingy.'

'When I planned this holiday I didn't bank on you spending 4,500 francs on a lot of feathers.'

'I'm going to bed too,' said Yvonne. 'With Baby on the way, I don't want any late nights.'

'I want to go to Verdi's Requiem.'

'Well, you can't.'

'Why don't we compromise?' said Nicky reasonably. 'Let's go to the fair and win some cheap plonk at the shooting range, and have a party back in our rooms.'

Only Yvonne wanted to go to bed. It would have been like missing the last act of a thriller. After they'd been to the fair, they all congregated in Nicky's room.

James, who proved a surprisingly good shot, had won a large teddy bear, a china Alsatian and two goldfish, who were swimming around in the bidet.

Imogen sat on the floor, too stunned by the hostilities at dinner to say anything. Nicky was filling tooth-mugs. Matt lounged on the bed blowing smoke rings.

Cable, who was extremely drunk by now, was pacing up and down, determined to keep everyone's attention. She tossed back one mug of wine, and was about to pour another one, when Matt got up and took away the bottle.

'You've had enough,' he said quietly.

'I have not!' she snapped back.

She rushed over to Nicky and flung her arms round his neck.

'I'm as sober as a judge, aren't I, darling?'

Nicky grinned and pulled her on to his knee.

'I don't care what you are,' he said, 'but I like you.'

'There you are,' Cable said triumphantly. 'Nicky says I'm lovely. I'm glad someone appreciates me.'

'Cable, baby,' said Matt, 'at this moment the whole neighbourhood is appreciating you, particularly the people in the next door room. Keep your voice down.'

Cable slipped off Nicky's knee and went over to the dressing table and picked up the transistor.

'Let's have some music,' she said, turning it up full blast. 'Imogen did a strip-tease last night. Now it's my turn. I'm going to do the Dance of the Seven Veils.'

She kicked off her shoes and started to sway to the music.

'There's one veil gone.'

'Atta girl,' said Nicky.

'What's the next veil?' said James.

'My watch,' said Cable, taking it off without stopping dancing.

A muscle was going in Matt's cheek.

'Cable,' he said in a voice of ice, 'turn that transistor down.'

'Why should I?' she said. 'I'm sick of being ordered about. Veil number three coming up.' She started undoing the buttons of her blue shirt.

James's eyes were out on stalks.

Matt got to his feet, went over to the transistor and turned it off.

Cable seized his wrist. 'Why are you such a wet blanket?'

'Go to bed and stop making a fool of yourself.'

'All right,' said Cable defiantly. 'I'll find some decent music somewhere else.'

She opened the window and put a foot out.

'Oh, don't Cable,' cried Imogen. 'It's terribly dangerous.'

'I'm going,' said Cable, starting to climb down the wall.

'You mustn't let her,' said Imogen, running to the window and catching Cable's hand.

'Turn on the transistor,' screamed Cable, who was hanging from the window.

Imogen turned, pleading to Matt, 'Please stop her.'

'Leave her alone. She's just showing off,' he said.

'Oh, let her go,' said Nicky. 'I'm fed up with her tantrums.'

Reluctantly, Imogen let go of her hand.

Cable started to clamber down the wall, then missed her footing and crashed to the ground.

'Are you all right?' called Imogen, worried.

Nicky and James started to roar with laughter.

'She's sitting in the middle of the road,' said Imogen, giggling in spite of herself. 'I hope she doesn't get run over.'

'Most unlikely,' said Nicky. 'It's a very deserted road, unfortunately.'

'For goodness sake forget her,' said Matt. 'She'll get bored soon and come in.'

'But she might have hurt herself,' said Imogen.

'Cable yells her head off if she even pricks her finger,' said Matt.

James put on Cable's wig, and a pair of earrings and started to do a tango with the Teddy bear. Everyone got slightly hysterical.

'She's all hunched up,' said Imogen. 'I think she's crying. I'm going down to her.'

'Not by yourself,' said Matt, taking her arm. 'I'll come with you.'

As they turned down an alley to reach the back of the hotel, Imogen stumbled. Matt caught her and suddenly she was in his arms, her eyes wide, her heart pounding.

As if by instinct, he bent his head and kissed her, and once she started she found she couldn't stop. She was powerless to do anything but kiss him back.

It was Matt who had to prise her fingers away from his neck. 'Easy, sweetheart. We've come to look for Cable not the end of the rainbow.'

He groped for a cigarette and, as the match lit up his face, his features were expressionless. Shattered, mortified, Imogen walked beside him. How could she have let herself go like that?

They found Cable lying in a huddle in the street. She was sobbing quietly. Matt was across the road in a flash. In the moonlight Imogen could see that her ankle was grotesquely swollen. Matt dropped on his knees beside her.

'Oh, God, darling, I'm sorry. I didn't realise.' There was no mistaking the tenderness and concern in his voice.

'Please don't go,' said Cable, through gritted teeth, and as he picked her up to carry her inside, she fainted. When the doctor arrived next morning he said she had broken her ankle.

Chapter Seventeen

And that, thought Imogen dully, was that. In the simplest, if most painful, way possible, Cable had drawn Matt back to her side again. Once more she was the centre of attention. Nicky and James – mortified at having laughed at her last night – brought her huge bunches of black grapes. Yvonne, peeved at having missed a drama and furious with James for not coming to bed, was only too keen to take Cable's part.

Cable, once her ankle was set, took every opportunity to wring every ounce of pathos out of her situation.

'The terrible thing was,' she told Yvonne, 'that when I was in such agony all I could hear was drunken laughter.'

'Disgusting!' said Yvonne. 'How could they have been so heartless?'

After last night's heartlessness Cable had gone off Nicky again, but she insisted on Matt dancing attendance on her.

'I think I could just manage a little soup. Could

you possibly close the shutters a little? Is it too soon for another pain killer?'

She's got us over a barrel, thought Imogen angrily, and then felt ashamed of herself. Matt, who was looking tired and on edge, drove everyone out of the bedroom in the end.

James, as a penance, was made to clean the car. Yvonne and Nicky went waterskiing. Rather half-heartedly they tried to persuade Imogen to join them. But she said she preferred to sunbathe. In fact, she just wanted to be alone.

As she lay on the beach she wondered if she'd ever been more unhappy in her life.

After yesterday's day in bed her suntan had settled to a deep tawny brown, without any red in it. Her hair was streaked with gold. The beach was packed with week-end trippers. Man after man sidled up and asked her to come for a drink or a swim.

She was wondering how much longer she could stand it when a silky voice said, 'Your sun lotion has spilled.'

'Oh, go away,' she snapped and looked up into the wicked brown face of Antoine de la Tour.

'Antoine!' she said, her face lighting up. 'How lovely to see you.'

'And you, ma petite.' He sat down beside her, his eyes running over her body.

Imogen told him about Cable.

'Serve her jolly well right,' he said. 'And now she mangle the commiseration out of everyone. I know 'er sort. Mimi has gone back to Paris,' he added, looking at her out of the corner of his eyes. 'I am poor boy on my own. 'Ow about the two of us spending the day together.'

Imogen drew circles in the sand, and decided it didn't really matter what she did now.

'I'd like to, Antoine. Can I just tell the others?'

But for reasons best known to herself, she didn't go up and tell Matt where she was going. Instead she left a hastily scrawled note at the desk.

Hours later, she sat drinking brandy on the terrace of Antoine's villa. The moon, grown slimmer since last night, was pouring white light on to the sea. Fireflies flickered in and out of the orange trees. The Milky Way rose like smoke from the dark hillside. Antoine sprawled in a hammock, smoking a cigar.

The day had passed in a dream. They had ridden along the sand for miles. They had swum and they had dined in a four-star restaurant.

Antoine had been a constantly amusing companion. But although he hadn't lifted a finger in her direction, she knew he was playing a waiting game. And this time she was dealing with a professional, not a larky amateur like Gilmore. It was like spending the evening with a tiger.

He drained his glass of brandy, stubbed out his cigar and stood over her, very tall, very dark.

'Let's go inside,' he said.

This isn't really happening to me, thought Imogen, as she sat down on a huge sofa, covered in leopard skins. In about two minutes he's going to seduce me and I don't give a damn.

Antoine sat down beside her. He put a warm hand on her throat and slid it very slowly along her cheek to her ear and removed an earring.

'Pretty, pretty girl,' he said. 'Would you like me to make love to you properly?' He swiftly removed the other earring. 'Improperly, I mean.'

Oh God, thought Imogen, it's like being in the dentist's waiting room! The hi-fi began to swell soft music. Antoine put her earrings on the table and began to stroke her hair.

'You're just too good to be true,
Can't take my eyes off you,' sang Andy Williams.

Imogen burst into tears.

'Darling, ma petite, please don't cry.' She was sobbing in his arms. 'It is Matt, is it not?'

She nodded miserably.

'I thought that was the way the gale was blowing. And what does he feel?'

'Nothing, nothing at all. He loves Cable. They fight like mad but you should have heard his voice when she hurt her ankle last night.'

Antoine nodded. 'He is strange mixture. Always he joke and give impression 'e take nothing seriously except the horses and the betting. But beneath, he care about things very deeply. And even at Ox-fawd, he was always one-woman man. Though why 'e choose that 'orrible Cable, I can't imagine. I go to Rome tomorrow,' he said. 'Come with me. I show you nice time. I make you forget.'

She shook her head sadly. 'It wouldn't work.'

'I give you part in my film.'

He picked up one of the leopard skins and draped it across her shoulders, and stood back with half-closed eyes.

'You make beautiful slave girl.'

After that they drank a lot more brandy, and Antoine got out his photograph album and showed her stills from his films, and lots of snaps of himself and Matt at Oxford.

'I think I ought be getting back,' said Imogen.

'Hélas,' said Antoine, ruefully. 'I'm not tired. I think I'll drive as far as Milan tonight. Just wait while I pack a luggage.'

Outside the hotel, he took her in his arms and gave her a very thorough kissing.

'Pretty girl,' he said. 'Tell Matthieu I behave with honour. The sheep in wolf's suiting, I think. Are you sure you don't want to come to Rome?'

Imogen shook her head. 'No thank you.'

As she climbed the stairs, she was surprised to see a light on in her bedroom. She pushed open the door to find Matt lying on the bed. The ashtray on the bedside table was brimming with cigarette butts.

'Where the hell have you been?' he said. It was the crack of the ringmaster's lash.

'Out with Antoine,' she faltered. 'I left a note.'

'It's nearly two o'clock,' he said, getting to his feet and towering over her. His eyes were almost black.

'Did you think I'd turned into a pumpkin too?' she said with a nervous giggle.

'You wrote that note ten hours ago. I just wondered how you filled in the time.'

'We went riding.'

'And?'

'We swum and had dinner.'

'And?'

'We talked and talked.'

Matt lost his temper. It was as though a thunder-storm had broken over her head. Seizing her by the arms, his fingers biting into her flesh, he swung her round to face the mirror.

'Just look at yourself!'

Her lipstick was smudged, her hair rumpled, the two top buttons of her dress had come undone. Hastily, she did them up.

'He was just kissing me good-bye,' she said.

'Sure he was – ten hours after he'd kissed you hullo. And your dress is covered in fur. Talk yourself out of that if you can.'

A slow anger was beginning to smoulder inside her.

'He draped a leopard skin over my shoulders. He wanted to see what I'd look like as a slave girl.'

'Oh boy – what you lack in morals, you certainly make up for in imagination.'

'We were talking. We were talking,' said Imogen, her voice rising.

'You're repeating yourself, kid. You really want to lose it, don't you? First you try Nicky, and he's not having any, so you switch to me. Then you try Gilmore and then when that doesn't come off you fall back on Antoine.'

'I don't,' shouted Imogen.

'You picked the wrong guy,' he said viciously. 'Antoine'll have forgotten you by tomorrow.'

Imogen saw red. 'Why won't you listen?'

'Because I've had enough of your blarney. Oh Matt, Nicky's so mean to me. Oh, Matt, I'm so unhappy. Oh, Matt I'm such a constant nymph.'

'Get out! Get out!' shrieked Imogen. 'It's nothing to do with you what I do. Just because you're tied to Cable's apron strings, you can't bear anyone else to have fun.'

'Leave Cable out of this.'

But she was quite hysterical now. All the pent-up rage and jealousy of the past few days came pouring out of her. She didn't know what she was saying – every vicious hurtful thing that came into her head.

Matt grabbed her wrist.

'Shut up, shut up, shut up!'

'Now who's repeating himself?' she said.

For a moment she thought he was going to hit her. In the long silence that followed, she could only hear his rapid breathing and the pounding of her heart. Then he turned round and went out of the room.

Imogen stood, stunned and terrified, trembling like a dog on Guy Fawkes Night. How could she have said all those terrible things? She collapsed into a chair and sat hunched up, her face in her hands. Then she gave a low moan. Her earrings were missing. They were pearls and belonged to her mother. They were still on the table at Antoine's house. She'd have to go and get them.

Putting on a sweater she tiptoed downstairs. The moon was setting. Drunks were swaying in the streets. She had no difficulty finding the road.

But it was further than she thought. She passed two men who looked at her curiously and called out to her. But she ran stumbling on. At last there was Antoine's house gleaming like an iced cake. No windows open at the front. She ran round to the back. If she lugged one of the magnolia tubs underneath and climbed on to it she could just reach. She was wriggling inside when everything round her was suddenly floodlit. Someone seized her by the ankle and pulled her to the ground. A man grabbed her arm and started gabbling at her in French. Struggling and shrieking, she was carried to a waiting car and thrown into the back, where another man pinned her arms behind her back.

She was being kidnapped. She'd never see Matt again, never see her family. She redoubled her struggles. It was only when the car drew up outside the police station that she realised she'd been arrested.

'Je ne suis pas un burglar. Je suis friend of Antoine de la Tour,' she said to the fat gendarme who was sitting behind a desk. But he just laughed and threw her into a cell.

At first she screamed and rattled the bars. But the fat gendarme came up and leered at her. He got out his keys. His meaning was quite plain.

Imogen shrunk away. 'Oh non, non – please not that!'

'*Ferme ta gueule, encore.*'

She sat on the narrow bed trying to stifle her sobs. No one would ever find her. She would be there for years like the Count of Monte Cristo. It was suffocatingly hot. She dripped with sweat, but was too shattered to think of taking off her sweater. The blazing row with Matt, the horror of her arrest were beginning to take effect. She couldn't stop shaking.

The hours crawled by. Light was beginning to seep through the tiny window, when there was a commotion outside. She heard a familiar voice.

'Matt!' she shrieked.

He came straight over and took her hands through the bars.

'Imogen, are you all right?' His face was ashen.

'Oh, please get me out of here. They think I'm a burglar. I was trying to climb into Antoine's villa to get my earrings.'

She didn't understand what Matt was saying to the fat gendarme. But he spoke very slowly and distinctly, waving his Press card back and forward, and the tone of his voice put a chill even into her heart. She was released in two minutes. She fell sobbing into his arms.

'It's all right, you're safe. Everything's all right.'

It was light in the streets as he drove back to the hotel.

'How did you find me?' she asked in a small voice.

'As soon as I cooled down, I realised I'd come on too strong. I came back to apologise and found you'd done a bunk. I toured the town for a bit, then I tried Antoine's house and found the place seething with police and Alsatians. It was simple after that.'

She hung her head. 'I'm dreadfully sorry. You seem to have spent your holiday getting me out of trouble.'

'Skip it. I had no right to shout at you. My lousy Irish temper, I'm afraid. Yesterday was a bit trying. Cable – upstaging like nobody's business. Nicky – sulking. James and Yvonne – at each other's throats.'

Poor Matt,' said Imogen. 'You haven't had much of a holiday, have you?'

Then she tried again. 'We weren't doing anything, Antoine and I. Truthfully we weren't.'

'It doesn't matter. What you get up to is your own affair.'

'But . . .'

'Let's drop it, shall we?'

This weary acceptance was far worse than his earlier blinding rage.

Chapter Eighteen

As soon as she got back to the hotel she went to bed, lying for a long time in a state of coma before she fell asleep. When she woke it was afternoon.

Listlessly, she dressed and wandered along the passage to Cable's room. Chaos met her eyes. Clothes of every colour of the rainbow littered the bed. Suitcases lay all over the floor.

'What are you doing?' said Imogen, aghast.

'What does it look as though I'm doing?' snapped Cable. 'Packing, of course. Since you're here, you may as well help me. Get those dresses out of the wardrobe – take the coat-hangers too. This beastly hotel can afford them – and put them in this case. My foot is hurting so much, I can't tell you.'

She sat down on the bed.

'But where are you going?' said Imogen.

Cable gave one of her sly, malicious smiles.

'All roads lead to Rome, darling. But I'm going by way of Milan.'

Imogen looked horrified. 'But that's where Antoine is.'

'Right first time,' said Cable approvingly. 'You're

getting perceptive in your old age. Rebel's collecting me in half-an-hour.'

'But I thought you loathed Antoine.'

'Did you now? Well, I'm entitled to change my mind. I never said he wasn't attractive. And he's mad for me, which is half the battle. He telephoned this morning, absolutely gibbering, my dear, and said ever since he met me on Wednesday he couldn't get me out of his mind. He knew I wasn't happy with Matt. If I came to Rome, he'd give me the best time in the world. Don't forget those bikinis hanging from the window. He's going to give me a part in his film – as a slave girl.'

'And what about Matt?'

Cable's face hardened. 'Don't talk to me about Matt,' she said stonily. 'I'm through with him for good. If anyone deserves his come-uppance, it's that guy.'

'But what's he done?' said Imogen.

'He's impossible, that's what. He was in the most vile temper all yesterday, quite unsympathetic about my foot which, incidentally, is absolute agony. Then he swans off for most of the night. God knows what he was up to – that blasted Casino, I suppose. Then he comes in at some ungodly hour this morning, just as I'd taken two more sleeping pills. Put all those bottles in my make-up case, darling. It's that trunk over there. Where was I?'

'You'd just taken some pills.'

'So I had. Well, I was very uptight, so I began to tell him a few home-truths. Very gently, mind you. And do you know what he said?'

Imogen shook her head.

'He said, "Why don't you shut up about your bloody foot. It would have been better for everyone if you'd broken your jaw."'

Imogen buried her face in the bottles to hide a smile.

'And then without giving me a chance to retaliate, he charges out of the room to watch some forest fire that's broken out in the mountains.'

There was a knock on the door. Cable jumped nervously.

'Answer it, will you?' she said.

A sleek black face appeared round the door. It was Rebel.

'Oh, hullo,' said Cable with relief. 'I won't be long. Could you take these cases down? I'm afraid you'll have to make two journeys.'

As soon as Rebel had left the room Imogen pleaded, 'You can't leave Matt like this. OK – so he blew his top. But he'll calm down. He's worth a million of Antoine. Antoine's just a lovely playboy.'

'And I'm a lovely playgirl,' said Cable, wriggling into a green dress that looked faintly familiar.

'But Matt really loves you.' Imogen was almost in tears.

'He shows it in a most mysterious way,' said Cable.

'But he'll be shattered.'

'Won't he just!' said Cable gleefully. 'Men hate it so much more when you take off with one of their mates. Well, if he loves me so much, he can

311

come and get me. And this time it'll be marriage or nothing.'

She got an envelope out of the chest of drawers.

'I've written him this letter telling him everything,' she said, spraying it with scent. 'Will you be sure to give it him?'

Rebel appeared at the door. 'You can carry me down this time, darling,' said Cable.

Rebel picked her up.

'Lovely,' said Cable, feeling his muscles and smiling up at him. 'I don't think we'll bother to go as far as Milan.'

Fear and desolation crept slowly through Imogen's stomach like a cold wind. She went downstairs and ordered a Coke. Madame came waddling over in carpet slippers.

''Ave you seen Monsieur O'Connor?' she asked, putting the Coke tin and a glass on the table.

Imogen explained about the forest fire.

'Ah,' said Madame. 'Well, I 'ave his plane tickets.'

'Tickets?' said Imogen slowly.

It was as though another layer of ice was being placed over her heart.

Madame nodded despondently. 'Tonight he go. I think 'e meant to take that one back to London for her foot, but she seems to 'ave gone already. Always Monsieur O'Connor stay for two week. But this year, I think he not happy.'

Mindlessly picking up her Coke tin, Imogen left Madame in full spate and went out into the street.

She was numb with horror. It was like some terrible dream. To be suddenly faced with life without Matt. A grey drab expanse stretching to infinity. Tears streaming down her face. Oblivious of the people in the street, she walked blindly to the far end of the cove, and stood there for a long time, looking at the sea frothing like ginger beer on the sand.

A car was hooting insistently. Blasted French, why did they always drive on their horns.

'Imogen,' yelled a voice.

She looked up as the white Mercedes drew alongside her.

Matt leant across.

'Jump in,' he said. 'There's something I want to show you.'

In a daze she got in.

He looked at her closely. 'Poor little love, you look done in.'

His face and hands were grimy, and his eyes bloodshot, but otherwise he seemed in excellent spirits. But not for long, thought Imogen. Cable's letter was burning a hole in her pocket.

As he swung the car off the coast road and headed for the mountains, she said, 'Matt, I've got something to tell you.'

'And there's something,' he said, taking the Coke tin from her and helping himself to a great swig of it, 'that I must tell you. In spite of her hundred per cent guaranteed sun protection lotion, Yvonne is peeling like a New York tickertape welcome. It's coming off her in festoons.'

313

Imogen couldn't help giggling.

'How was the fire?' she asked.

'Raging merrily, but they expect a storm tonight, so no one's very worried about it. I got a good story, though. Port-les-Pins fire brigade spent all morning bravely fighting the fire, but come lunchtime, like all good Frogs, they downed tools and returned to the town. When they got back three hours later, they found their fire engine burnt to a frazzle.' His shoulders shook.

She'd never seen him so happy – it wrung her heart. Oh damn, damn Cable.

They drove past vineyards and olive groves shimmering like tinfoil, past Braganzi's fortress and up into the mountains. When they'd gone as far up as the car could go, Matt got out.

'Come on,' he said, taking her hand and leading her up a steep path to the top.

Below them stretched a mountainous waste of Old Testament country. The sun moved in and out of the clouds lighting up village and farms. To the right like a judgement on an ungodly people, a great furnace was licking over the hillside. Bits of ash fluttered like snowflakes through the air.

'It's beautiful,' breathed Imogen.

'I always make a pilgrimage up here every year,' he said. 'It's sort of insurance that I'll come back again.'

The highest rock was smothered in undergrowth. Matt pulled away the brambles and the wild lavender to reveal a plaque with a list of names on it.

'Who were they?' asked Imogen.

'The local resistance fighters in the last war,' he said. 'I ought to add your name, oughtn't I?'

'My name?' she said in a stifled voice.

'Yes, sweetheart, for resisting the advances of three of the most formidable wolves in the business. Not that you were exactly resisting Larry the other night.'

She had a feeling he was laughing at her again.

'What are you talking about?' she muttered.

He sat down in a hollow in the rocks and pulled her down beside him.

'Matt,' she said desperately, 'there's something I must tell you.'

'Tell away then.' He put his hand under her hair and was gently stroking the back of her neck.

'Don't do that,' she sobbed. 'I've got a letter for you – from Cable.' She pulled it out of her pocket and almost flung it at him.

He picked it up, studied it lazily and tore it into little pieces which the wind scattered in an instant.

'Now arrest me for being a litter-bug,' he said. 'I know what's in that letter. I don't even have to open it. Cable, driven to distraction by my appalling behaviour and lack of consideration, has pushed off to Rome with Antoine.'

Imogen looked at him in bewilderment – a faint hope flickering inside her.

'I tried not to get uptight about you and Antoine,' he said. 'But in the end I knew I'd go crazy if I didn't

315

have it out with him. So I rang Milan. He gave me a run-down on last night, corroborating your story word for word. He said you were enchanting, but entirely preoccupied with someone else.'

Imogen blushed.

'I'm sorry I was so bloody to you last night, little one. It's that Coleridge thing about being wroth with one we love working like madness in the brain. But I'm glad it happened. It showed me how hung up on you I'd got without realising it. I never felt a fraction of that white-hot murderous rage when I caught Cable being unfaithful.'

His voice was as soft as an Irish mist, and as he took her face in his hands, they smelt of wood smoke and wild lavender.

'Funny little Imogen. You were like a little girl, running after the rest of us crying, "Wait for me,"' and he bent his head and kissed her very gently. Next moment she flung her arms round his neck.

'Oh, Matt! Oh, Matt!'

Much later she said, 'But I don't understand. I thought Antoine and Cable loathed each other?'

'Did they? Animosity as intense as that often means the other thing. Neither will trust the other farther than they can throw them, which seems a good basis for a relationship.'

'But she's expecting you to follow her.'

'She's got a long wait in front of her then. If you keep turning a light switch on and off, on and off, like Cable did, the fuse blows in the end. There's nothing left.'

A suspicion crossed Imogen's mind. 'Matt, you didn't put Antoine up to it?'

He grinned. 'Not exactly. Let's say I planted the seed.'

'And what about Nicky?'

'Rumour has it that Nicky has been casting covetous eyes at some nymphette at the waterskiing school. And Tracey's due back this evening, so I don't think he'll be inconsolable for very long. Which leaves you and me.'

Imogen looked down at her hands. 'But you're going back?'

His face became serious. 'I've got to, darling. The Foreign Desk rang me this morning. This business in Peru's going to explode at any moment. They want me to fly out tomorrow.'

Imogen went pale. 'But you might get hurt.'

'Not I. Matt the cat with nine lives. Besides I've got something to come home for now, haven't I? I got a ticket for you too. I'm sorry to rot up your holiday, but I can't leave you here alone at the mercy of every passing wolf and gendarme.'

'You're taking me back to London with you?' she asked incredulously. Everything was crowding in on her. She couldn't take so much happiness at once.

Matt picked up the Coke tin that had fallen on to the ground and wrenched off the silver ring used to open it.

'You can go home to Yorkshire if you like. Or better still,' he looked at her under drooping lashes, 'you can shack up in my flat and look after Basil

317

and make up my mind where you want to go for a honeymoon.'

Imogen opened her mouth and shut it again.

'It's all right. Don't rush into anything. Kick the idea round for a bit. You might not like being hitched to a journalist. It's a rough life. But I warn you, I don't give up easily. Anyway, people keep telling me I ought to hang on to you – Gilmore, Antoine, the Duchess, Braganzi, Tracey. You've got a lot of fans, sweetheart.'

'I have?' she said in amazement.

'Yep, and I'm the biggest one.'

He picked up her left hand and slid the Coca-Cola ring on to her wedding-ring finger. Then he pulled her into his arms and kissed her.

'I love you,' he said softly, 'because you're gentle and good, and because I know you love me.'

He looked at his watch. 'Christ. We'd better step on it, if we're going to catch that plane.'

Imogen grumbled and snuggled up to him, wanting to be kissed some more.

'Come on,' said Matt, pulling her to her feet. 'It's a great day for the Irish, but I can't answer for my actions if we stay here necking much longer, and I can't have you getting blasé.'

As he drove back into the town, she sat, her fingers clutched over the Coca-Cola ring, half-stunned with wonder at what was happening.

As he stopped the car outside the hotel, however, she looked at him with troubled eyes. 'Matt, are you sure you're over Cable?'

'Darling,' he said, flinging his arms out in a fair imitation of Al Jolson. 'I'd run a million miles from one of her smiles. Come here, if you don't believe me.'

It was a few seconds before they realised Yvonne was tapping angrily on the window.

'Matt! Matthew!'

Matt turned round. 'Yes?'

Yvonne looked in horror, suddenly realising it was Imogen he was kissing. 'What on earth's she doing?'

'Just getting into training.'

Yvonne pursed her lips. 'Where's Cable?'

'I'm not quite sure.'

'Well, most of my wardrobe seems to be missing . . .'

THE END

A LIST OF OTHER JILLY COOPER TITLES AVAILABLE FROM CORGI BOOKS AND BANTAM PRESS

THE PRICES SHOWN BELOW WERE CORRECT AT THE TIME OF GOING TO PRESS. HOWEVER TRANSWORLD PUBLISHERS RESERVE THE RIGHT TO SHOW NEW RETAIL PRICES ON COVERS WHICH MAY DIFFER FROM THOSE PREVIOUSLY ADVERTISED IN THE TEXT OR ELSEWHERE.

15255 2	LISA AND CO	£6.99
15250 1	BELLA	£6.99
15249 8	EMILY	£6.99
15251 X	HARRIET	£6.99
15252 8	OCTAVIA	£6.99
15256 0	PRUDENCE	£6.99
15055 X	RIDERS	£6.99
15056 8	RIVALS	£6.99
15057 6	POLO	£6.99
15058 4	THE MAN WHO MADE HUSBANDS JEALOUS	£6.99
15054 1	APPASSIONATA	£6.99
15059 2	SCORE!	£6.99
14850 4	PANDORA	£6.99
14662 5	CLASS	£6.99
14663 3	THE COMMON YEARS	£5.99
99091 4	ANIMALS IN WAR	£6.99
04404 5	HOW TO SURVIVE CHRISTMAS (Hardback)	£9.99

All Transworld titles are available by post from:
Bookpost, PO Box 29, Douglas, Isle of Man IM99 1BQ
Credit cards accepted. Please telephone +44(0)1624 836000, fax +44(0)1624 837033,
Internet http://www.bookpost.co.uk or
e-mail: bookshop@enterprise.net for details.
Free postage and packing in the UK.
Overseas customers allow £2 per book (paperbacks) and £3 per book (hardbacks).